Other books by Kirt Hickman

Fiction

Worlds Asunder

Non-Fiction

Revising Fiction: Making Sense of the Madness

For Children

I Will Eat Anything

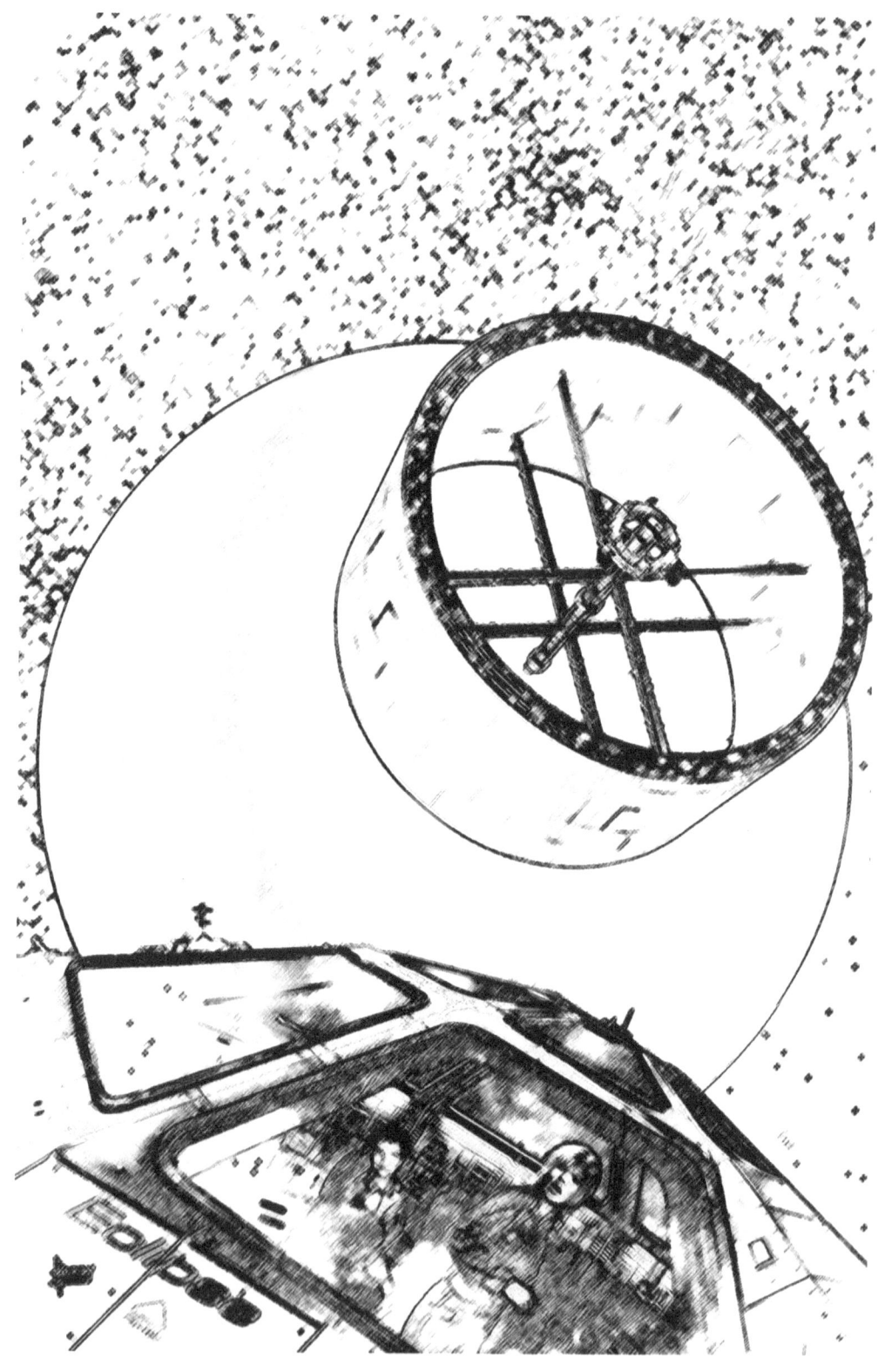

VENUS
RAIN

WORLDS ASUNDER: BOOK II

Caught between a cold-hearted killer
and cold, hard space. . .

Kirt Hickman

QP Quillrunner
Publishing

Published in the U.S.A. by
Quillrunner Publishing LLC
Albuquerque, NM

Printed in the U.S.A.

Cover art by David A. Hardy

Book design by Janice Phelps Williams
Typeset in Palatino10/14

Cataloging-in-Publications Data is on file with the Library of Congress.
Library of Congress Control Number: 2008931112

ISBN 978-0-9796330-3-4

For Lisa, who always knew I could.

Acknowledgments

A book like this can't be created by one person alone. It took the tireless effort of many people to make *Venus Rain* a reality. My thanks go out to all of you.

To my network of critiquers and test readers: Keith Pyeatt, Erle Guillermo, Gerry Raban, Laura Beltemacchi, Lisa Hickman, Ben Valerine, Tom Lemp, Larry Koch, and others. Special thanks to David J. Corwell for catching the things that the rest of us didn't.

To my editor, Susan Grossman, for ensuring that *Venus Rain* is the best that it can be.

To all my peers at SouthWest Writers, for your constant moral and technical support. I've learned so much.

To David A. Hardy and Janice Phelps Williams, for exceeding all my expectations for book and cover design.

To my wife, Lisa, for giving me the time and encouragement to begin, to endure, and to finally complete *Venus Rain*. I couldn't have done it without you.

And most of all, to God, for blessing me with the necessary time and talents.

Prologue

Kelly Baker, just nine years old, sat on the sofa and stared, open-mouthed, across the coffee table at her parents, who looked back with expressions of pity and . . . something else—something Kelly couldn't quite identify. She said nothing. What was she supposed to say in a situation that couldn't possibly be real?

Divorce.

"We both love you very much," her mom had said. "We just don't love each other anymore."

That's when Kelly knew it wasn't real. Love didn't just go away, so her parents couldn't have stopped loving each other.

Thus, all the questions they probably expected escaped her until the following day. Then she asked them. She didn't understand the answers she got, let alone believe them, but it was clear her parents hadn't changed their minds. So Kelly kept asking, over and over, in every way she could think of. When that didn't work, she screamed at them. She pleaded. She tried to bargain with her parents, both individually and together.

She begged her dad to stay.

A month later he left, not just the dorm, or even the space station. He went all the way to Jupiter. The lifeblood of the solar system, people called it. To Kelly, it was just some mythical place that existed only in school lessons and vid-stories, a place no more real than her parents' divorce had been the day they'd announced it.

Over time, her questions changed. Did grown-ups really stop loving?

Was it something you outgrew, like wearing diapers or playing with dolls? Would her parents stop loving her someday? Maybe they already had.

Two years later, Kelly sat on that same couch, staring across the same coffee table, now littered with thinpads that contained her completed homework. Her eighteen-month-old brother slept peacefully, finally, just beyond his bedroom door. His toys cluttered the living room, waiting for Kelly to pick them up. The dishes in the sink and the shopping list on the breakfast table also demanded her attention.

Now that their mother had begun commuting to the planet surface, it seemed like Kelly was always alone with her brother. It wasn't fair. Friends her own age couldn't baby-sit yet, and here Kelly was raising an infant who needed parents even more than she did.

She wiped tears from her eyes with the back of her hand, and then with her fingers. All her questions about their parents flooded back into her mind. She considered them in light of the ways she herself had changed since the divorce.

Maybe they were right about love. Maybe you did outgrow it.

Chapter 1

Kelly Baker pushed her new boyfriend into a cramped electrical junction room and pressed her lips against his.

Mark's hands found their way into the back of the micro-blend denim shirt that she wore open to expose the bra beneath, which she'd chosen for its color: black. Mark always wore that color. Not old goth, which Kelly would have preferred, but a black polo shirt with the Telnet Services logo and canvas work pants, a little too stiff in the front buttons.

"Mmmmm." The sound came unbidden. She hadn't known Mark for long, yet he had some indefinable quality that unsettled her in strange and wonderful ways, especially when it made her think of him at times she didn't want to. Maybe it was the way he believed in her, despite her wretchedness.

Maybe it was just his age: twenty-four. Like the way Kelly wore her shirt and the neon-pink highlights in her straight platinum hair, Mark's five-year age advantage gave Kelly one more way to drive her mother into a flat spin. It would, that is, if she ever let her mother meet him. The risk was, her mom might actually like him.

Warmth radiated from the electronics racks around them. Finally, Kelly came up for air. "Let's get sweaty."

Mark pushed her gently away and checked his watch. "We're late."

"Who cares." She dug into her pocket for her tin of synth.

"Kelly, don't." He reached for it, but she jerked away. She scraped a pinch of flakes from the tin and settled them under her tongue. Her mouth went at once numb and tingly, her sinuses cleared, and her mind reached zero-g.

13

Mark snatched the tin from her hand.

"Hey!"

He squeezed it in his fist and brandished it before her face. "You don't need this."

"It's only synth."

"I don't care what it is. You—"

"Synth, Mark. It's not addictive." A smile crept across her face as she stared into his eyes and wrapped her arms around his slim waist. "It's the high without the tie, the trip without the grip. You know, the sting without the string. It's even legal."

"I think it's more addictive than you realize." He grabbed her wrist and pulled her from the junction closet onto the facilities deck, the outermost ring of the spinning cylinder that housed all of *Venus Rain*'s residents. Dust, brought to Facilities by the cylinder's artificial gravity, scattered beneath them as Mark dragged her toward the stairs that led to Planet U, the solar system's premier planetary science university.

"Where're we going?"

"To the ceremony."

She resisted his pull enough to tell him she didn't want to go but not enough to frustrate his effort to get her there.

"This is a big deal for La Roche. For everyone, really." Just before the stairs, they passed a reclaim dump and Mark tossed her tin of synth down the chute.

"Hey!" It disappeared before she could lunge for it. *Asshole.*

One flight up, they pushed their way into a crowded corridor. Businesses had closed early to allow employees to attend the event, and the auditorium had overflowed into the halls.

Nobody seemed to notice the way Kelly wore her shirt. Although this ceremony warranted more conservative dress, an exposed bra was far from the raciest attire one could find on the university deck on any given day.

The only one who reacted was Mark. At the entrance, he glanced at her bra, drawing a smile from her, and pecked her on the lips. They pushed their way through the crowded doorway and down one of the side aisles.

". . . on this thirtieth anniversary of the Venus Terraforming Project." Professor La Roche spoke from the stage, hunched like an invalid over the podium. His voice, raspy with age, carried through the speakers to every corner of the room.

Over the stage behind him loomed a two-story hologram of one of the Project's massive atmosphere processors, with its giant gas reaction tower and bank of exhaust stacks, surrounded by the yellow-brown soil of Venus's surface. The image, converted from a 2-D painting commissioned for the cover of a publicity brochure, stood much more picturesquely than any real processor, if Kelly could believe her mother's firsthand accounts.

Halfway to the stage, Mark found an opening along the wall for them to wedge themselves into for the duration of the speech. Kelly turned her attention to La Roche, who instructed two of her classes that semester.

". . .has dropped fifty degrees since we brought the first processor online. As we strip the oxygen from carbon dioxide and combine it with imported hydrogen to form water, we reduce the greenhouse effect."

Most of the residents knew at least that much of the basics of terraforming. La Roche was addressing the reporters who had arrived yesterday with the supply convoy.

Oversized molecules floated in the air above the holo-emitter, splitting and recombining in diminishing waves of symbolic heat. Kelly stepped in front of Mark, wrapped his arms around her bare abdomen, and enjoyed the feel of his fit body against her back.

La Roche continued. "The falling temperature slows the rate at which water decomposes. Meanwhile, the output of the processors remains constant. This will result in an exponential increase in the rate of temperature decline. Though it has taken thirty years to bring the temperature down by fifty degrees, we will dissipate the remaining four hundred degrees in just twice that time."

Applause filled the auditorium.

"Venus began—" La Roche waited for silence while the image changed to that of a morphing planet surface. "Venus began drier than any desert known to humankind, but when the process is complete, we will have produced enough water to create oceans on the surface and clouds in the sky. Imagine, Venus rain."

The thunder of the audience's approval shook the floor.

La Roche shouted over the din. "The average surface temperature will exceed that of Earth by a mere twenty degrees."

A commotion at the back doors pulled Kelly's attention from the stage. Angry shouts drifted over the heads of the audience. People standing in the doorway were shoved forward from behind.

"Humans will live there without the benefit of an artifi—"

Half a dozen men marched in from a door to La Roche's left. Three stopped at the entry. The rest continued onto the stage.

These were not the civilian police who kept peace on the station—they would have worn red jumpsuits embroidered with yellow stars and carried Lancaster pulse guns. These men were genuine Chinese military, with army uniforms and deadly projectile rifles. Illegal weapons, by international law.

La Roche backed away from the podium as the soldiers approached.

One of the men crossed the floor-mounted emitter, disrupting the holographic image, and waved awkwardly toward the dignitaries seated along the back of the stage. "Bleed the innocence from their hearts." He spoke softly in Chinese, but the audience had grown silent and the stage microphone picked up his voice and fed it to the speakers for all to hear. And although the international inhabitants usually spoke English, *Venus Rain* was owned by an international consortium dominated by Chinese companies. Anyone who lived there picked up enough of the language to get by.

A man beside the leader stepped toward the dignitaries. Tall for an Asian, with black hair halfway down his back, he didn't fit the military prototype. From a distance, his eyes appeared closed, or nearly so, as if he was in a state of meditation, hypnosis, or drug-induced catatonia. His boots clomped on the hollow stage. He leveled a pistol at one of the women, a scarlet-suited East Indian named Raji Yanamandra, who worked for the Planet U administration.

The sound of the gunshot blasted from the speakers. A spray of gore exploded from the back of Raji's head. Her body flailed into a row of plastic folding chairs and thumped to the stage. The audio system dampened a whine of feedback to silence.

"Oh my—" Mark breathed into Kelly's ear.

People in the front rows retched onto the floor or fainted in their seats. Kelly's stomach soured. She tore her gaze away from the pool of blood that swelled beneath Raji's head as the military leader approached the podium. Though he moved quickly, his passage seemed to take an eternity. None of it seemed real.

As he stepped up to the microphone, the spotlight revealed a grotesque visage, red and raw across the man's forehead, the right side of his nose, and most of his cheek and jaw. Skin flaked from his face as though scorched by the Mercury sun and only beginning to heal. "Now I have your attention," he said in accented English. "I am Colonel Chang Chaozong." He held his right forearm level, with his fingers slightly cupped. His wrist rotated back and forth as though driven by an oscillating servo. "I claim this station for the People's Republic of China. Each of you will live or die by my command."

Soldiers herded La Roche and the other speakers and dignitaries from the stage. Chinese troops guarded the exits.

The shock of the violence cleared Kelly's head of synth. She loosened Mark's grip enough to look at him. "What's going on?"

Mark shook his head. His irises, nearly black in any light, were indistinguishable from his pupils now. "I don't know. Listen."

His grip tightened until it became painful, but Kelly welcomed it. She searched her pockets for more synth. They should have stayed downstairs. At least there they could find a place to hide, like . . . oh, God. Like her little brother Rod must be doing now. She shook herself loose from Mark.

A muffled clang reverberated through the walls. "As of this moment," Chang continued, "this station is locked down. Pressure doors have been sealed. Do not resist these conditions. My soldiers are immune to pleas and have orders to kill."

He pointed to Shou Jijin, the station director of *Venus Rain*. "Bring him."

A soldier pulled the man from the row of executives along the back of the stage. Shou's eyes went wide. His steps faltered as the soldier walked him out with Chang. Chang's longhaired crony followed, his heavy footfalls echoing behind them.

As soon as they were gone, La Roche hobbled to Raji's side and eased himself to his knees.

Kelly started toward the back of the auditorium, but Mark caught her arm. "Where are you going?"

"I've got to find my brother."

Mark surveyed the room.

"He's not here." She yanked her arm away and gestured toward the main doors. "He's out there somewhere, running around the station."

"You can't leave. You heard what Chang said."

"I don't care. I have to find him." With her dad gone and her mother off the station, nobody else would.

Mark grabbed her shoulders. "Think about this. There're a thousand people in here. If we just mind our own business, this thing will blow over. Everything'll be fine—"

"Fine?" She glared into his black eyes.

His face turned red and his grip tightened. "If we draw attention to ourselves . . ."

A smirk crossed Kelly's face despite the tension. "You're scared."

"You're damn right I'm scared. Jesus, Kelly, aren't you paying attention?" He stabbed a finger at the stage and raised his voice. "That woman is dead."

"Shhhhh," a man beside them hissed.

On the stage, La Roche climbed to his feet. The audience hummed with whispered questions, stifled cries, and muted hysterics. No one seemed to have singled out Kelly and Mark arguing against the wall.

"Listen to me." Mark's tone was calm now, full of concern. "How old's your brother?"

"Nine."

Mark put his reassuring hands on her shoulders. "If he's smart, he's hiding somewhere. You tell the guards you want to go find him, they'll keep you here and hunt him down. There's got to be another way."

Kelly's head ached from stress and the buzz of fading synth. She searched her pockets again, but the tin was still gone. "All right. What do you suggest?"

"I don't know, but we've got to sit tight until we come up with a plan."

"Great. You sit tight. I'll go talk to the professor."

"Kelly, no."

She ran down the aisle. Most of the audience had drifted away from the stage.

The old man staggered down the stairs to the front row of seats. "Professor La Roche." Kelly rushed to a stop before him.

His head jerked up from watching the floor. It took a moment for his moist eyes to focus on hers. "Miss Baker."

Mark ran up beside her.

La Roche's gaze oscillated between them as though he was confused by their presence together. "Mister Torben." He started to walk away.

"Professor. . ." Kelly didn't know what to say next, suddenly embarrassed that she thought this old man could help her. He had always gotten around slowly, limping with age, but now he looked broken. Broken in mind and spirit.

Nevertheless, she had to try. She'd spent enough time in his office arguing for higher grades, which her command of the material justified and which she would have earned if she'd put a little time and effort into her assignments. Though he never budged on the grades, she and the professor had come to understand one another.

Furthermore, La Roche was one of the most prominent and respected men on the Venus Project. Since he was the keynote speaker, killing him would have made the most effective demonstration of Chang's resolve, but the soldiers had spared him. Maybe that meant something. Maybe he held some sway with Chang.

"What's this all about?" Mark asked him, filling the silence.

La Roche shook his head. "I have to find something to cover Raji."

"But, Professor—"

La Roche's eyes flashed to Kelly's, knifed her with grief.

She looked at her feet. "Sorry."

"Come on." Mark put a hand on the old man's shoulder. "We'll help you."

Kelly followed them without a sound.

"Was Raji a friend?" Mark asked in a low, comforting voice.

La Roche's head bobbed. He ran his fingers repeatedly through his full head of silver hair, mussing it further with each stroke, then took off his glasses and wiped his eyes with his sleeve. "She was a good woman."

Kelly walked beside him to the media control room. Nobody stopped them when they went inside. There were no other exits. No way to escape.

"Here." She pulled a long red stage curtain from a cardboard box under a table. "How's this? It's fitting, I think. It matches her suit."

La Roche put on his glasses and waved his hand absently. "Sure, sure." His eyes, suddenly shrewd, swept the room as if looking for something else. He scanned the equipment, the floor, the ceiling.

Kelly stepped toward him. "Professor?"

"Yes. That'll do nicely." La Roche opened a parts cabinet full of spare electronics and cables, found a cardboard box of tools, and pocketed a few of the basics: a screwdriver, pliers, and wire cutters. He rummaged through the curtain box as if to assure himself that it contained nothing but fabric. Then he switched off the hologram emitter and stage microphone and moved back toward the door. "Come now."

His demeanor changed once more as he crossed the threshold, back into the defeated old man he'd been a few moments before.

The three returned to the stage, deserted now save for the body and a few friends stalwart enough to remain with Raji despite the recent violence. The crowd settled into an uneasy silence. Many reclaimed the seats they'd occupied during the ceremony. The soldiers at each exit stood at attention. Even the station's giant air handlers had gone still.

La Roche took the curtain, knelt beside Raji, and draped it over her body. Raji's other friends backed away to give him some time with her.

Kelly waited a few moments before she knelt too. "Professor? Professor, I need your help with something."

He stiffened as though he sensed the urgency in her tone.

"My little brother didn't come home from school this afternoon. He's out in the station somewhere. Probably scared. I just thought . . ." She faltered. This man had lost a friend and colleague. What right did she have to impose upon him? What did she expect him to do?

"What do you think they'll do if they find him?" Mark asked.

"Do?" La Roche glanced around the stage. The three were alone. "That depends on whether he causes any trouble."

Kelly cringed. Trouble was all he caused. Like the one Saturday morning when he was six. He hid their mom's company badge to prevent her from going to work, to make her keep her promise to take him to the zero-g playground. Their mother stormed around for two days whenever she was home. No matter what she said or did, Rod wouldn't tell her what he'd done with the badge.

It didn't work, though. Their mom went in anyway, got a temporary badge or something until the company replaced hers the following Monday. That was so like both of them. And neither had changed since.

"Why do you think they're doing this?" Mark asked.

"I don't know. Maybe it has something to do with the China Dominion Affair. Maybe it has something to do with the Project." He shrugged. "It could be something else entirely."

"You want to go find your brother?" he asked Kelly.

"I'm worried about him."

"I can help you." La Roche dug a utility knife, the kind with all the gadgets folded into it, from his front pocket and handed it to her. "There's an air vent in the ceiling of the media center." He gestured toward the room where they'd found the box of curtains. "Undo the screws and climb into the shaft. Don't forget to replace the grate behind you."

"Okay," Mark said.

"You going with her?" La Roche asked him.

"Somebody's got to keep her out of trouble."

La Roche's expression was all business once again. "I'll make sure you're not interrupted, but you've got to do something for me."

"Why would we be interrupted?" Kelly asked. "Nobody cared when we went in there before."

"Don't look, but there're two men on the catwalk above you."

Reflex turned her head. The walkway that provided maintenance access to the automated spotlights held two Chinese soldiers who watched over the whole assembly. Fortunately, their attention was elsewhere.

"They saw us enter the media room," La Roche continued, "and watched until we returned. If you go in there and don't come back out, somebody'll come looking for you."

"All right." Kelly swallowed hard. "What do we do?"

"There's a silver case in my dorm, number 2812. My code is F-105. The cupboard under the sink has a false bottom. The case is beneath it. Bring it here and leave it in the airshaft just inside the grate. Agreed?"

Mark nodded.

"We have to wait until they release the pressure doors. You won't get anywhere in the environmental system with them closed. The dampers are vacuum-tight."

"Chang must be using the doors to keep people from moving about the station," Mark said, "while his men use the manual overrides to round everybody up."

"Probably," La Roche said.

"Then we can't wait." Kelly's eyes snapped from La Roche to Mark and back. "We've got to do something now." Rod knew the recesses of the station as well as anyone, but he was a bit too brave for his own good. He was liable to do something stupid for fun and get caught in the process. "He'll run, thinking it's some kind of game."

"If he does that," La Roche said, "they likely will shoot him."

Kelly's thoughts grew more scattered and her muscles twitchier the longer they talked. "Do the dampers have overrides?"

"Of course," Mark said. "But activating them will show up on the maintenance panel in Center."

La Roche eyed him carefully.

Mark shrugged. "I used to work on the maintenance grid." He turned back to Kelly. "They'll be able to track our movements."

"Come on." La Roche climbed to his feet. "We'd better blend. The air's shut down until Chang reopens the pressure doors. With this many people in here, he can't leave them closed for long." He limped to the side of the auditorium, near the media room door.

For the next thirty minutes, Kelly and Mark hovered near him without speaking.

Kelly's shaking hands roamed over her clothing. Her parched mouth craved a pinch of synth. It wasn't addiction, she told herself. The motion just gave her something to do with her hands when she was nervous, and it calmed her mind enough to think.

She turned her back to Mark, pulled his arms around her chest, and squeezed them with her own, trembling.

Chapter 2

Amanda Baker heaved on a stuck valve in the helium cooling line of atmosphere processor thirteen. It refused to budge. Disgusted, she grabbed a two-meter length of titanium pipe and slid it over the end of the wrench to lengthen the lever arm. She put all of her weight onto the bar and bounced in Venus's Earthlike gravity. Instead of twisting loose, the valve stem sheared off. Amanda fell to the grid-metal floor. The wrench and cheater bar clattered beside her. Liquid helium whistled past the valve with the wail of a wounded banshee, 272 degrees below zero, cold enough to freeze human flesh in microseconds.

Amanda rolled until she hit the far wall, where the stream of evaporating helium dissipated into the heat of the temperature-moderated maintenance chamber. Just beyond the bulkhead, superheated gases, the lifeblood of the Terraforming Project, roared through pipes as big around as a docking collar. An incessant, numbing vibration shook the floor.

She retrieved and inspected the broken piece, then heaved it at the composite wall of the processor. Her whole body ached from stresses she couldn't begin to count. Safety protocol required her to have a buddy, but ever since the company transferred her partner—with years less seniority than herself—to a better assignment in data analysis, Amanda had done her work alone, and it always took longer than expected. For four hours, she'd labored in the lethal heat of the maintenance chamber and had already switched to the backup battery on her cooling vest. Now she had a busted valve to replace. That would take at least another half-hour.

It was a shit job. Amanda always got the shit job. That was the rub of being an American woman working for a Chinese company. Yet the money was good, or good enough at any rate. With overtime, it paid her son's medical bills and her daughter's tuition. So she worked her ass off, kept her mouth shut, and prayed she'd have enough at the end of the month for the rent, the sustenance charge, and the Project tax, which shouldn't have been levied against those working for the Project.

Amanda gritted her teeth and lurched into motion. If she allowed the coolant to escape the fresh helium tanks, she'd have to come back before next month's scheduled replacement.

Despite the heat, she jogged down two flights of stairs to the spare-parts bins for a replacement valve. Her lungs labored in the stifling air. Minutes later, she shut off the helium flow to swap the part, which she'd have little time to do. The hot greenhouse gases that burned through the stacks at a hundred thousand cubic meters an hour forced the processor's temperature to climb. If it got too high, thermal expansion of the jet rotors could crack one of the stacks. The processor would be down for months. And of the thirty-two processors, the company needed them all.

She disconnected the broken valve, twisted the new one into place, pressure-tested the line, and restored the helium flow. Dehydration parched her throat, so she sucked down a few gulps of tepid water from her flask and returned it to her waist.

By the time she got back to the shuttle, her cooling vest battery blinked yellow.

She stumbled into the pilot's seat and thumbed the comm. "VR-2 to *Venus Rain* Center. Request permission to return to station. Over."

Static hissed from the speaker.

"VR-2 to *Venus Rain* Center. This is Amanda Baker at number thirteen processor. Request permission to launch from Venus surface. Over."

Nothing. Her link didn't even pick up the background wash of transmissions leaking in from adjacent frequencies or the garbled chatter of messages coded for other ships. Just space static, as if *Venus Rain* had ceased to exist.

❧❦⟨○⟩❦❧

"That's it," La Roche said when the air kicked back on. "Wait here. Keep an eye on the catwalk. And above all, don't be seen."

He hobbled through the throng toward the back doors of the auditorium, which had become little more than a holding pen for the innocent—people ignorant of the daily political struggle that had taken place in some form or another since the dawn of humankind, or at least ignorant of its sudden volatility in places where it seemed absent.

But not everyone there was innocent. Certainly Raji hadn't been. Chang must have known she was a spy. There was no other reason he'd choose her to serve as the example.

The question was: Did Chang know La Roche was her partner?

The fact that La Roche was alive suggested Chang hadn't connected him to her, yet there was another possibility. Chang might need La Roche's technical expertise to keep the Project running.

He shuffled across the carpet, keeping his head down to prevent his aged legs from tripping, but also to hide his face, lest it betray his consternation.

The European Union had sent him to *Venus Rain* to perform a simple task: identify the facilities that supported China's illegal Mingyun satellites and to report any unusual activity to his superiors on Earth.

Nevertheless, the circumstances of Chang's presence raised additional questions. What was he after? And how did he plan to get it? He couldn't hope to hold the Venus system with just a few satellites. That meant he'd brought additional defense systems with him, that the Chinese had built defenses into *Venus Rain* itself, or both. Observation was no longer enough. La Roche must identify those systems, map them, learn what he could of their capabilities and deployment, and somehow, through the wall of jamming interference that Chang had almost certainly erected, communicate them to European Intelligence.

For this, La Roche needed resources of his own: tools, assets, and access to Chang's military information. The third required him to escape the auditorium, but he must do so in a way that fostered trust on the part of Chang and his men. He had to get Chang to *let* him out. Otherwise, the bastard wouldn't let him access so much as a food-vend, let alone a telnet terminal.

La Roche came to a stop behind the final screen of hostages. He was about to trade any chance he might have to cultivate Chang's trust for a pair of assets, Kelly and Mark. And he'd given them his utility knife, the most valuable physical tool on his person, leaving him with only the things he'd scrounged from the media room cabinet.

Already his dilemma seemed a tradeoff among the vital resources he needed. He saw no way to gain them all. He must settle for what he could get now and work on the rest later.

With a deep breath, he pushed his way into the space near the back doors. The two men there, a private and a private first-class, wore steel-gray combat gear, including helmets. Each had a comm link jacked into his ear, a special-forces patch on his sleeve, and a Chinese, military-issue, automatic rifle in his hands.

"Back," the PFC said in thick English.

"Hogwash." La Roche waved a dismissive hand and continued toward the door. "You may not recognize me, sonny, but I'm Doctor Dennis La Roche. I run the Venus Project." That was pushing the truth, but these grunts probably didn't know the difference. "I demand to speak to your superior."

"No."

"I'd even settle for that unpleasant, mealy-faced fellow who stole my stage."

The soldiers closed ranks and held their rifles before them like push bars.

La Roche pressed forward, his voice raised in his most sincere façade of anger. "Look here. I'll not be treated like a supply shipment of livestock." He reached for one of the six ornate sliding doors. "I'm no prisoner—"

A rifle butt smashed into his cheekbone. Pain exploded across his face and the station spun off its axis. When his vision cleared, he stared at the ceiling past the barrel of the PFC's rifle.

Shouts erupted from the crowd and the private tried to keep everyone at bay.

La Roche ignored the gun in his face, rolled over, and pushed himself to his knees, careful not to look at the catwalk. He collected his glasses from the faded carpet and examined them. The flexsteel frames and durapane lenses had survived the violence, so he settled them on his face and crawled to the back row of theater seats.

Using a chair back for support, he pulled himself to his feet, then stared down the PFC's rifle into the man's eyes. "Sooner or later you're going to have to let us through those doors. Unless you want to clean shit off the auditorium floor."

Kelly shivered despite the warming air and tugged the loose ends of her shirt closed over her midriff. The auditorium smelled of close bodies and stale vomit. The only sound was a muted murmur from the few prisoners brave enough to speak.

One of the men on the catwalk swept the room with his gaze, pausing occasionally to study something but never lingering on La Roche, as far as Kelly could tell, and never on her and Mark.

The other soldier was more troubling. He mostly watched the entrance to the media room, the only door left unguarded by the soldiers on the ground.

"Why soldiers?" Kelly asked, almost to herself.

"What?"

She loosened Mark's arms enough to turn her face toward him. "Why soldiers instead of station security? Why bring illegal weapons when Lancaster pistols would work just as well?"

"Because they wouldn't. With this many people, we could rush the door. They'd shoot some of us, but the Lancaster's a stun gun. With lethal weapons, nobody'll take the chance."

"You sure about that?" Kelly nudged her chin toward the back of the room, where La Roche emerged from the throng into the clearing at the main entrance.

The soldiers stiffened as he approached. La Roche said something, and then one of the men struck him with the butt of a rifle. The audible crack reached Kelly where she and Mark waited.

The crowd began to shout and press the guards.

"Now." Mark shoved Kelly toward the media room. The two slipped through the door and closed it behind them.

Mark rolled a chair under the vent in the center of the three-meter-high ceiling and took La Roche's utility knife from Kelly. He selected one of the gadgets it offered and pressed the button on the side. The power screwdriver whirred to life. "Nice."

Kelly steadied the chair while Mark removed the screws that secured the wire-mesh cover.

As the last one popped loose, the grate slipped from his grasp. "Look out."

Kelly got a hand on it, but the edge smacked her forehead before Mark caught it from above.

"Sorry. You okay?"

Kelly gritted her teeth. "Keep going." She probed the wound with her finger and her hand came away sticky with blood that had begun to run down her face. "Damn it."

Mark pushed the grate through the opening and slid it to one side. Then he folded the knife, stuffed it into his pocket, and hopped to the floor. "My God, Kelly. You okay?"

She nodded, her hand covering the wound.

"You sure?" Mark grabbed a napkin next to an empty coffee mug on the table. "Put this on it. We got to go." He urged her onto the chair and boosted her into the duct. Then he yanked the box of stage curtains in front of the chair and tossed a couple of them onto the floor, as if someone had been sorting through them. He pocketed a handful of supplies from a first-aid kit hanging on the wall and turned back to the chair. It rattled quietly as he climbed through the hole.

Kelly didn't bother to mention the blood she'd left splattered on the floor.

❧❨⭕❩☙

Mark replaced the grate in the media room ceiling. "Where are we going?" he asked Kelly.

"Station south." Due to the spin of *Venus Rain*'s cylinder, designers had established compass coordinates on the station as if it was a planet. South happened to be the end that pointed toward Venus.

"All the way to the observation hallway?" Mark asked.

"Yeah."

"You sure? Do you even know where your brother is?"

"I have a pretty good idea." She began to crawl away down the duct. When Mark hesitated, Kelly stopped. "What?"

"Let's get the case first. La Roche's room is just down the hall."

"Who cares about the case?"

"Shhh."

Kelly waited.

"It'll take forty-five minutes just to get to the south end, and we don't even know your brother's there. Besides, if we go traipsing back and forth across the station with him in tow, we'll probably get caught. We can get the case while we're here, and then when we find him we can just hole up somewhere."

Kelly shook her head and started off again.

"It'll take five minutes."

"Fine. You get the case. I'll go find my brother." She continued away, leaving a trail of red drops and hand prints behind her.

Mark let out a thick sigh. Kelly's need here was clearly greater than the professor's, but Mark had made a promise to La Roche that he didn't know how to break. Ultimately, it was the boy who swayed him. "Cripes." Mark hurried to catch up. Kelly couldn't even get out of the duct without the utility knife in Mark's pocket.

Together, they crossed the opening of a vertical duct that fed air upward from the facilities deck, and then they passed under several shafts leading to the upper floors of the habitation cylinder before coming to a grate that fed the interstitial between floors. Screws had been mounted from the outside, where Mark couldn't reach them, so he drilled them out using a bit from La Roche's knife. He set the grate aside and climbed through the hole.

They'd have to crouch all the way and climb over or around pipes and utility conduits hanging from the ceiling and crisscrossing the floor. Nevertheless, it was faster and quieter than trying to get around in the flimsy duct, where every echo carried through the vents to any room it fed.

Kelly followed him through and kept going.

"Wait up." Mark tacked the corners of the grate back into place with a welding laser on La Roche's knife and then hurried to catch up.

The thin, aluminite floors were sufficient to hold their weight but would communicate their footsteps to anyone below. So they tried to step on pipes and ceiling support trusses whenever they could.

At one point, Mark found a pinlight on the utility knife, clamped it between his teeth, and turned Kelly to face him. "Let me see your head."

A trickle of blood ran down her pretty little cheeks. Their softness, combined with the small point at the end of her nose, gave her face a quality that Mark thought of as, "cute that won't quit."

"Mark Torbin, are you flirting with me?"

"Always." Mark spoke around the pinlight. "Let me see." He brushed the hair away, tugging the pink strands that stuck in her dried blood.

"Ow." Her face crinkled. The synth was beginning to fade from her green eyes. "How bad is it, doctor?"

A deep laceration cut through the hairline above her left eye. "It's not bad, but you'll need some dermaplast." He ripped open a strip of gauze from the supply in his pocket and handed it to her. "It's still bleeding. Hold this on it."

She did. "Can't you just kiss it for me?"

Mark couldn't tell if it was the synth talking. He pecked her on the lips. "That'll have to do. We've got to keep moving."

La Roche touched his bruised cheek tenderly as he squeezed his way back through the crowd to the media room. A stab of pain pierced his face. The bone was cracked. It must be.

Kelly and Mark were nowhere near the door and no sound came from inside, so he entered the room as though he didn't know that the guards on the catwalk were watching him.

The kids might as well have ransacked the place. Leaving the chair and box in the middle of the floor was bad enough, but they'd also set the grate crookedly over the vent hole. A red handprint marked the ceiling beside it, blood spattered the floor, and first-aid supplies littered the tabletop.

A soldier barged in behind La Roche. "Sir, there's no exit here. Please come into the main room."

La Roche glanced up to let the man see his crushed face, hoping the sight of it would keep his attention from the floor and ceiling. "I'm not looking for an exit." He spun back to the first-aid kit, kicking one of the curtains across the worst of the blood spatters on the floor, and rummaged through the supplies until he found the Deadzone painkillers. He popped open the cap, swallowed two capsules, and made a show of stuffing the bottle into his front pocket.

The soldier wore suspicion like a mask. He looked over the scattered medical supplies and then at La Roche. La Roche schooled his expression to neutrality, inclined his head politely, and walked past him toward the auditorium.

The soldier grabbed him and thrust a finger at the handprint on the ceiling. "Who went through there?"

"How should I know? I was getting my head spun around just for trying to talk to your boss. Which I still intend to do." If he couldn't make the man believe him, La Roche would never get back in to retrieve his case.

The soldier shoved him into the auditorium and keyed the comm link in his ear. "Get me Lieutenant Han."

Chapter 3

When Colonel Chang climbed down the ladder from *Venus Rain*'s stationary axis into the partial gravity of the spinning control room, his men had already secured the place. Six of the eight civilians who'd been working in Center now stood behind their chairs with their hands shackled. The other two, the man at the engineering console and the woman on comm, slumped in their seats, executed without warning to prevent them from shutting their stations down or broadcasting a mayday.

"Gentlemen of *Venus Rain*," Chang said, "I have no need of your services." He motioned forward two of his own guards. "Get them out of here."

Once they were gone, Chang's men brought in station director Shou Jijin.

"Give me the access codes for station operations and security," Chang said.

Shou stiffened. "I will not."

"Are you loyal to the People's Republic?"

A brief pause. "Of course."

"Are you loyal to President Li?"

"Yes."

"Good. I'm here upon direct orders from President Li Muyou," Chang said. "You will give me the access codes."

Shou hesitated. "Can you prove that claim?"

Chang slapped the man's face, nearly hard enough to knock him down. "I am in control here."

"Not without the codes." Shou faced him defiantly, a red flush brightening the assaulted side of his face. "Without them, you can do nothing."

Chang's men had captured many of the terminals with accounts still logged in. That would help in the near term, but it was unlikely that the civilians had left Chang access to everything he needed. He leaned forward, placing his grotesque face within inches of Shou's, his voice low and threatening. "You think I came here without a plan? I don't need your codes. I merely hoped you would save me time."

He drew his pistol from its holster and clicked off the safety. "I'm going to ask you one more time. Give me the codes."

Shou's internal deliberation took longer than expected. Chang knew as much about the man as anyone could without having actually met him before. Every file, record, and scrap of information about Shou had been compiled and uploaded to Chang's ship before it even left Earth, as had those of every other resident of *Venus Rain*. The flight had given Chang two weeks to study them.

In that time, he'd at least skimmed every document. For those of the more important persons on station, including Shou Jijin, Chang had practically memorized the file. Unfortunately, he had no point of leverage against Shou, no family on or off the station that he could threaten, no monetary asset worth treason—except for maybe Shou's career, and Chang had already cost him that. Shou would refuse.

"No."

Chang slammed the butt of his pistol against Shou's temple and the station director dropped, unconscious, to the floor. Chang turned to the soldier who had escorted Shou in. "Take him to the hold." To the rest of his men, he said, "Those of you with logged-in terminals, take your stations."

Private Huang and Corporal Ming each had to shove a body out of his seat before he could sit down.

"Is comm logged in?" Chang asked Huang.

"Yes, sir."

"Shut down all relays. No outgoing transmissions of any kind. Private Qin and those of you without access, follow me."

"Rod could be in any one of three places." Kelly ducked a waste pipe that ran across the ceiling of the interstitial. The place was quiet, save for the characteristic vibration of the floor, the hum of the shafts, and an occasional gurgle from the pipes. No footsteps came to them from the rooms above. No voices found their way through the thin aluminite ceiling on which the two walked. It was as if the station itself had been stunned to silence by the brutality of the lockdown. "He likes to watch the guys run the facilities equipment. There's a window at the south end of the station that overlooks the maintenance deck."

"I've seen it."

"Or he could be in one of the lounges that look out on the planet. He got his allowance day before yesterday. He might have bought an ice cone and gone there to eat it. I swear he's going to be a planetary or facilities engineer someday." She fell silent. The southern ring had dozens of observation lounges among the pubs, restaurants, and dignitaries' quarters that hogged most of the view. Her brother could be in any of them.

"And the third?"

"Huh?"

"You said there were three places he might have gone."

"If he's out with a friend, they probably went to buy candy on the Concourse." The Concourse was two floors up. "If he did that, they could be anywhere by now."

Two more soldiers arrived in the auditorium. La Roche clenched his jaw. One, identified by his uniform as Lieutenant Han, was the man who'd shot Raji. The soldiers, along with the one who'd confronted La Roche over the bloody handprint, drew him once again into the media room. The other newcomer, a small man in full combat gear—a private by the insignia on his arm—stripped his helmet and flack jacket and climbed into the environmental duct.

Han came at La Roche with a kubaton, a short rod no longer than his hand. He shoved La Roche against the workbench, pressed the shaft of the weapon across his throat, and peered through half-closed eyes. "Who went through the ceiling? Where did he go?"

La Roche could only gurgle and choke in reply.

Han eased up on his windpipe. "Answer."

"I . . ." La Roche gasped for breath. "Don't know."

A 13-mm pistol appeared in Han's hand. His eyes widened momentarily and a sneer of suppressed glee pulled at the corners of his mouth. He pressed the gun between La Roche's eyebrows and pushed his head back. "Who is he?"

La Roche glanced at the handprint and forced calm into his voice. "What makes you think I have any idea? It could've been anybody."

"You created a diversion," said the corporal who'd found the handprint. "Then came here to see if your friend escaped."

"I came for the first-aid kit." His back and neck began to protest. "That print could have been there for weeks, for all I know, made by some maintenance worker."

"The blood on the floor is sticky."

"Let's assume—" La Roche forced the words past his stressed larynx. "Let's assume for the sake of argument that I know who left it. Shooting me isn't going to get you an answer."

Han grabbed the front of La Roche's collar and hurled him into the parts cabinet with a crash, denting its aluminum doors.

La Roche lay there for a moment, waiting for the Deadzone to react, wishing he'd taken more of the pills.

The private who'd crawled into the airshaft dropped to the floor and spoke to his lieutenant in Chinese. "It's no good. Someone left the shaft about thirty meters down and welded the vent closed behind him."

La Roche, as always, pretended not to understand Chinese. Whenever he was asked why he never learned the language, he spouted some crap about European nationalism. Otherwise he just let people attribute it to the arrogance of the French.

Han spun on the corporal and responded in the same language. "Where do you suppose he got a welding laser? From a planetary science teacher? Why do you think the professor knows something?"

"I . . . I just thought . . ."

La Roche lay gasping on the floor. The Deadzone was beginning to work on both his nerves and reflexes.

"Corporal?" Han prompted.

"I thought he was just creating a distraction at the door. He came straight here—"

"Start the DNA scans. Account for everybody on the station." Lieutenant Han left the room in three heavy strides.

The private collected his gear and headed into the auditorium.

La Roche climbed stiffly to his feet and followed. He didn't take an easy breath until the corporal accompanied him out and closed the door.

Kelly stood over the access hatch to the southern corridor of the rotating cylinder that formed the skin of *Venus Rain*, hesitant to leave the safety of the interstitial.

"You okay?" Mark asked.

"Yeah." She pulled the gauze from her forehead. "Has it stopped bleeding?"

He glanced at the wound. "For the moment."

Kelly searched the area for a place to stash the gauze until Mark stuck out his hand. She lay the soaked dressing in it, unwilling to touch more than a corner of the bandage.

Without hesitation, Mark wadded it up and stuffed it into his back pocket, wiped the blood from his hand onto his pants, and swung the hatch open. He poked his head through the opening and scanned the hallway below. "It's clear."

There was no ladder, so he lowered his body through until he hung by his hands, then dropped the last half meter to the floor. After that, he helped Kelly down.

The cylinder had a dozen observation lounges on this deck alone and there was no guarantee her brother would be in any of them. "How will we find him?" Mark asked.

"Let's try the maintenance deck first."

Kelly jogged down the empty corridor without seeing so much as a custodial robot. She and Mark paused to check each adjoining hall for Chang's soldiers before crossing. The station seemed deserted.

They stopped at one of the lounges. A nut bar and packet of real beef chips from the nearest food-vend littered the end table. A mug of coffee had overturned onto the blue and gold upholstery of one of the cushioned sofas. The immense orb of Venus loomed in defiant majesty beyond the floor-to-ceiling windows, daring humanity to try to build a life on its sweltering surface.

Mark plucked a thinpad from the floor near the pot of a plastic-looking philodendron plant. "Whoever this belongs to is still logged in."

"To the telnet?"

"Just this document." He handed Kelly the small electronic pad. The file looked like a half-finished project report.

"Figures." She threw it onto the sofa. Like everybody else on station, the author obviously didn't know how to leave his work at work.

"Come on." She hurried to the maintenance observation deck, where a single window offered a view of the machinery and operations on the deck below, provided by the station's architect for the benefit of touring politicians and dignitaries—anyone who might provide funding for the Venus Project. This hall, too, was empty.

"Damn." Kelly stopped and scrubbed her hair. Pain knifed through her when she touched the forgotten wound on her forehead. The synth was gone now, her mind clear. Still, she couldn't think. The usually-teeming halls of *Venus Rain*, as deserted now as a derelict vessel, were too disorienting. Too much like a nightmare. "Where is he? Where is everybody?"

"In lockdown."

"No, look." Kelly gestured to the deck below. "They left the equipment unattended. There's not a soul down there."

Mark shrugged. "I guess Chang's afraid of sabotage."

Kelly's head began to throb dully. Pain radiated from the laceration like veins of fire in her forehead. Her hands roamed her pockets once more. If she had it, synth would kill the pain. "Where is he?"

She walked the length of the window, pressing the heel of her fisted hand against the bridge of her nose. Her brother could be anywhere. She really had no idea where he went after school. This had been a guess, nothing more.

When her jaw began to ache, she unclenched her teeth. "Damn it. Where is he?"

"Shhhh." Mark ran to her. He grabbed her by the shoulders and pressed her into one of the cushioned benches that lined the wall opposite the window. "Relax for a minute. We'll find him."

"If they haven't gotten him already."

"So what if they have? Look at me. Kelly, he's nine. They're not going to hurt him."

Tears moistened the blood on her cheek. "He must be scared. Look at my hands shaking. I'm terrified. What's a kid going to think?" She lowered her head and sobbed into her palms. "They shot her. She was standing there, and they just shot her."

Mark sank to his knees and hugged her close until her body stopped trembling and the tears subsided.

She leaned away from him. "I don't know what they'll do to him. I don't know what they'll do to any of us. I just want to know he's safe."

Mark glanced up and down the corridors, then at the security scanner down the hall. Two bathrooms and a third door broke the smooth line of the wall opposite the windows. A small maintenance door that stood unobtrusively beside the vast window provided ladder access to the deck below. "If he's hiding, he won't be out here in the hall. Let's check the bathrooms."

Kelly took his hand and let him pull her to her feet. She lifted her chin toward a security scanner near the ceiling. "Think they're watching?"

"Probably." Mark pushed open the door to the men's room, drew Kelly in, and checked the stalls. Then he led her to the ladies room and entered without knocking.

Kelly grabbed a handful of paper towels and activated the sink. Blood caked her left cheek. Makeup smeared both sides of her face and a deep cut gaped open on her forehead. Her pink-streaked hair stood out in shoots and tangles. A weak laugh escaped her throat, but by the time it passed her lips she was crying. "Look at me."

Mark came up behind her, wrapped his arms around her waist, and kissed her neck. "You're beautiful."

"If you're going to lie, at least make it convincing."

"Turn around." He took the wad of towels from her hand, set half of them on the counter, and ran the other half under the warm faucet. He wiped the blood from her face and the makeup from beneath her eyes. Blood had dripped onto the bare skin of her chest and abdomen. He wet the towels again and scrubbed her clean. The warm sensation sent tingles up Kelly's neck and down between her legs.

She took a deep breath.

"Feel better?"

She nodded weakly.

He pulled a wad of packets and bandages from his front pocket and dropped them onto the counter. Several tumbled into the sink. Mark ignored them. He soaped a wet towel and cleaned the cut on Kelly's forehead.

She stiffened her neck and jaw against the pain and tried to hold herself still while he finished. Mark ripped the top off a foil tube of dermaplast and squeezed it into the wound. Instantly, the anesthetic in the salve soothed the pain. He pressed the wound closed, held it for a few seconds for the dermaplast to set, and stretched a bandage across it.

He gazed at her as though she really was beautiful.

She smiled. "Thanks. You make—"

His wet lips covered hers. His probing tongue cleansed her mind of whatever she'd been about to say. For a moment, the whole absurd lockdown and the brutal events that started it really were nothing more than a dream.

Then the bathroom door crashed open.

CHAPTER 4

"Let me talk to them," La Roche told Lieutenant Han. "They respect me. I can make your job easier."

Chang's executioner eyed him for a long moment through his half-lidded eyes.

"You don't have enough men to watch the doors, collect the samples, and enforce segregation of the people you've scanned from those you haven't. You're going to need their cooperation."

Still Han hesitated.

La Roche let him. This was the man he must get past or through in order to get to Chang. Helping with the scans, a task Han would complete in any case, was at least one small step La Roche could take toward gaining his trust.

Han's gaze swept the assembly hall, in which nearly a thousand people milled, and then went to his handful of soldiers.

With the auditorium filled beyond capacity, he couldn't simply force everyone to sit down while he carried the DNA scanner from aisle to aisle. He was going to have to form some sort of line and manage everyone through it, which served La Roche's purpose better. He needed Han to stay put.

If you talk to them yourself, La Roche wanted to say, *they'll fight you.* But he kept his mouth shut. That conclusion would be more compelling if Han came to it on his own.

"What are you going to say?"

"That it's in their best interest to get themselves scanned."

"It *is* in their best interest."

"You and I know that." La Roche gestured at the audience. "Who's going to tell them? You?"

Han was sold. La Roche could see it in his eyes. "I'll need the microphone." He climbed painfully onto the stage. "It's turned off in the media room."

Han keyed the link in his ear. A moment later, the soldier at the media room door stepped in to turn on the audio. La Roche suppressed a smile. He now had an excuse to go into there later and retrieve his case.

When he reached the microphone, he tapped on it with his finger, sending dull thumps throughout the auditorium, until the room went silent.

"Ladies and gentlemen, please, may I have your attention."

Nearly every person in the room met his gaze, expectant faces hungry for news.

"General Chang is taking roll, making sure everyone is accounted for. His men want to scan the DNA of everyone on station, starting with this room."

Grumbling came from the audience. Several people shouted complaints or disparagements, but La Roche couldn't make them out. He raised his hands, palms out, and gestured for silence until most of the crowd was listening again.

"No harm can come from this," he continued. Except to Kelly and Mark, and anyone else who might try to oppose the lockdown. But Chang would identify the stragglers soon enough anyway. If Han's trust came at a price to those kids, that was a tragedy La Roche would have to endure, but they must deliver his case first.

"Colonel Chang undoubtedly has access to *Venus Rain*'s manifest. He knows you're all on station. Don't cause trouble for yourself. Get yourself accounted for. Otherwise he'll consider you a fugitive."

The audience grumbled again, more subdued this time.

"Half the station's population must be in this room. The sooner we get this done, the sooner Chang can move us to more comfortable quarters."

"Like home?" someone shouted.

"Yes. Like home." La Roche gestured at Chang's executioner. "Here's the offer Lieutenant Han has made."

Han stiffened at the edge of La Roche's vision. He'd made no offer.

La Roche refused to look at him. "As soon as he's scanned everybody, he'll start escorting us in groups to the bathroom." Han was going to have to address bladder and bowel relief sooner or later anyway, so he might as well agree to the proposal now. The way La Roche offered it, it provided an incentive for the audience's cooperation. Furthermore, it delayed the lavatory visits until after the scans, when Han might have the resources to provide escorts. It was a boon all the way around. If La Roche was lucky, Han would recognize that.

Han leaned forward as though he wanted to storm the stage, but he held his position and said nothing.

"So here's what I'd like you to do," La Roche continued. "Those of you who had seats, return to them. If you were standing for the presentation, line up along the left-hand wall." He pointed to clarify that he meant the audience's left, not his own. "Han will scan you first, and then he'll start the rest of us filing by rows down to the front of the stage." He motioned for Han to set up his team there.

"I don't like this any better than you do," he added so a few of them might not think he'd sold out to the Chinese. "But I don't see a downside at the moment and I'd hate to see what'll happen if we make them do this the hard way." Raji's covered body still lay behind him on the stage.

La Roche led by example. The soldiers already knew who he was. Since he was the keynote speaker for the ceremony, fliers and banners all over the station displayed his name and image. He presented his forearm to the scanner. The device, not much larger than a thinpad, sampled a few of his skin cells, hummed for a moment, and displayed his name and image. If the man had scrolled down, he'd probably have seen La Roche's entire life history, at least those portions that had been fabricated for public consumption.

La Roche motioned for the first of the attendees to come forward. As they did, he returned to the podium and waited in silence until he was sure none of the soldiers were watching. Then he fished blindly beneath the lectern for the wires that fed the microphone cutoff switch. He yanked them from their fasteners to give himself room to work. With the wire cutters he'd taken from the media room, he stripped the insulation from both leads and returned the tool to his pocket.

La Roche surveyed the soldiers before continuing. None seemed to care what he did as long as he stayed on the public stage, where they thought he couldn't cause any trouble.

He twisted the stripped leads together, shorting the circuit and hard-wiring a bypass to the microphone switch.

The speakers crackled as the leads touched and Han's head whipped around.

"Sorry." La Roche backed away as though he'd accidentally bumped the microphone pickup. He stood there until Han turned his attention elsewhere. Then he moved forward as if to observe the progress of the scans.

Chang and three of his men, including Private Qin, a young soldier recruited out of the Ministry for State Security, rounded a final corner at the extreme north end of the station's cylinder. A sign on the door before them read, LOGISTICAL RESOURCES, AUTHORIZED PERSONNEL ONLY. The department title included all the qualities necessary for a cover organization, including vagueness of purpose and implied justification for the very real security measures that surrounded the place. Most important, it was completely boring.

The door, controlled by a card scanner and numeric keypad, barred access even to Chang. The only two people who knew the code were the man and woman who worked there—a Chinese counter-intelligence team, the people who had tipped off Chang's government to the clandestine activities of Raji Yanamandra.

Chang keyed the intercom.

"May I help you?" a voice said through the speaker.

"The chickens come home to roost," Chang said.

The man in Logistical Resources asked, "Where do they roost?" It was all part of the protocol.

"In a forbidden rice paddy."

"One minute."

Chang extracted his badge from his uniform pocket, held it before him, and waited until a chime sounded and the door slid open.

The employees of Logistical Resources, who also served as the local Mingyun satellite operation cell, confronted Colonel Chang and his men with automatic pistols that could pump out a thousand rounds a minute.

The woman reached cautiously forward and snatched Chang's badge. While her partner covered the visitors, she fed it into a card slot for authentication. It came back positive.

"They're clean," she said. "Please excuse our offensive protocol, Colonel. We didn't come up with it."

"You've done well." Chang took back his badge. "We may enter?" It wasn't quite a question.

The woman motioned them in. "Please." Beyond her, a floor-to-ceiling window revealed a spectacular view of space.

As soon as the door closed, Chang addressed the counter-intelligence team. "We need the back door. I assume it's still in place."

"Of course. But like everything else, there are protocols."

Chang motioned to Private Qin, and the boy stepped forward. Once his badge was authenticated, he and the woman sat down to work.

"I'll be in Center," Chang told them. "Let me know when we have access."

"Aww, gross, man!" Rod yelled as he barged into the bathroom.

"Rod!" Kelly nudged Mark away and ran to her little brother. He looked good. His blond hair was tousled, but no more than usual. His quick smile seemed absurd, given Chang's lockdown, though at that moment it couldn't have been beaming more than her own. All at once, she scooped him into her arms.

"Eww." He squirmed free.

"Mark, this is my brother."

"I gathered."

"His name is Henry."

The boy stuck out his hand like a grown-up, though his scrawny body stood no taller than Mark's shoulders. "I go by Rod."

Mark cocked an eyebrow at Kelly.

"He thinks it's cool or something. His name's Henry."

"Henry's some old guy's name. When I'm sixty, I'll go by Henry." He waved his arms in exasperation. "Why do you always do this? If I want to go by Rod, I can go by Rod."

"Cause it's gross." She winked at Mark.

"I hate to break up this touching family reunion," Mark said, "but we have to go. Scanner in the hall, remember?"

"I know where." Rod launched himself through the bathroom door and into the hall.

"Wait!" Kelly tried to catch him, but he was already gone.

Rod yanked open the door beside the observation window and climbed down the ladder to the facilities deck. "There's lots of hiding places down here."

Mark and Kelly followed him down.

The walls and floor vibrated with the hum of the equipment around them: air-circulating blowers, fluid and vacuum pumps, waste incineration furnaces, banks of electrical cabinets, power conditioners, junction relays, and equipment-cooling fans. Those were just a few of the labels Kelly read as she passed.

She stopped in front of an internal air processor, banks of pumps and filters that scrubbed CO_2 from the air—stripped the carbon from the oxygen—and kept the atmosphere in this octant of the station breathable. She didn't have to read the label here. She'd seen it before, on a field trip of sorts, during her first semester at Planet U. But then she'd seen it only through the observation window. Up close, it was massive. "This is so important to station operation and human survival. They should've left someone to watch it."

"If anything changes, something goes wrong or someone tampers with something, it'll show up on the maintenance grid in Center." Mark was trying to reassure her, and it was working. But there was another message in his words: Don't touch anything.

"Hey, guys," Rod yelled over the hum of the equipment, "check this out."

They walked around the air scrubber. Rod stood near an open port on a waste furnace that, according to the readouts, burned at a thousand degrees centigrade. An open rack of O-ring gaskets stood nearby. He picked one up and launched it like a rubber band into the opening of the furnace. It vaporized in midair before it reached the other side.

Rod laughed and shot another one. "Pretty cool, huh?"

Kelly grabbed his shoulders and spun him to face her. "Did you open this?" She had to shout over the noise.

"What do I look like?"

"Did you open it?"

"No." He brushed her hands off him. "Geez."

Mark grabbed them both and yanked them behind the scrubber. "We've got company."

Kelly crossed behind the machines until she found a piping rack with gaps large enough to see through to the observation window. Two soldiers looked down from the floor above. One had his finger on his ear, activating his comm link.

As far as La Roche knew, there was no accurate record of who had actually attended the anniversary ceremony. Han wouldn't be able to identify the missing until he ran everyone on station through the scanner, not just everyone in the auditorium.

Yet with the scans only half done, Han stopped to key the link in his ear. "Yes, sir," he said after a moment's pause. "I understand." He began to key codes into his thinpad.

La Roche stepped close enough to see its screen and stood respectfully, as though waiting for Han's attention.

An image from one of the station's many security scanners appeared. Kelly, Mark, and a boy of maybe ten years ran across a wide, empty corridor. La Roche caught only a glimpse before Han turned the screen away. La Roche pretended to neither notice nor care.

Han handed the thinpad to a subordinate. "Kelly Baker." He slurred the l's like r's, making the name nearly unrecognizable. "Henry Baker and Mark Torben. Make an example of them."

A moment later, Chang's voice came over the station-wide intercom. "Attention, residents. My name is Colonel Chang. I speak to you from Station

Center. Upon the authority of the People's Republic of China, I have placed *Venus Rain* under martial law. Make yourselves comfortable. If you are a Chinese national, you will be soon cleared and allowed to resume your duties."

La Roche listened carefully for anything Chang might let slip through his word choice or inflection.

"The rest of you will be moved to your quarters. You are prisoners of war, and you will remain such until current political developments between your countries and mine have been resolved. When a peace is negotiated, you will be also released."

Current political developments? Developed by whom? Chang's statement had included all non-Chinese personnel, regardless of nationality. If this was between China and some other single country, the instigator might have been in question, but this was between China and the rest of the worlds. Therefore, China was making some sort of power play.

"In the meantime," Chang continued without emotion. "I will permit no incoming or outgoing transmissions or space traffic. Upon completion of this message, station intercom will be deactivated.

"Anyone who fails to cooperate will be killed. Raji Yanamandra, a European spy, has already been executed. Heed that as your only warning."

As soon as Chang finished, Han spun on La Roche. "What do you want?"

"I'd like you to begin escorting us to the bathroom. I'm an old man. I haven't got the control I used to."

Han's mouth smiled, but his cold eyes remained shrouded by their lids. "I might like to see you piss in your pants."

His subordinates stood stone-faced or eyed La Roche's shattered features with hints of compassion.

"Take them," Han said to his men in Chinese. "If anyone escapes, I'll hold you personally responsible."

La Roche gave no hint that he understood the words. He waited until the guard motioned him toward the door before he thanked Han. This would at least get him beyond the confines of the auditorium. From there . . . well, from there . . . who knew?

"Did they see us?" Kelly asked.

"I couldn't tell." Mark led them around a series of tanks that held some of the station's recycled water supply. "But they know we're down here. They'd have seen that much on the scanner."

The three ran past what must have been fifty or a hundred tanks, each thousands of liters in capacity, until they'd moved well beyond sight of the observation deck and beyond much of the noise. The faint beeping of a status alarm reached them from somewhere ahead.

At one point, they found blood on the floor, smeared as though something had been dragged through it. Kelly's eyes followed the stain to a small space between two power conditioners. A body lay there, wearing the red jumpsuit of a station security officer.

Without a word, Mark took Kelly by the hand and started out again. They didn't get far before Chang's announcement came over the comm.

"Shhh," Kelly hissed when Rod tried to speak halfway through.

"But—"

"Shhh!"

As soon as Chang finished, Rod said, "Mom's on Venus."

Mark looked at Kelly. His dark eyes grew wide.

"She'll get back," she said.

"How?" Rod asked. "That Chang guy said no space traffic."

"They'll let her come home," Kelly said. "She's no threat to them."

Mark squatted next to Rod and put a hand on his shoulder. "She's no good as a hostage if they let her die down there." He tried to sound reassuring, but something in his voice betrayed his doubt.

"Come on." Kelly turned roughly away. "Let's keep moving."

Mark caught up, leaving Rod several paces behind, and whispered, "Do you know what the temperature is down there, even inside the processors?"

"Yes." More angry than afraid, Kelly glanced back at Rod to make sure he was out of earshot. "She'll be fine."

"No, she won't. Not for more than a few hours. How long has she been down there?"

"I don't keep track. And she doesn't bother to tell me."

"We've got to do something."

Kelly stopped. Her voice rose higher than it should have. "Fine. She's down there. We're up here. What are we supposed to do? At this point we'll be lucky if we can keep ourselves alive."

Rod came alongside and looked back and forth between them.

"I don't know," Mark admitted. "For starters, let's get the professor's case."

Kelly grabbed his arm before he could turn away. "How can you even think about that? We need to find a place to hide, or better yet, get back to the auditorium before they figure out we're gone. Who cares about the case?"

"I do. La Roche helped you find Rod. And we promised we would."

"That was then. Things are different now."

"How? You got what you wanted and to hell with the rest? Is that it?"

Kelly crossed her arms over her chest and said nothing.

"You do what you want," Mark said. "I'm going for the case."

A message from Chang, coded for every station in the Venus system, came over Amanda's comm on *VR-2*, where she'd taken refuge from the heat.

". . . For the duration of the standoff, no space traffic or communication will be allowed. Armed satellites patrol Venus space. Any ship in flight without my prior authority will be destroyed. You have been warned."

The comm channel cleared for maybe half a second when Chang stopped speaking, and then the squeal of jamming noise returned. No wonder she couldn't reach anyone on her comm.

"Well, that's that," she said aloud as she set down the mike, her throat raw from hailing the station for the past four hours in the parched air of the shuttle. She should have taken off as soon as she'd finished her maintenance. Chang couldn't very well hold her responsible if she'd been in flight before his announcement. But station and company protocol prohibited her from launching without clearance.

Now she was stuck here, and Kelly and Rod were somewhere on station. They were all prisoners of the People's Republic. Prisoners of war. Hostages, no matter what Chang chose to call them.

In fact, he'd taken the entire Venus system hostage. The people of *Venus Rain*, sure. But also those of *New Hope* and *Hera*. The stations, satellites, ships, even Venus herself, was a hostage.

What the hell gave him the right? She punched off the comm and powered down *VR-2*'s environmental system. The short-range bird had been designed for a single purpose, to withstand the pressure and temperature of the Venusian atmosphere. With typical flight times of less than six hours, it hadn't been built for endurance. The battery had already reached redline. If Amanda drained it further, it wouldn't have enough juice left to run the startup sequence if she ever did get permission to launch.

The problem was, Chang didn't know she was there. He wasn't from the company. He couldn't comprehend the maintenance required to keep the Terraforming Project in motion. When he did find out, and when someone explained the deadly conditions on the surface, he'd authorize her return. Oh, he'd watch her closely, and the guns of his satellites would target her all the way back, but he would allow her to return.

Then she could at least comfort, if not help, her kids. Kelly might be coping. No, she was a wreck. Rod was probably doing better than she was. In truth, Amanda didn't know how her children would handle Chang's presence. She didn't even know what their circumstances were, where they were being held, or how they were being treated.

When it came down to it, she didn't really know them at all. She'd been such a peripheral part of their lives for so long. Yet that had been necessary since their father left. The cost of living was bad enough, but Amanda insisted that Kelly and Rod finish their education. In three more years, Kelly could get a job with the company. Not a lucrative job, perhaps, but enough to get by. Enough to live on station or to take her someplace she actually wanted to be.

Maybe then Amanda could cut back her overtime and get to know her son. Hopefully before he reached that critical age. Before Amanda's absence from his life drove him to Kelly's justified bitterness. Before he too shut out his mother for good.

The air in the cabin began to grow stale. If she had a pressure suit, its cooling system might be enough to keep her alive until Center realized she was there, but the company shuttles didn't carry them. So she popped the hatch and climbed out into the sweltering processor. She'd have to find another way to survive.

⮜⟨○⟩⮞

Kelly hurried to keep up as Mark wound his way through the interstices of the machinery, avoiding the many alleyways that were monitored by security scanners.

"I thought you were going back to the auditorium," Mark said.

"I can't just walk in. I'll have to climb through the vent."

They passed a panel with a beeping LN_2 alarm. Liquid nitrogen. Something was running out of coolant. That would get somebody's attention.

When Mark stopped, he did so in front of a lift. "Let me ask you something. You ever keep a promise? Even once in your life?"

Kelly shrugged. "I don't make promises."

Rod reached for the lift button and Mark grabbed his arm. "They'll see its movement on the grid." He grabbed Kelly's hand and led them both around the corner. They passed a machine shop, a bank of supply and parts cabinets, and a rolling toolbox.

Mark pointed to an aluminum ladder leaning against the wall. "Grab that." Instead, Rod picked up a laser scribe and engraved swirling patterns on the wall.

Kelly snatched it from his hand, slammed it onto the workbench, and went to get the ladder. By the time she got back, Rod had recovered the scribe and drawn a stick figure with angry eyes and long fangs. He labeled it, "Princess Kelly."

"Damn it, Rod." She snatched the scribe again and threw it into a nest of coiled electrical cables. "Come on." She took him by the wrist and yanked him after Mark.

The three doubled back to an access hatch that led to the interstitial and set up the ladder beneath it.

"Hey!" The shout came down the alleyway. A Chinese soldier pointed his pistol at Kelly. When she turned to run, he fired.

Chapter 5

United States President Victoria Powers walked into the Situation Room, leaning heavily on the cane she usually carried on her arm, followed by her massive Chief of Staff, Warren Parker. Secretary of Defense Dan Norton, Thomas O'Leary from the CIA Office of Asian Pacific Analysis, and two of his aides were already there.

The scene was all too familiar to Powers. Too familiar and too recent. It smacked of the conflict, in which she herself had played a part, over China's Mingyun satellite program four months before. By the time that crisis had ended, the United States had destroyed the missile satellites in Earth orbit and China had agreed to retrieve and dismantle the one orbiting the Moon.

But there were more. As a show of good faith, or so Powers had thought, China disclosed a number of other missile satellites around Mercury and Venus, and still more within the Jupiter system. Because of the time and preparation needed to retrieve a deployed satellite, Powers had given China a year to take them all down.

Since that disclosure, the lunar satellite was the only one China had actually recovered.

Norton and O'Leary stood when Powers entered the room, their chairs scraping the hardwood floor. Usually annoyed by such displays of respect, especially from Norton, whose gestures lacked even feigned sincerity, Powers was too absorbed in her own thoughts to retort.

"Where's your staff?" she asked Norton.

"On its way."

Warren Parker pulled out the president's seat but made no move to help her into it. She wasn't nearly as decrepit as this crisis made her feel. She leaned her cane against the edge of the table and sank into the chair. Just then, a dozen military officers and analysts poured into the room and sat down.

"Let's get started." Powers' voice was strong and, like her features, had the aspect of granite—hard and immovable—when she exercised her authority. "Briefly, what do we know?"

Norton motioned to an aide, who stood and slid a data card into a slot in the tabletop. The hologram emitter in the center of the table came to life. An image of Venus hovered over it, surrounded by a swarm of colored dots, all but three of which orbited the planet.

"This is Venus as it looked yesterday," the aide began. "The three incoming ships are a supply convoy for the Chinese station *Venus Rain*." He pressed a button on the console and the station jumped in size, out of scale with the rest of the image, until it grew large enough for Powers to make out the spin of the habitation cylinder.

"Because China has led the Terraforming Project since its inception, they own most of the hardware around the planet." He pressed another button and over half of the orbiting swarm turned red. Three of the dots blinked. "These three are Mingyun satellites. With them, China covers all of Venus control space.

"Our station is here." One blip grew to show the awkward spurs of *New Hope*, large enough to house a hundred people but too small to generate its own artificial gravity. "The majority of our assets are communications or atmospheric analysis satellites. Some have imaging capability, but at the moment, we can't talk to them. China's jamming the signals." He didn't have to point out that none of the American assets were military in nature.

"This is what long-range scans show of Venus today." O'Leary spoke with a slight brogue. He pressed a button and the dots in the swarm grew at least tenfold in size, representing the limited resolution achievable from Earth. The enlarged image of *Venus Rain* disappeared, lost in a cloud of red. "China appears to have shifted the orbits of all its satellites and deployed enough chaff and decoys to make their real assets indistinguishable from the clutter."

A long-range missile strike was obviously impractical. And the ultimatum that had come to Powers directly from Chinese President Li Muyou had threatened the hostages should anyone try to approach Venus. But Li assumed China would see them coming.

"What's the status of our Covert Armed Tactical Spacecraft?" Powers asked Norton.

"We have four CATS ready to fly: *Jaguar*, *Snow Leopard*, and the two new ships: *Cheetah* and *Black Panther*. But we won't have an orbital launch window for Venus for seventeen months. We do have a window for Mercury. With a solar orbit of only eighty-eight days, it'll catch up to Venus in just four months."

Secretary of State Tony Mariano walked in. His deep-set eyes scanned the assembly from beneath dark, hairy brows. As he took his seat, everyone fell into silence. "Sorry I'm late. Are we discussing military options already?"

"No," Powers said, despite Norton's nod and the statements Mariano had obviously overheard. The last thing she could afford was to overreact. "We're assessing the situation and taking an inventory of assets. What have you heard from the embassies?"

"The European Union received the same communication we did, nearly verbatim. President Hunt has offered to send a delegation here, so they might work with us to 'resolve the standoff.' Those are his words."

"And Russia?" Powers lay her cane across her lap and began tapping the end with her wedding ring.

"This is where it gets interesting." Mariano shifted in his seat. His mustache twitched on his lip. "Li's offered Petrov a deal. If Petrov recognizes China as the sovereign owner of Venus, China will issue Russian companies exclusive contracts to supply hydrogen for the Terraforming Project—"

Norton slammed his palm on the table. "He'll never go for it."

"Dan?" Powers prompted.

"The Terraforming Project is temporary. He'll never give up Russia's piece of Venus for a few decades of economic prosperity."

"I'm not done." Mariano's brows came together over his eyes. "China has very little ore industry in the Jupiter system, or anywhere else for that matter. They've also offered Russia exclusive contracts for ore and ice for all of its country's extraterrestrial needs, including those on Venus, indefinitely."

Parker let out a long, low whistle.

"Still," Norton said. "We're talking about an entire planet here. As soon as China's established on the Venus surface, it can supply its own needs."

Mariano continued. "We're talking about shutting the United States and Europe out of the ore, ice, and hydrogen markets, and the resources and real estate of Venus. It'll take nearly a century for China to become self-sufficient on Venus. The prosperity Russia can attain in that time could squeeze us out of the international economic and political arenas for good."

Both men were exaggerating, yet both had valid points. The truth was, no one could predict the consequences of such an agreement. The best of economic and political projections, compiled or calculated by the most respected experts with a wealth of computer models and historical data, were mere speculation. Interplanetary dynamics shifted too greatly, and too often, for models to be of more than vague predictive value. For proof, one only had to look at the politics of the Venus Project over the past twenty-four hours. The best anyone could do was to run a multitude of simulations, over a wide range of assumptions, and play the averages.

Nevertheless, their arguments laid out the strengths and weaknesses of the military and economic options for the four major political powers—the four countries with expansive space programs, which every other country paid into for the privilege of claiming its piece of the extraterrestrial pie.

"There's an awful lot of bargaining room to be had in the next hundred years," Mariano said. "Russia will be in favor with China and they'll have the wealth and resources to offer virtually any price for the right of settlement on whole continents of Venus."

Powers banged the butt of her staff on the floor. "That's enough, gentlemen. We've ventured too far into speculation. I need something concrete. How did Petrov respond?"

"He hasn't."

"Then we have time to influence his decision. In the meantime, we can take economic steps against China."

"We certainly can." Norton punched a command into the hologram generator. The image changed to a diagram of the solar system with each planet shown in its current position relative to the others.

He stood and made his way to the front of the room. His appearance was artificial, the product of hair implants, dye, and dermal regeneration, but his youthful exuberance for all things martial was real, and a little overstated for Powers' taste. Norton's love of military options drew him to creativity and ambition in his planning, which was the reason she had appointed him to her cabinet.

But her memory of the China Dominion Affair, and the interplanetary war it nearly sparked, urged her towards caution.

"China needs hydrogen to produce water on Venus," Norton began. "That's the crux of the Terraforming Project, its Achilles' heel. Without it, China can't terraform. And without terraformation, Venus is a dead rock.

"The hydrogen comes from Jupiter's atmosphere, from which there's a direct orbital launch window to Venus every eight months. But they ship most of the hydrogen via Mercury, which provides a window every three and a half months. If we send the stealth fleet to Mercury, we can shut those shipments down." His face lit with the possibilities.

Mariano shook his head. "Some of those shipments are Russian. If we stop them, Petrov will view it as an act of war."

Norton leaned forward with his fists on the table. "I suppose you have a better idea?"

The corner of Powers' mouth crept up. Watching these two was like watching a pair of grade-school kids deciding whether to play tag or catch the shooting star.

"Send the CATS to Venus," Mariano said. "Address the problem with the Chinese. Leave the Russian shipments alone, at least until we can negotiate a deal with them."

"Aren't you listening? We just missed our window for Venus. We won't get another one for seventeen months." Norton raised his brows, waiting to shoot down Mariano's next idea.

Mariano was undeterred. "How about a Trojan horse? China claims any ship approaching Venus will be viewed as a threat. But Venus has three manned space stations. If this thing drags out for months, and I don't see how it can't, China won't have the stores to supply them all."

O'Leary cleared his throat. "That's right. If China put troops on *Venus Rain* to pull this off, those troops arrived on yesterday's supply caravan. We can get troops in the same way."

"We're talking about Li Muyou," President Powers said, "the man who perpetrated a sterilization crusade upon his own people. We can't count on his sense of human compassion to allow a supply ship in. I think he'll stop the supplies to force a quick resolution. The way he'll see it, we'll have to back down or let our people starve."

"Besides," Norton added. "What are the troops going to do when they get to New Hope? Watch Venus Rain from across the void?"

"Send stealth ships with the freighters," Mariano suggested.

Norton thrust a finger at the hologram. "We'll have to base them on Mercury until we get a window from there to Venus. China's Mercury base is less than a hundred kilometers from ours. They can watch the CATS land."

"Don't land them," Mariano said. "Land the supply ship. That's what a normal freighter would do—but hide the stealth ships in orbit."

One of the military aides spoke. "Have you seen the crew compartment in a CATS? They're fighting ships, designed for interplanetary travel, yes, but that takes only weeks. You can't ask a crew to sit aboard one for four months."

Deflated, Mariano sat back in his seat.

"We've got another problem," O'Leary said. "Stopping the hydrogen shipments at Mercury is only a temporary measure. If we want to also keep the direct shipments away from Venus, we'll have to stop them at their source."

"Gentlemen." Powers' quiet voice carried enough authority to silence everyone. "I've listened to your arguments. What we need are viable options. Tony, you work on Russia. Go through the embassy, but work your way up to President Petrov if you have to. We need Russia behind us. They're the only ones with the leverage to bring this to a peaceful conclusion. I'll contact President Li directly and see if he's amenable to humanitarian shipments to New Hope. Warren, arrange for the arrival of the European delegation. Their stake in this is as big as ours. We'll bring them in on the meetings. That proved pivotal last time around."

"Yes, Madam President."

"O'Leary." President Powers brought up the previous hologram of the long-range scans of Venus. "Penetrate that cloud of deception. Locate the Mingyun satellites. And generate an inventory of strategic resources in the

Venus system. Food, water, oxygen, hydrogen, anything we can leverage. If we can't supply *New Hope*, I want to know what our deadline is."

Powers fixed her gaze on each of her staff. She'd promised herself she wouldn't overreact, but there was no way she was going to let Li Muyou, or anybody else, hijack Venus. "Remember, people, *viable* options."

Within minutes, Tony Mariano was back on the comm. Having already spent an hour talking to Russia's ambassador to the United States, he asked for, and was granted, a conversation directly with Foreign Affairs Minister Dmitry Zhukov.

"I understand hydrogen is a lucrative business," he told Zhukov. "But withholding it from the Venus Project is the strongest form of political sanction we can apply."

"I don't believe you do understand." On the screen, Zhukov's gray eyes burned beneath the few scraggly strands of silver that still clung to his scalp. He adjusted the square-rimmed glasses on his bulbous nose. "Hydrogen is more than a 'lucrative business,' as you put it. The industries of Jupiter provide the funding for all of Russia's extraterrestrial endeavors, as well as supplying our country with natural resources for which we would otherwise depend on other nations."

"That's true for America as well, and for the European Union." In fact, it was a matter of international law. The Third Outer Space Treaty prohibited nations from depleting Earth's own resources to fund or supply space stations. Space exploration and population must be self-funded, self-supplied efforts. After all, the objective of the space program for every country in the world, whether it participated actively or not, was to ease the human burden on Earth, not to increase it.

"We're not talking about ore," Mariano continued. "We're talking about hydrogen. And only hydrogen destined for Venus. You can still bring shipments to Earth for hydrogen fuels, or to other space stations for fusion power."

"You are familiar with the Jupiter Union of Mining Personnel?" Zhukov asked.

"Of course." JUMP was the workers' union that encompassed all major industries in the Jupiter system: ice, ore, and hydrogen.

"JUMP links the industries together. If we disrupt one, the workers will shut down the rest."

Exasperation crept into Mariano's voice. "I'm talking about a short-term disruption."

"You're talking about a political gambit, but you have no idea how long it will take to convince President Li to back down." Zhukov paused and scratched at his blubberous upper lip. "Let me ask you this. How long can your Venus station survive without supply? And if China runs out of hydrogen, how long do you think Li is willing to suspend the Terraforming Project to win sovereignty over the planet?"

"Under no circumstances will we allow China sovereignty over Venus. And neither should you."

"I'm just saying time is on his side. He can wait you out. Stopping the shipments will not bring you victory."

"Then we'll fight." Dismissing Zhukov's valid point, Mariano changed tacks. "Li has offered you exclusive supply contracts for supporting his claim of sovereignty?"

"That's correct."

"Why would you accept such a deal?" Every other planetoid in the solar system was just rock. Rock with resources, but rock nonetheless. They'd never be habitable by humans in any real quantity, never habitable without the benefit of an artificial environment. But Venus . . . Venus was a sister Earth, a brand-new start. It would become a world that lived and breathed. "Countries have gone to war, century after century, for small tracts of land on Earth. Why would you not fight for your share of an entire planet? Surely that's worth a temporary economic disruption, however long it might last."

Zhukov straightened in his seat. "We have not accepted the Chinese proposal. Attractive as it is, there is much room for negotiation. China cannot hope to win against the three of our countries—"

"That's my point."

"Venus is a big world. We might yet carve out whole continents for Russian occupancy before this deal is done. And frankly, we've grown tired of Western arrogance. We'll no longer be pushed around by our larger neighbors. China has made an offer, and we will negotiate with them."

CHAPTER 6

A scream ripped past Kelly's throat as the bullet ricocheted off a pipe near her head. Adrenaline shot through her body, a high greater than synth, but she was too panicked to enjoy the sensation.

Another shot rang over the hum of equipment. The report scattered her thoughts until only one remained: *Run!* She sucked air into her lungs and fled, every breath her last—every step her last—until the bulk of a hydro-pump came between her and the soldier. Yet it didn't matter. She couldn't outrun him. He was too fast.

Mark turned another corner, grabbed a pipe wrench from the top of a toolbox, and ducked behind a massive water filter. "Keep going."

Fool. Kelly took another step.

Then Rod stopped.

Shit. Another step.

"Rod!" She threw the plea over her shoulder. "Run!"

As the soldier rounded the corner, Mark swung the wrench at his head.

The man blocked the blow with his gun hand, and his pistol sailed away. He gripped Mark's arm and twisted it behind his back. In the same motion, the soldier slammed Mark's head into the stainless steel bulk of the filter housing.

Kelly's mind raced ahead. *Get away,* it shouted, but her feet had already stopped.

Mark was the one who had chosen fight over flight, the one who, so full of testosterone, took a swing at the soldier. If the man crushed his skull, maybe it served him right.

But it wasn't just Mark. It was crazy, dumbshit Rod, with his worthless white belt in karate. Kelly could say a lot of things to her mother, but she couldn't tell her she'd gotten Rod killed.

Mark's head lolled on his shoulders. A gash that spanned the width of his cheek poured blood down his jaw. It sprayed the machinery crimson as the soldier flung him away.

"Rod." Kelly's voice was a strangled whisper.

The soldier drew a combat knife from his belt.

A gap between machines was open to Kelly's right, but Rod was caught in the corridor. He took up his best *tae kwon do* fighting stance.

"Don't try to run," the soldier said in Chinese. He flipped the knife to grip the blade, ready to throw it if the boy gave him cause.

Rod brandished his fists. "I ain't a-scared of you."

Kelly turned pleading eyes on the soldier and spoke in his own language. "Don't hurt him. He doesn't speak Chinese." That was true. But Rod certainly understood it well enough.

Mark groaned and twisted his head. He rolled as if he was trying to locate the ceiling but had forgotten which way was up.

When the soldier glanced down at him, Kelly darted into the side passage.

"Ha!" Rod yelled in authentic karate fashion.

Shit. Shit. Shit. What did he think? That three months of karate made him a pro?

Rod grunted, and Kelly heard him hit the floor.

She circled the machine and snatched up the soldier's gun. "You son of a bitch, get away from him."

She pulled the trigger to make sure the safety was off. The shell ripped a hole in the side of the filter, and water, rainbow-streaked with lubricant, streamed to the floor.

The soldier stared her down.

She aimed the gun and tried to look like she could kill him. Tension tightened her gut and synth withdrawal frayed her nerves. Adrenaline pumped need into her veins—the need to run. Her hands shook visibly. "Drop the fucking knife!" She didn't know if the man spoke English, but she couldn't force her mind to translate her words into Chinese.

The soldier loosened his fingers and the knife clattered to the floor. He relaxed his expression, put his hands over his head, and took a step toward Kelly. "You ever killed a man before?" He spoke in his own language, his tone calm and mocking. "I wouldn't have harmed you. Or the boy."

Mark lifted his head from the pooled water, dripping rivulets of blood into the puddle, and climbed to his knees.

Rod rounded the corner of the machine, holding his gut, and stood beside Kelly.

"There, you see." The guard took another step forward.

Kelly stepped back. She tried to squeeze the trigger, but the life in the man's eyes froze her finger. "Stay where you are."

He took another step.

Mark came to his feet slowly, his face a wet smear of red and his black clothes and hair dripping with coolant. Blood welled from his cheek with every surge of his pulse. A feral grimace turned his expression malicious. But his dark eyes seemed unable to focus.

"Stop," Kelly yelled again.

"Careful," the man said.

Kelly saw only his eyes, fixed and unblinking. He was just out of arm's reach and Kelly had come to the wall behind her. She gripped the gun with both hands and searched for the will to take his life.

"*Aaaghhh.*" The man's features twisted in pain and he collapsed onto one knee.

Mark yanked the knife from the soldier's thigh and kicked him in the back of the head. "Come on." He stepped around the man, grabbed the gun from Kelly's hand, and slid it under a network of conduits where it wouldn't likely be found, then gripped Kelly by the arm and pulled her away.

"What'd you do that for?" She glanced back to make sure Rod was with them.

"We don't need it."

She yanked her arm from his grip and stopped in the corridor. "What else are we supposed to fight with?"

Mark stopped. He spun to face her. "You planning on killing somebody?"

"He would have killed us."

"Not if we'd have stopped."

"You don't know that."

Rod caught up, no longer showing his pain. "Quiet, you guys."

"He's right." Mark moved down a side passage, but his wound slowed him. He spent more time looking at things than he should have needed, and his balance faltered.

"Come on, Rod." Kelly hurried after Mark.

They came to the same electronics room she and Mark had made out in earlier. Mark opened it and scanned the equipment. Arrays of lights covered the panels, some off, others blinking. Most burned steadily. Cryptic lettering, Chinese symbols, or Arabic numerals labeled each light with some meaningless identifier.

"What are you looking for?"

"Give me a minute." Mark unfolded the pinlight from La Roche's utility knife and shone it down the gap between the last panel and the wall. He traced something he saw there up toward the top of the rack. Then he stowed the light and got out the laser.

"What are you doing?" Kelly whispered harshly.

Mark didn't answer.

"Guys?" Rod said.

Mark fired the laser into the gap. Something in the crack sizzled. Smoke wafted into the closet air with the smell of burnt insulation. The myriad lights flashed. Some went out altogether. A status alarm beeped a steady cadence and a beacon over the door began to strobe.

"That ought to slow them down." Mark ran for the nearest staircase. He stopped one flight up, just before the door.

Kelly hurried to catch up. "What did you do?"

"The maintenance grid tracks the status of lifts, pressure doors, airlocks, and other safety devices. Now Center is blind to those systems for this octant of the station. It doesn't affect the security scanners, but it'll hide some of our movements."

Mark pressed the manual override for the door at the top of the stairs and slid the panel open a crack. He peered into the corridor for a moment before ducking back behind the door. "Soldiers," he whispered. "Looks like they're walking prisoners to the bathrooms." He closed the door again and waited. "Chang'll have to find somebody to fix the grid."

Kelly's mouth wouldn't seem to close. What Mark had done was brilliant, but what he was about to do seemed downright stupid. With the auditorium down the hall, was he planning to just walk in?

"There aren't as many security scanners on this deck as there are in Facilities." He cracked the door again and peeked out. Then he stuck his head through and looked down the length of the corridor. "It's clear. Come on."

They jogged through the deserted halls to the first corner and turned left, then slowed down. Mark checked each corridor before they entered or crossed until they'd moved away from the auditorium and into the staff dormitories. Mark found suite 2812, La Roche's room.

Of course. The case. Maybe he was right. The case would at least give Kelly a way to feel like she was fighting back. She entered the key code and the door slid open.

A bar-style window and three padded aluminite stools separated the kitchen from a large living area. Along one wall sat a miniature railroad, a model of the proposed Transatlantic Rail or maybe the London-Paris hypersonic subway. A portion of it ran through an aquarium that contained a dozen live fish.

"Cool." Rod ran into the room.

"Leave it alone," Kelly warned.

Mark headed for the kitchen. "I'll go find the case."

Kelly grabbed him by the hand and pulled him into the lavatory. His face looked like it had passed through a synth grinder. Blood soaked the front of his shirt. His cheek and brow had begun to swell, distorting the side of his face and forcing his eye closed. "Sit."

Mark lowered himself onto the commode, muffling the hollow hiss of suction it emitted, while Kelly ransacked the cabinet for Deadzone and bandages. "He doesn't have any dermaplast."

Mark set down the combat knife, dug into his pocket, and handed her the pouch he'd taken from the first-aid kit in the media room.

Kelly soaked a towel in the sink and knelt before him. The whole side of Mark's face would turn purple by morning. She looked into his good eye with as much sympathy as she ever remembered feeling for anybody. The truth was, she couldn't have found her brother without him. "Sorry I got you into this. You want the Deadzone first?"

He picked the bottle up from the countertop, dispensed a pair of pills, and swallowed them dry.

A high-pitched *whir* reached them from the other room. "Cool!"

"Rod!" Kelly leapt to her feet and darted into the living room. She snatched the controls to the bullet train, shut it off, and pointed to the stools at the bar. "Sit."

Rod faced her squarely. "I ain't gonna break it."

"Damn right you're not. Now sit down."

"You're not my boss."

She grabbed him by the arm and launched him at the chairs. Two of the three skittered across the floor as Rod stopped himself against the bar. "Bitch," he said under his breath.

Kelly's fists bunched at her sides and she came at him. "What did you call me?"

"Hey! Hey! Enough," Mark said from the bathroom doorway. "What are you, nine?" Self-applied dermaplast sealed the rent in his cheek.

Kelly pointed. "He is."

"Then he has an excuse." Mark's face, marred by swollen tissue, looked threatening, but his tone was merely condescending.

Rod crawled onto one of the stools and sat with his hands folded in front of him, his head down as though he hoped to be forgotten.

Mark put a hand on Kelly's shoulder and drew her into the kitchen. "I know you're upset. We all are. We've gone through hell, but we have to keep our heads. Let's find La Roche's case and get out of here."

Kelly focused her energies on Mark. She met his dark gaze and drew him to her. "What's so important about the case?" She was going to say, "The *damn* case," but she didn't want him to think she was just being stubborn or petty. "We're safe here." She glanced at Rod. "All of us. If we go out there for the sake of this case, we risk getting caught." Her stomach became a knot. "We'd risk our lives, Mark." She looked away, afraid he'd recognize the difference between her usual opportunistic flirtation and the deeper emotions she was beginning to feel for him. "How can you think about leaving this room?"

Mark breathed a sigh. She sensed him turning from her. When he spoke, he sounded farther away. "He helped us find your brother."

She wheeled on him again. "Fine. So he helped us. Big deal. Is that worth getting killed over?"

"Is your brother?"

Heat rushed to her face. She couldn't begin to put a value on Rod's life.

Mark didn't give her time to recover. "La Roche thought so. He let a soldier crack him in the face to give you a chance to find him."

"He didn't do it for Rod. He did it to get his precious case."

"Then it must be that important." Mark put an arm around her shoulders and held her against his chest. "Listen. I don't know what this case is all about, but whatever it is, he's hiding it from Chang—"

"Let's open it," Rod said hopefully.

Mark ignored him. "And now Chang's here in illegal military force, taking hostages and killing people."

Kelly pushed herself away enough to meet his gaze. "You think this is about the case?" If it was, the soldiers would come looking for it.

Mark shook his head. "I don't know. But now, all of the sudden, La Roche doesn't want to hide it anymore. Now he wants it in his hands."

"Let's open it," Rod said again, more seriously this time.

What could the case contain that La Roche could use in the auditorium? He didn't even have a computer terminal, unless they let him into the media room or unless he intended to plug into the podium, right there in front of everybody. "We can't get it to him," she said. "We can put it in the duct, but how will he get it out?"

Mark shrugged as well as he could without releasing her from his arms. "He asked us to leave it in the duct. How he gets it is his problem."

She stepped back and nudged him toward the sink. "If Chang might be after it, we'd better hurry."

Mark ripped open the cabinet and shoveled everything out. He rapped on the bottom of the cupboard and on the kitchen floor. They sounded the same, hollow, like aluminite with an interstitial beneath. "It's not here."

Rod climbed onto the bar and sat cross-legged where he could see.

Kelly squeezed in next to Mark and stuck her whole head inside the cabinet. The floor of the cupboard was the same height as that of the kitchen, with no room beneath for a hidden compartment.

She checked the top of the cupboard. The sink was there, the contour of the bowl, the drain pipe, everything. No hidden space. "Shit."

"Ooh, ooh, ooh." Rod jumped down as if the bar had suddenly become too hot to sit on. He ran in excitement to the sink and sprayed sterilizer into his hand.

Kelly backed away with Mark. "What is it?"

Rod held out his soaped hand. His eyes gleamed at her with a wicked sparkle. "You said a bad word. I get to wash your mouth."

Mark dismissed him with a shake of his head.

Kelly was less amused. "Go sit down. This is serious." Then to Mark, she said, "What're we going to do?"

"I don't know." Mark took Rod's wrist and led him into the other room. "Go rinse your hands. I've got to talk to your sister."

"You gonna kiss her?"

Kelly ignored him. She dug the utility knife from Mark's front pocket and crawled back under the sink. With the pinlight, she lit the inside of the cupboard and searched for anything unusual: seams in the aluminite paneling, gaps, or hinges. She cleared out the cabinet beside it and compared the depths to the back wall. Nothing.

"I want to watch," Rod said from outside the door.

"I'm not going to kiss her." Mark's voice held a tremor of impatience.

"Rod!" Instantly, Kelly regretted her volume. The thin walls of the station did little to dampen sound from one dorm to the next. "Now."

Rod humphed and walked away.

Kelly cleared the rest of the cabinets. None had compartments she could find. "What did he say, exactly?" she asked Mark.

"Rod?"

"La Roche. What were his exact words?"

Mark pulled his butt onto the bar and dangled his feet over the edge. He pinched the bridge of his nose and tried to think.

"Come on," Kelly said. "I wasn't listening. What did he say?"

"Give me a minute."

"Mark—"

"Damn it, will you let me think?" He didn't look at her. He couldn't see the hurt in her eyes.

If anyone else had talked to her that way, she'd have stormed from the room and not come back. Instead, she stood in mute apprehension.

Mark's mouth moved as he tried to piece together La Roche's words. "He said, 'There's a silver case in my dorm, number 2812. My code is F-105. The cupboard under the sink has a false bottom. The case is beneath it. Bring it here and leave it in the airshaft just inside the grate.'"

"You're sure?"

Mark shrugged. His face had swollen more, destroying the beauty she'd once seen in it. Still, she felt drawn to him. "That's what I remember."

There's a false bottom in the cupboard under the sink. The case is beneath it. "It's got to be here."

"And yet it's not."

The life went out of Kelly's limbs as the exertion of the past few hours caught up to her all at once. Mark beckoned her. She leaned back against him, facing the open, ransacked cabinets, and stared at them for a moment, devoid of thought. She closed her eyes. "I don't want to do this anymore."

Mark rocked her back and forth as if she was a baby in his arms. "I know."

"Hey guys," Rod said. "Got any handcuffs?"

Mark's body shifted. Kelly must have fallen asleep. It took several seconds to register what her brother had said. *Handcuffs?*

"'Cause it seems like I should handcuff this to my wrist or something." Rod strode into the room with a duralloy briefcase that looked like it could survive a nuclear blast. Electronic cipher locks adorned the edge where latches should have been. "It was under the sink in the bathroom."

Kelly should have been relieved. Instead, she was terrified. Now that they had the case, Mark would insist on delivering it. Worse, its construction and the sophistication of the locks made it obvious the case was dangerous. She had the sense that whatever it contained was the reason for the lockdown.

Either that, or it would determine its outcome.

Chapter 7

Colonel Chang paced the central corridor of the tight, rotating cylinder that formed the floor of *Venus Rain* Center. So far, everything was progressing according to schedule. His signal-jamming microsats, chaff clouds, and other defensive countermeasures had been deployed. He'd commandeered the station, gained access to all of the onboard computer systems, and instituted the lockdown. As soon as everyone was accounted for, he could breathe more easily. The hard part would be over.

Suddenly, flashing lights lit up the engineering station. Error messages scrolled on the display. He marched up the corridor between the two rows of consoles. "What is it? What's happening?"

The engineer, Corporal Ming, shook his head and punched commands into the board. "We lost part of the grid." Ming, military to the core, right down to a crew cut so short he might as well have been bald, pulled up a diagram of the entire station. A ninety-degree arc of the southern half of the habitation cylinder flashed yellow. "The whole octant just went down. It must be a comm error somewhere in the system."

Chang grunted. Tension flared in his clenched jaw, irritating the exposed nerves of his raw face. This was no accident. The failure had created a blind spot big enough to fly a freighter through. And with the lockdown incomplete, his men were too tied up with other duties to respond.

"Compile a list of residents in that octant."

"Yes, sir, but it won't be complete. We haven't finished accounting for everyone yet."

I know that, Chang wanted to shout, but he stifled the impulse. "Understood."

"Sir," Ming said a few moments later. "The auditorium is in that sector, along with maybe half the residents."

That couldn't be coincidence. Chang keyed Lieutenant Han. "What's your status?"

"Taking roll now. Estimated completion in fifteen minutes."

"Is everything under control down there?"

"Yes, sir. Is there a problem?"

"We just lost the maintenance grid in your sector." Chang paused. "You ever find those kids?"

"No." Han's tone suggested a shrug.

"Then we can guess who the saboteurs are. Find them."

Chang's hand pivoted at the wrist in nervous cycles as though he couldn't decide between palm up or palm down. "Close the safety doors in the corridors only," he told Corporal Ming. "Leave the environmental ducts open. Shut down all lifts."

"Done," Ming said a moment later. Unfortunately, without communication, Chang couldn't confirm that the systems had actually responded.

∿⟨○⟩∿

Amanda stumbled through the docking port of her shuttle. Heat exhaustion hadn't taken hold of her yet. Her disorientation stemmed from her own shit luck and the circumstances of the lockdown.

If she died, who would care for Rod? Kelly? Ha! Kelly's idea of babysitting was to put Rod in front of a vid-file while she got high or got laid. She had no income of her own and had never once, as far as Amanda knew, considered getting a job.

No. Amanda had to get home. And her engineering mind had already begun to work the problem.

Somehow, she had to let this Colonel Chang know she was on the surface. She could do that. The numerous alarms and safety indicators of the atmosphere processor were continuously relayed through a network of satellites to the Project hub on *Venus Rain*. Amanda could do something to the reactor, set off a warning that someone on station would see.

If anyone up there bothered to watch the panel.

In the meantime, she could bleed coolant from the processor to keep herself alive for a day or two before the supply dropped to critical levels.

And if she shut down the flow for a short time . . . yes. That would do it.

With a clear course before her, Amanda rushed to the helium shutoff valves. She closed them down by slow increments, keeping an eye on the temperature of the reaction tower. Several of the zones began to increase. Ten degrees. Twenty degrees. Fifty.

She closed the valves further. The upper zones reached redline. Counting on the safety margins, she let the temperature climb higher. The lower zones rose into warning range as well.

When the highest reading touched the top of the scale, she backed off, let the temperature drop a few degrees, and watched. Over the next thirty minutes, she tweaked the bank of valves until every reading sat firmly in the red, with enough coolant flow to keep it from rising but not enough to bring it back to normal.

That reduced the demand on the helium source for the time being, but it raised the temperature in the maintenance chamber. It increased the toll on Amanda's body. Already the headache had set in. Thirst and dizziness would follow.

She perforated a length of flexible hose, connected it to a bleed tap in the cooling line, and ran it along the framework overhead. Then she cracked the bleeder valve. Helium hissed from the holes and evaporated in the room air. The frigid vapor drifted down as a fine white mist. Amanda adjusted the flow until her own little region of the processor settled at a comfortable twenty-five degrees centigrade.

She sat with her pipe wrench in one hand, the other cupped over the comm link in her ear, and let the processor do her work for her. First, she'd let Chang know she was there. Then she'd hold the processor hostage, if necessary, to gain her ticket home.

However important the briefcase might be, Kelly couldn't put it into La Roche's hands without knowing what was inside. It wouldn't take a very big bomb to rip the last two floors of the habitation cylinder out from under the auditorium and kill a thousand people. The thought of the quaint old professor with a bomb seemed absurd. Then again, it seemed less so when the quaint professor just happened to be the technical lead on the most ambitious endeavor humanity had ever undertaken.

Besides, the nature of the case belied the quaint-old-professor image. Still, a bomb somehow seemed unlikely. "We should open it," she said.

"I don't think we can." Mark examined the case more closely. "This is a cipher lock. It takes an eight- or ten-digit key code. A decoding worm could cycle through the possibilities, but even if we had such a program, there's no way to download it. The manual keypad is the only input." He twirled La Roche's utility knife in his hand. "If we cut through, he'll know we opened it."

"What do you think it is?" Rod grabbed the case and started pressing buttons.

"More to the point," Kelly said, "what do you think *he* is?"

Mark looked up. "La Roche?"

Kelly didn't answer.

Mark shrugged. "I don't know. He seemed pretty close to Raji. If I had to bet, I'd say he's on our side."

What side was that? This was some sort of political game. Beyond the ability to name a few public figures who frequently appeared in the news-blips, Kelly knew nothing—let alone cared—about world or interplanetary politics. La Roche was European. So, in relation to the United States, whose side *was* he on?

Mark reached for the case. "Let's get this to La Roche before your cat burglar here enters enough false codes to disable the real one."

Rod turned his back to them and continued his efforts to guess the code. "What's Mom's birthday?"

Kelly humphed. "Why would it be Mom's birthday?"

"La Roche's birthday?"

"Too easy," Mark said.

"The date of the French Revolution?"

"Do you know it?" Mark asked him.

"How about the year of the Apollo Eleven landing?"

"Not enough digits," Kelly said.

"1969." Rod entered the number twice. Nothing. "Oh, I know. 55378008. Upside down, it spells BOOBLESS."

"Give me that." Mark snatched the case and headed for the door.

"Hang on." Kelly retrieved the combat knife from the bathroom. Then she and Mark made a quick sweep of the place for anything else that might become useful later. Kelly found a thinpad in La Roche's bedroom. She lacked a pocket large enough to put it in, so she handed it to Mark.

La Roche apparently used his second bedroom as an office. The room contained two telnet terminals on a large sim-wood desk, the backside of the aquarium, and a section of the model rail layout. Mark exhumed a second thinpad from a stash of unrecognizable electronic gadgets.

"What is all this stuff?" Kelly asked.

Mark picked up several devices, one at a time. "Waveguide taps, listening devices, a micro-fiber scanner . . ." He shook his head at the rest. "You got me."

"What do you think it's for?"

"Who knows." Mark went to the kitchen and shoveled everything that had come out of the cupboards back into them.

When he finally palmed the panel by the door, it failed to open. It just beeped, as though he'd entered an invalid command. He keyed O-P-E-N and pressed the ENTER key. Another beep. His shoulders slumped.

"What is it?"

"Looks like Chang's locked all the residential dorms from Center. We can't open it from inside."

Chapter 8

"We've found one, sir," Lieutenant Gou told Chang over his shoulder. He pushed his glasses up on the bridge of his nose. "Lin Anni. She's a Chinese citizen, an electrician transferred here from a Jupiter hydrogen ship, the *Gansu*, three years ago. She's logged maintenance on the grid at regular intervals since then and should be qualified to make any repairs."

"She worked for JUMP?" Chang asked.

"She worked for Weixin. All their employees are Union."

Chang frowned. Though Weixin was a Chinese company, the Union was international, political. "Clear her."

"That'll take time. Her history with the Union makes her loyalties uncertain."

"Then find someone without a Union history."

"It's a small station, sir. Only four people have logged repair or maintenance on that part of the grid. One of the others is Chinese, Wong Zude, but his father was one of the protesters killed in the Fertility Riots in Nanjing. The other two are foreign. One of those is Mark Torben. That leaves Lin."

Chang wanted a Chinese citizen, one not tied to JUMP, but he wasn't about to let the others get near anything important.

Nanjing had been the bloodiest of the Fertility Riots, and Chang himself had led the offensive to suppress it. His men killed hundreds of civilians. Chang still heard them screaming when he closed his eyes some nights.

Yet that wasn't his only chronic reminder of the battle. The raw nerves in his face flared at the memory of a protestor who'd gotten too close with a makeshift bomb of ammonium nitrate, diesel fuel, and beryllium biosulfate, the corrosive that still ate away at the flesh of his face and prevented it from healing. Chang's wrist swiveled habitually as a result of the physical therapy he'd undergone for years after the same bomb shattered his elbow.

"There may be others who are capable of troubleshooting the grid," Lieutenant Gou continued. "But it'll take time to identify them. And they'll still have to be cleared. It depends on how long you want the grid down."

"Where's Wong?"

"According to station records, he was on shift at the start of the lockdown. He may have been on the maintenance deck. We're holding those workers in a conference room on the deck above."

"And Lin?"

"Off duty. Probably locked in her dorm or the auditorium."

"Pull two of Han's men. Have one locate Wong. Escort him to the security hold and confine him there. Find Miss Lin. Have her repair the grid. Make sure she's watched every moment."

"Yes, sir."

"What do you want?" Han growled as soon as the men Chang had recalled were gone.

La Roche leaned close. "The microphone is still on." He shot a glance toward the crowd. "They can hear you."

A low rumble escaped Han's throat as he launched himself onto the stage with his long hair flying like a black flag behind him. He marched to the podium and flipped the audio switch.

La Roche hurried after in his painful, shuffling gait. He tapped the microphone pickup with his finger and loud thumps filled the auditorium. "That switch hasn't worked for years."

Han was down to just four men to execute the DNA scans and to guard a thousand prisoners. The entire scanning process had stopped as soon as Han moved to the podium. One of his men marked the next person in line. His soldiers were stretched too thin.

La Roche began limping from the stage.

"Wait," Han said.

La Roche turned, a neutral expression on his battered face.

Han's heavy-lidded eyes narrowed further. He pointed his pistol at La Roche. "Go turn it off."

La Roche shrugged. "You can put the gun away. I can't fight you."

Han keyed his link and told his men to let La Roche into the media room. He was an old man, practically an invalid. He couldn't possibly pull himself through a loose grate in the ceiling.

La Roche continued to exaggerate his limp until he reached the crowd and Han returned his attention to other duties. Then he hurried the rest of the way, as well as he could on his aching joints.

Once inside, he breathed a heavy sigh and pondered the open hole in the ceiling. This might be the last chance he'd have to get in here alone. The case had better be there. He shoved the chair into place beneath the opening, stuffed the curtains back into the box, and lifted it onto the seat. Still, he needed more height.

He grabbed a stack of equipment from the desktop, three consoles maybe half a meter in combined height, and yanked the plugs from the wall. That would kill the audio from the stage. He carefully balanced them on top of the curtain box. The resulting tower, unstable from its rolling base, was probably high enough for him to reach the duct, but it had taken too long to build.

The stack of consoles rocked in the box as soon as he put his hand on them. When he placed his foot on the seat, the chair rolled. Not far, but enough to shake La Roche's balance. Panting now, he took a moment to steady himself. He continued to climb until he was perched on his hands and knees on the pinnacle of the tower.

Aware a fall would shatter bones that, at his age, would never heal, he began to ease himself to his feet. The seat shook. The consoles wobbled. His aching joints labored to compensate. His whole lower body trembled in an effort to dampen the tower's oscillation. The wheels of the chair rattled, unable to decide which way to roll.

Slowly, La Roche came erect, gripped the edges of the vent hole, and stuck his head through. The duct was empty.

He muttered an oath. Damned kids these days, never held themselves responsible for anything. Especially the Baker girl. Yet even that trait was something he could use.

Mark rifled through La Roche's dresser.

Rod was in the other room, playing with the model train. It was safer than letting him use the telnet terminal for games or vid-file downloads, which Chang's men might detect.

"What if this isn't about the case?" Kelly lounged on the professor's bed, beneath an environmental vent too small to crawl through. "I'll bet Chang doesn't even know it exists. If he did, he would've shown up by now. Right?"

Nothing in the back of the drawers. "Probably." Only half listening, Mark moved to the closet.

"Then we should be safe here. They can't link us to La Roche and it'll take a dorm-by-dorm search to find us." She rolled onto her side and watched him. "If we go out there, they can catch us any number of ways."

"Maybe." Mark pushed the hanging jumpsuits all the way to one side and began to search the pockets, one by one.

"Mark?"

He finished the jumpsuits and went on to the sports coats and slacks.

"Mark, let's stay here? At least for the night."

Nothing in the coats. He pulled a chair into the closet so he could reach the top shelf. "We've been through this. I promised to deliver the case."

"It's late. I'm tired. We can deliver it in the morning."

"We may have to." Mark left the bedroom and went to La Roche's home office.

Kelly showed up in the doorway a few minutes later. "What are you looking for?"

"A Gauss driver." He wouldn't find one. The tool was issued only to maintenance personnel who needed access to the inner workings of electronics and computer equipment, like the control panel for the lock on La Roche's door. Mark had one in his toolbox, but that was packed away in his locker at work.

There was no reason La Roche would need a Gauss driver, yet he had too many odd items around for Mark to rule out the possibility.

"If I have to, I'll cut into the circuit with the welding laser, but if someone comes looking for the case, I don't want them to know we've been here. And

I don't want to incriminate La Roche. Whatever he's up to, it's better that he maintains the illusion of an ordinary professor." Mark searched the desk, then turned to Kelly with a huff. "You could help."

She shrugged. "I don't know what a Gauss driver looks like."

"It's got a shaft like a screwdriver. The head has a groove cut across the middle like the top of a screw."

Instead of moving toward the file cabinet or the office closet, Kelly slunk up to Mark, slow and sexy. Her open shirt invited him to undo the bra clasp between her breasts.

"Kelly. . ."

When she wrapped her arms around him, he nearly pushed her away. Instead, he glanced at the open door to La Roche's living area. She wouldn't go far with her little brother in the next room.

Kelly didn't kiss him, however. She stuffed her hands into his back pockets and dug out La Roche's knife.

She stepped back and began unfolding and inspecting the attachments. The distribution of Gauss drivers was universally restricted to prevent unauthorized access to sensitive equipment. Nobody would put one in an ordinary utility knife. Mark turned to the file cabinet and yanked open the top drawer.

Then again, La Roche's knife was anything but ordinary. He turned back as Kelly unfolded an attachment that had been concealed by the knife's outer casing.

"Like this?" Kelly displayed the tip.

Mark shook his head in disbelief, snatched the knife from her hand, and headed for the door.

"Shut it down," Kelly told Rod. "Apparently we're leaving."

Rod gave Mark a sour look as he walked by, but said nothing.

Using the Gauss driver, Mark tripped the four interior, magnetic latches that secured the cover plate to the door's control panel. "Hope the grid is still down." He shorted the switch contacts with a knife blade and the door slid open.

Mark grabbed the case and turned to leave. Pressure doors sealed both ends of the hallway outside. "That'll make it harder for anyone to spot us by accident."

"Yeah, but how do *we* get around?"

"As long as a door has similar pressure on both sides, the manual override will open it. And if the maintenance grid is still down, Chang won't see it happen."

They cycled through two doors, closing each behind them, and came to a lift. Rod reached for the button, but Kelly grabbed his wrist. "You sure the lift is on the bad maintenance circuit?"

"No, but we won't be using the lift. Grab that side." Mark took the combat knife, wedged it between the doors, and pulled to the left. Kelly tugged on the right side. The crack widened and Mark jammed his fingers into it. He tripped the safety sensor and the door panels separated.

The hole beyond dropped ten meters to the facilities deck. Above him, it continued out of sight. It gave him the sensation that he might fall a thousand meters up the shaft.

Kelly caught his arm and yanked him back. "You all right?"

"Yeah. Yeah, I'm fine."

Rod looked down. "Cool."

"See that?" Mark pointed to a vent grate in the shaft wall, about four meters up. "That's where we're going." He climbed into the shaft and onto the ladder beside the door. Kelly and Rod followed, letting the door close behind them.

The vent was more than an arm's reach from the ladder. Mark had to stretch out with one leg dangling over the drop to reach the screws. He started to remove them one at a time.

Before he finished the second one, a whispered hum sped down the shaft. A lift car descended on bearings of air, driven by magnetism on frictionless rails.

He swung back to the ladder and flattened himself against it as the car swept by. Its descent slowed as it passed and the car came to rest just below them on the facilities deck.

Mark put a finger to his lips and waited several minutes for the passengers to vacate the lift and to see if it would return, before leaning out to work on the grate again. When the last screw fell, the grate, too distant and too heavy for him to catch, tumbled with a crash onto the sliding door on top of the lift car.

Kelly gasped.

Wasting no time, Mark tucked the utility knife into his pocket and leapt for the lip of the vent opening. He caught it by the tips of his fingers and levered himself up until he could get his elbows inside it. His arms straining, he pulled himself into the interstitial beyond.

No sound came from the lift car.

Mark braced himself and stretched his arm through the hole, back into the shaft to help Rod.

Kelly held one of her brother's hands from the ladder. "Watch your arm."

"I'm okay." With his other hand, Rod clasped Mark's wrist and Mark heaved him up.

Kelly took a deep breath and said her own form of prayer. "We're all going to hell anyway." It wasn't that she didn't believe in heaven. She just didn't think, in this day and age, that anybody actually got there.

From there, they crept back toward the duct that fed air into the media room.

Mark rounded the corner of the auditorium, which rose through both the interstitial and the next habitation level. On the duct, next to the grate Mark had welded into place earlier, sat a Chinese soldier.

Kelly's hand roamed her pockets—probably looking for synth.

"What now?" Rod mouthed.

There was no way past the guard. The flimsy aluminum ducts would make too much noise for Mark to enter farther down and try to sneak past. One bad shift of weight would give him away. "The bathrooms."

Kelly looked up from her pocket search. "What about them?"

Mark grabbed Kelly's arm and pulled her away until he was sure they could talk without being overheard. "Chang's men were taking people from the auditorium to the bathroom. I can leave the case there."

"And just hope La Roche is the one who finds it?"

"I'll send someone back with a message for him."

"Then what? He's supposed to carry it to the auditorium right in front of Chang's men?"

Mark shrugged. "It's the best we can do. Then we've got to hole up before Chang gets the grid back online."

CHAPTER 9

Lin Anni froze when the soldier appeared in her doorway.

"We need your help," the man said.

Help? She nearly said, *Go to hell*, but the hard face of the soldier, and the illegal pistol on his belt, stopped her. "And when you no longer need my help?"

"We're not murderers," the soldier said. "Part of the maintenance grid has gone offline. You must repair it. When you're done. I'll bring you back here."

Her gut clenched at the thought of helping President Li, who'd had Anni's own mother and sister forcibly sterilized during his "crusade." Yet if she didn't do it, somebody else would. There were any number of people on board who could probably locate the problem, whatever it was, and still more who could repair it, given enough time to study the schematics. The fact that Chang had chosen her—he must be aware of her history—spoke loudly of the urgency with which he wanted it fixed.

The question was: should she do it?

"We may be on this station for a long time," the soldier continued, "We'll need your help as long as you don't resist us."

Oh, she wouldn't. Not outright. At least not until she found a way to do it without getting caught. "I won't resist. But I'll need a terminal." She had one in her dorm, on a small desk in a corner of the living area, but she had been afraid to use it since the lockdown began.

"Can you run your tests from here?"

She nodded, hesitantly at first, then with more confidence. "Yeah . . . sure."

The soldier stepped into the room and the door slipped closed behind him.

Anni's gut tightened. She felt physically ill as she considered the things this soldier could do, alone with her in her dorm.

But he did nothing. He stood behind her, unnaturally silent, and watched the monitor.

Trying to hide her fear, she swallowed hard and focused on her task. It took three tries before she finally keyed her access code correctly.

Once she did, she needed only minutes to determine where the problem was located. "There." She pointed to a schematic of the facilities deck in which a maintenance closet flashed red. Her diagnostic didn't report the extent of the damage, however. Or its nature. It could be as simple as a pulled plug. On the other hand, someone might have blown the closet to splinters.

The guard motioned Anni toward the door and followed her into the hall.

The damage was so localized, and the effect so broad, that someone must have done it deliberately. And for a specific purpose. If the damage was substantial enough, Anni might delay the repair long enough for the saboteur to accomplish whatever he'd sabotaged the grid to do.

She glanced at the soldier and stepped onto the lift. He kept his hand on his pistol, as if she could somehow resist him physically.

A moment later, the lift settled to a stop on the facilities deck. The door slid open and Anni stepped out. She went first to her locker for tools, then proceeded to the repair.

As she approached the closet, her dilemma became more immediate. The closed door appeared undamaged. Only the flashing beacon above it hinted at sabotage. That ruled out a bomb or fire, so the damage was probably repairable. If it was more than a pulled plug, the decision would be real indeed. And hers to make. Should she fix it?

Regardless of what she thought of President Li personally, or of his policies, it was her country he led. And Li was old. He'd forfeit his power soon enough. To oppose him now, for the sake of a political grudge, might mean opposing her country's future.

Come to think of it, she wasn't even sure Colonel Chang was working for Li. If the headlines were true, his brother, General Chang Lei, wasn't working for Li when he perpetrated the China Dominion Affair. By opposing Colonel Chang, Anni might actually be supporting Li Muyou.

She opened the maintenance door, half-expecting to find widespread damage, the panels gummed with fire suppressant, or the electronics smashed, but she didn't. Status lights flashed their uncertainty, and a strident whine cried plaintively for attention. Beyond that, the hardware looked fine. The air carried a faint scent of burnt polymer.

Anni inspected the panels and readouts. Every piece of equipment had power. The covers showed no signs of tampering or forced removal. The saboteur had done this without accessing the insides of the equipment. It was possible that someone with access to a Gauss driver had opened the panels without damaging them, but she ruled out the possibility. This room contained dozens of consoles, and all flashed distress. It would have taken too long to remove and replace each cover. No. This was done externally.

The guard watched her from the doorway, leaning this way and that to keep Anni's hands in sight, as if he thought he could tell by looking whether she was repairing the equipment or doing additional harm.

She shone a work light into the gap between the equipment and the wall. From there, the damage was obvious, so much so that even the guard would understand it. She waved him over and showed him the severed leads. He nodded.

"Simple enough," she said. "But it'll take time to fix." She waved her hand at the nearest tower. "I'll have to disassemble and remove this whole rack just to get at it. That alone may take an hour."

Her captor frowned but said nothing.

"And I can't just splice the wiring. Each of these cables—" there were dozens of them— "carries thousands of microfilaments. I'll have to replace each entire cable."

The soldier stared at her dumbly.

"To do that," she continued with a slight huff, "I'll have to remove all of the racks. And part of the wall. It'll take at least ten hours."

"That's not acceptable," her captor said.

Anni raised an eyebrow at him. "Then you fix it."

The man's distress was so palpable she had to suppress a grin. Enemy or not, she didn't agree with the way Chang pursued his goals. She would enjoy any measure of discomfort she could inflict on him or his men. The fact that she didn't create her captor's plight did nothing to diminish her enjoyment of it.

Yet she committed herself to repairing the grid as quickly as possible. That decision would drive her actions from here on out, at least until she knew more about what Chang was up to.

When the soldier didn't answer, Anni turned toward the equipment rack, pulled the Gauss driver from her tool belt, and got started. "If you get me some help, the work will go faster."

The man keyed the link in his ear and began mumbling into the pickup.

A soldier escorted hostages to and from the lavatories, in groups of five, sometimes men, other times women. If his pattern held, Mark would have about thirty seconds between groups—not enough time to get into and out of the bathroom, which, fortunately, the guard never seemed to enter.

When the way was clear, Mark sprinted down the hall, into the men's room. He locked himself in the last stall, held the case in his lap, and pulled his feet out of sight.

Moments later a bunch of men walked in. "It's about time," one said.

Mark set the case in the corner, where it wouldn't be seen unless someone looked under the stall door. He keyed a quick note to La Roche on one of the professor's own thinpads to tell him where to find the case. Mark also mentioned the things they'd taken from the room and promised to return or replace them later. Then he walked out of the stall.

"How'd you get—" one of the prisoners, a man with a thick black beard, began.

Mark's finger shot to his lips.

The man's brow creased. He continued in a lower voice. "Who messed you up?"

"Do you know Professor Dennis La Roche?"

The man's eyes narrowed. "I know who he is."

Mark shoved the thinpad into his hand. "Give this to him."

The man glanced nervously at the bathroom door.

"You don't have to say anything. Just give him the thinpad. And don't let Chang's men see it."

At that moment, the guard walked in. Fortunately, the man stood directly between him and Mark.

"Yeah, but I was here first," Mark told the bearded man. "You'll get your turn." He held his hand in front of his face and pretended to dig something from his eye while he turned to a hissing urinal. The solder might not remember the appearance of each prisoner, but he'd have noticed someone with Mark's ruined face. He'd know Mark didn't belong there.

The guard stepped up to the next urinal and stared at Mark, who kept his head down and hoped the bruises hadn't spread to that side of his face. He took deep, slow breaths in an effort to calm his racing heart.

"Got a smoke?" the soldier asked in Chinese. Surely he knew cigarettes were prohibited—he'd have learned that before he launched from Earth. Either the guard didn't care, or he was baiting Mark.

Mark didn't look up. The soldier glared at him. Mark could see that much through the corner of his eye.

He finished his business, turned away from the soldier, and moved to the sink as quickly as he could. He buried his bruises in a handful of wet towels so the soldier wouldn't see them in the mirror.

Another prisoner emerged from one of the stalls. If the guard counted them now. . .

Mark held his breath until another man pulled the guard's attention by approaching the lavatory door. Then he bolted into an empty stall and pulled his feet onto the commode. The pounding of his heart began a renewed throbbing in his bruised cheek. He prayed the guard wouldn't check the stalls before he left.

President Li Muyou was an old-school dictator who refused to learn the Western language that had begun to dominate the realms of Earth and space. When Powers finally reached him on the comm, they had to converse through translation software.

Dan Norton sat in the Oval Office with her, as did Warren Parker. Though Powers had instructed them to stay off the scanner and remain silent, she let them make their own interpretation of Li's motives. However Li came across, Parker would advise further negotiation. Norton would recommend a hard-line course of military action. An angel on one shoulder. The devil on the other.

No. She cast the metaphor aside as unfair. Norton would advise force because that was his job, to lay out the military options, to cite martial resources, to bring to the forefront of the President's mind that the United States had a strong sword arm, ready to fight if she chose to employ it.

In truth, that's where Powers' tendencies lay. Li was a hardcore tyrant, despite such titles as "President" and "People's Republic." He was a hundred and fourteen years old, stubborn as a badger, and valued achievement above all else. His mission for the past three decades had been to lift from his country the burden its own population placed upon it. Venus could do that, and would in any case. But if Li could claim the entire world for China . . . what a feat that would be.

"Ahh, President Powers," Li said the moment he appeared on the screen. The wrinkles in his face were deep chasms, the line of his mouth almost indistinguishable among them. "How may I assist you this—" He consulted a chronometer on his desk and a look of false concern filled his eyes, the only part of his face still capable of expression. "This must be a matter of great concern for you, Madam President, to be up at this hour." The English was relayed, impassive as Li's visage, by the software, but his muted voice was audible in the background so Powers might interpret any inflection or change of tone. The combination made Li particularly difficult to read.

You bet your ass it's of great concern, you malicious bastard. "Grave concern would be closer to the mark, Mr. President." The title grated her heart like sandpaper.

"Then perhaps I would be courteous to skip the pleasantries of state and allow you to speak of that which troubles you."

Powers' fist whitened around her cane. *You know damn well what troubles me . . .* She took a deep breath before opening her mouth to reply. "Let's be clear, shall we?"

"Of course."

"You've taken Americans hostage, not only on *Venus Rain*, but on *New Hope* as well."

"This is what troubles you? Madam, the solution is so simple I fear you would think me mocking you if I say it out loud. But I can't bear to see you distraught, so I'll risk that misunderstanding." He set his elbows on his desk. "Simply acknowledge China's sovereign ownership of Venus. We will release the Americans on *Venus Rain* and allow you to vacate *New Hope*."

Powers' temples throbbed at the absurdity of his demand and the ease with which he spoke it. Was he that confident?

"You know I can't do that."

Li leaned forward. "Can't? Or won't?"

"The United States and the European Union will take any actions necessary to ensure our continued interests in the Venus Project. We're negotiating with Petrov to stop the hydrogen shipments that support it." Her voice crept up in volume, and tension laced her tone. "Your arrogant threats serve only to delay Venus's habitability, possibly by decades."

Li nodded but said nothing as he listened to a computerized voice translate her words. He took his glasses off, laid them on his desk, and steepled his hands in front of him as though in deep contemplation. "In the decades General Chang Lei served me, he did a lot of things, upon my orders, that appalled the Western world—things that you don't understand were necessary. And he did some things even I didn't approve."

Confused by Li's unexpected digression, Powers waited for him to get to the point.

"I do not condone the actions of General Chang Lei or those of his China Dominion." Li seemed to be talking to himself. "He acted outside my knowledge and authority and risked interplanetary war for the sake of a demonstration." If he expected Powers to believe Li had been unaware of Chang's conspiracy . . .

"Nevertheless," Li continued, "Chang did convince me of one thing." He put his glasses back on and his gaze returned to the screen. "He convinced me of the strength of China's military position in space and the inability of the United States and Europe to face that threat. Furthermore, Petrov has assured me the hydrogen shipments will continue."

"You underestimate our capabilities."

"Perhaps you underestimate mine."

They talked for several minutes, but despite President Li's sticky-sweet tone, he refused to soften his position. "I'm touched that you would so inconvenience your schedule to contact me at this social hour. I'll keep you no longer, Madam President." He bowed his head respectfully before closing the channel.

"God," Powers exclaimed as soon as the screen went dark. "He's insufferable."

Dan Norton sat, looking at his hands, which he'd folded in his lap. "There is a saying in some Asian cultures." He raised his gaze to meet Powers'. "If your enemy is polite to you, it means he's about to kill you."

Chapter 10

"We need to find a place to hide," Kelly said when Mark returned to the stairwell, "until we decide what to do next."

"We can go back to the auditorium now," Mark suggested. "The hostages seem like they're being well treated. I don't think they'll shoot us if we give ourselves up."

"I thought you didn't want to go back there."

"I didn't, not until we delivered the case. Obviously we couldn't just walk in with it, but La Roche should find it now. We don't have to hide anymore."

"You heard what Chang said. He'll execute anyone who fails to cooperate."

"If we give ourselves up freely—"

She gripped his shoulders. "You sabotaged the maintenance grid. You think he'll just let that go?"

Mark shrugged. "They'll fix it."

"You stabbed one of his men—"

"To keep you from killing him."

Kelly grabbed his arm and pulled him down the stairs to the facilities deck and toward the lift.

Rod followed, his eyes wide.

"I spared his life," Mark continued. "That should count for something."

They passed a metals reclaim bin. From it, Kelly grabbed a length of stainless steel pipe with a flattened end. "You want to go back? Fine." She'd faced one of Chang's soldiers already because that's what it took to save Rod's life. But now the danger had passed. Somehow they'd all come away in one piece. She wasn't about to face them again. Not if she had a choice.

She came to the lift, jammed the flattened end of the pipe into the slot between the doors, and pried them open. With a mere glance to make sure the lift wasn't descending upon them, she leapt to the floor of the shaft and pulled Rod in behind her.

Mark followed them and let the door close. "Okay. Suppose you're right. What do you plan to do?"

She wheeled on him with such vehemence that he recoiled. "Hide. Fight if I have to. But I won't submit to execution." Kelly waved the pipe like a wand at the vast height of the shaft. "The interstices of this station go on forever. We can hide for weeks if we have to."

Mark sighed. He glanced toward the lift door and took a long look up the shaft. "Okay, but we've got to get out of this sector, get to one with a working grid. They won't think to look for us there." He reached for the pipe. "I'll hold that while you climb."

Kelly snatched it away. "You've taken everything I've picked up, like you think I'm not safe with it or something. I'm hanging on to this." She thrust it into her belt and launched herself up the ladder.

Together, they climbed to the top floor of the habitation cylinder. There weren't many security scanners on the housing levels, and if the closed safety doors were any indication, the grid was still down. They could move freely as long as they kept an eye out for Chang's patrols.

Rod stopped at one of the public restrooms. "I got to pee."

"We'll all go." Without waiting for a reply, Kelly led the way into the men's room. She walked into the nearest stall, keyed the latch, and pulled her pants to the floor.

The guys finished first. "Is Rod your middle name?" Mark asked her brother.

"No." His voice sounded small against the background of suction from the toilets and the pressure spray of the hand cleaner. He didn't elaborate. He liked to keep the nickname his own funny secret.

Kelly rolled her eyes as she pulled up her jeans. She opened the door. "Go ahead. Tell him. I dare you."

Rod's indignant look met her gaze in the mirror. "You can't dare me."

She moved to the sink and turned on the sterilizer spray. "I just did."

"It doesn't count unless it's something you can do too, 'cause you have to take the dare if I do."

"I can tell him." When her hands were clean and dry, Kelly walked toward the door.

"Wait," Mark said. "Now I want to know."

Kelly gave Rod a questioning look. "You gonna tell him?"

Rod shook his head emphatically.

She shrugged. "I guess he's embarrassed."

"Am not."

She opened the door, checked the hallway, and stepped outside. Together, they raided a food-vend, returned to the lift shaft, and climbed into the overhead interstitial.

Once inside the space, which was smaller than the one over the facilities deck, they crawled two-thirds of the way around the cylinder. There, Kelly found a pocket between an environmental duct and one of the lifts, where they settled in and waited for someone to find them. In truth, the station wasn't that big. No matter where they hid, Colonel Chang would find them. And despite what she'd told Mark, it wouldn't take him weeks to do it.

European President Peter Hunt keyed the console on his desk to silence the Mozart that infused the room while he worked. "Come in, come in. Sit down."

Andrew Yates, the director of the European State Department, strode across the rich carpeting to the president's marble-topped desk in the Executive Mansion in Brussels. "Good evening, Mr. President. My shuttle leaves for the States in a few minutes. I need to know what aid we're prepared to offer."

Hunt frowned. "Yes. That would be the question, wouldn't it?"

"It would seem so."

Yates' unusually subdued mood struck a cord of worry in the president that he couldn't quite identify. Nevertheless, Hunt was resolved in his decision. "They're going to war over this thing, then?"

"They're discussing a blockade of Russian hydrogen shipments. I don't see how such an action could result in any other outcome."

A smile tugged at the corners of Hunt's mouth before he forced a more suitable expression. "Offer them ships and troops. Whatever they need." He stood, placed his knuckles on the desk, and leaned over them. "But be absolutely clear on this point: Do not, under any circumstances, disclose the Centurions."

Yates' eyes saddened. "Anything else, Mr. President?"

"Support the blockade. A disruption of trade will get expensive for everyone. But I'm no more willing to give up our share of Venus to Li Muyou than Powers is to give up hers."

"Well then," Yates said with some of his usual spirit. "Let's rattle Li's cage a bit, shall we?"

Professor La Roche hadn't found a way to escape his bathroom guard. Yet the privilege of traversing that short stretch of hallway gave him a vague hope he couldn't quite define . . . until he received Mark's terse message. The boy was a genius.

La Roche slipped the thinpad into his pocket and hobbled to the auditorium doors. The line for the restrooms had dwindled and he reached the front by the third group.

"Didn't you go already?" the soldier asked him.

"Now I've got to shit."

The man's face soured as he motioned La Roche through the door with the others.

When he got there, his case sat on the floor of the last stall, next to the head. He didn't have long, but he took time to examine the case, which appeared undamaged. He pulled a Deadzone capsule from his pocket, cracked it open, and poured the contents into his hand. Gently, he blew some of the powder onto each of the case's electromagnetic latches. Oils from somebody's skin had left fingerprints on the keys. Someone with small fingers, like Kelly or her little brother.

Short of missing items from the case's contents, however, La Roche had no way to know if the kids had actually succeeded. But the odds against it were more than ten billion to one, unless they had some means to guess the code, which was why he'd used a different, purely random number—totally unguessable—for each latch. The fact that the kids had tried was useful information, nothing more.

He laid the case across his lap and typed in the access codes. With a faint whine, the circuit drained the electromagnets that held the case shut. Each latch released with a muffled pop and La Roche pulled the case open.

From inside, he pocketed a petite 9-mm pistol, a silencer, a spare magazine, a thinpad, a data card, and a pocket utility knife like the one he'd given to Mark, all issued to La Roche by the European Intelligence Agency when they assigned him to *Venus Rain*.

He'd finally taken the second step. He had the tools he sought. Now he must find a way to build on the slim foundation of trust he'd begun when he helped Han with the DNA scans. Unfortunately, no aid he could give the Chinese from within the auditorium would be significant enough to convince Chang that he could let La Roche wander freely about the station. La Roche needed something more, some sort of lucky break.

"Sir?"

Chang didn't look up from the list of Mingyun satellites, signal-jamming microsats, radar buoys, chaff clouds, and other countermeasures he'd deployed around Venus, checking coordinates and orbital vectors, looking for a weakness in his defenses. "Yes, private?"

"We've accounted for everyone on station except four people, who include the Baker kids and Mark Torben."

Now Chang looked up. He clenched the handles of his chair to keep from scratching the pain in his face. "Who's the fourth?"

"Amanda Baker. She's a planetary engineer. The kids' mother."

That couldn't be coincidence. "Where's their father?"

"According to her personnel file, the mother's divorced."

"She must be with the others. Find them. Look up their dorm and search it. I want to know who their friends are, where they might have gone. Use anybody you need. Just find them before they cause any more damage." With the lockdown and headcount complete, Chang could finally spare the resources.

He turned to Lieutenant Gou. "Begin clearing the Chinese nationals. Start with the Project and station facilities personnel. As soon as we find the last four hostages, release the cleared workers to their duties. Move everybody else to their residences." They'd be more comfortable there.

Chapter 11

Kelly lost track of time. She was bone tired and her mind was frayed. Synth would help, if she had it. She clasped her hands in her lap to keep them from searching her pockets for the umpteenth time. Though she closed her eyes, her nerves were stretched too taut for sleep.

"What are we gonna do?" Rod asked.

Mark didn't answer.

Kelly could feel his eyes on her. She pulled the flaps of her shirt over her chest and held them tight. "Sleep."

"Sleep?" Rod sounded disappointed. "I've never been in this part of the station before. I want to look around."

Kelly smiled despite herself. Leave it to Rod to find the grand adventure in everything. "It's not safe." She opened her eyes and found Mark's. "What do you think?"

He nodded. "It's too dangerous."

"Not that." She slapped his arm with the back of her hand. "About what to do next."

"That depends on whether they really will kill us if we turn ourselves in."

Kelly sighed. "I think it's safest to assume they will."

What was that? A rational, logical thought? Her mother would never have believed her capable of it. And Kelly had done everything she could to promote that belief. But now, too drained to connive or manipulate, she fell back on her base traits. And as much as she hated to admit it, she'd inherited her mother's analytical mind.

Mark continued to watch her.

She lacked the energy to flirt with him, but she did spare a smile for his look of concern. "We need to know what they're after and why they're willing to kill for it. What do we have, or know, that they want?"

"Well, let's see." A hint of sarcasm crept into Mark's voice as he ticked his points off on his fingers. "We stabbed one of Chang's men. We sabotaged the maintenance grid. We broke into La Roche's apartment and delivered a case that contains God knows what . . ."

Kelly shook her head until his voice faded to silence. "They shot at us before we did any of those things. They probably don't even know about the case."

Mark bit his lip, chewed it for a moment. "We escaped from the auditorium. Maybe they know that. If they do, they must assume we did it for a reason."

"To find Rod."

"They don't know that." Mark's voice rose in frustration.

"Shhh." She put her finger to her lip and glanced at the thin aluminite floor.

Mark sighed and settled himself more comfortably into their alcove. "I don't know what Chang's up to. But whatever it is, it's important enough to break treaties. He's brought weapons into space. The last time somebody did that, it started a war."

Kelly's heart leapt, suicidal, into a blind chasm. Chang was the name of the man who'd started that war. She never paid attention to politics, or even the newsblips for that matter, but even the most disconnected person couldn't have missed the China Dominion Affair. She tried to recall the details, but all she could remember was something about terrorist attacks and some illegal Chinese satellites. Kelly grabbed Mark's arm. "You don't think Chang works for the China Dominion?"

"Whoever he is, he's willing to take hostages from every major country in the world. He's isolated China. That means the stakes of his game are incredibly high or—"

"Or he's desperate."

"I'm still hungry," Rod said. "We should have eaten at your teacher's."

Kelly ignored him. "Do you know if China has those satellites around Venus?"

Mark nodded slowly. He'd been following the newsblips. They had interrupted more than one intimate moment. "Venus. Mercury. Jupiter. I don't remember how many, but I know China's been stalling their recovery."

"I heard the soldiers say something about Venus," Rod said.

Kelly shushed him. Her heart hadn't stopped falling. It hadn't found the bottom of her own fear and desperation.

"Fine." Rod got up and stormed off.

Mark was on his knees before Kelly could rise. "I'll get him."

He clambered after Rod. The low ceiling and cramped quarters of the crawlspace hampered his movements, but Rod slowed before either of them left Kelly's view.

"She didn't mean it," Mark told him. "This thing is hard on all of us."

Rod huffed. "Nobody ever listens to me."

Mark put a hand on his arm and turned the boy to face him. "*I'm* listening." He met Rod's eyes for a long moment, gave him time to believe it. "What did you hear? What did the soldiers say?"

Rod frowned. He looked back to where Kelly still sat in the alcove. He probably thought she couldn't hear him from there. "Why should I tell you now? You didn't care before."

"I did care. I do care. You stormed off before I could say anything."

Mark sat cross-legged before the boy and urged him to sit. "We need your help. It'll take all of us to figure this thing out. And what we decide affects you too."

That got to him. Kelly could see it in his eyes. Rod wanted them to know—wanted her to know—he had a stake in this. He was in as much danger as she and Mark. But she'd understood that from the beginning. Otherwise, they'd have stayed in the relative safety of the auditorium.

"She loves you, you know," Mark said.

"Who?"

"Kelly. You may be the only thing in the worlds that she does care about."

"She doesn't care about anything."

"She risked her life to find you, to make sure you were safe."

Rod grunted without looking up from the floor. "She never listens to me."

"She's been looking out for you since before you were old enough to make your own decisions. Sometimes people don't realize how much others have grown up."

Rod looked at Mark. He'd probably never heard those words, *grown up*, in reference to himself. He certainly hadn't heard them from Kelly or their mother.

Mark put a hand under Rod's chin and lifted the boy's gaze to meet his own. "We need your help. What did you overhear?"

For a moment, Rod said nothing. When he did speak, he looked almost embarrassed. "Not much, really. One of the soldiers got a comm on his link. After he finished, he said something to the others, something about space."

"Try to remember."

"Something about moving *Venus Rain* to a higher orbit, radar jamming, and Mingyun satellites. Stuff like that. Then he said, 'When we get to Center, prepare communications to send a message to President Li.'"

"That it?"

Rod shook his head. "Somebody else said, 'I guess that means Venus is ours.'"

Now Kelly's heart hit bottom. Chang was no terrorist. He was working for President Li, and he was here to hijack the entire planet. The stakes were *that* high. And she, her brother, and Mark had gotten into the middle of it.

Chang sat in the command chair of *Venus Rain* Center with his head back and his eyes closed. Only the incessant pivoting of his right hand betrayed his consciousness. He'd been up for twenty-four hours, but he had no intention of sleeping until he brought *Venus Rain* firmly under his control. For that, he must find the four missing residents.

"Colonel?"

"What is it, corporal?"

"I've found something in Mark Torben's financial account."

Chang didn't reply.

"He made a purchase from a food-vend about one o'clock this morning." After the lockdown had started. Even after he'd sabotaged the grid, which had just come back online.

Chang raised his head, squinted into the harsh glare of Center's solid-state lighting, and glanced at the chronometer. The transaction had taken place hours ago. But it gave him a place to start. He keyed his comm.

"Chang to Han. Mark Torben hit a food-vend last night. Corporal Ming will relay its location."

"Thank you, sir. That helps."

Another soldier arrived with a technician in his late fifties or early sixties, who fidgeted in his dark blue company jumpsuit.

The tech stumbled to a halt and stared in horror at Chang's ruined face.

For that alone, Chang could have thrown him out the nearest airlock. No matter how long he lived with his deformity, he never got used to the ignorant reactions of others. It had taken a decade of practice to temper his own response. "You work for the Project?"

The man nodded slowly.

"What's your name?"

"Chen Tongyi."

"What do you do for the Project, Mr. Chen?"

"Nothing." The man shifted his weight from side to side as if he wanted to run but didn't dare move his feet. "I monitor the systems. I watch the readouts and contact my supervisor if something alarms. That's all. I don't know anything."

"It's okay. You're not in trouble. We just need someone who knows what he's looking at to keep an eye on the processors while we sort everyone out."

The man's eyes widened. "Sort out?"

"Relax. We've already checked your background. You've been cleared to return to your duties. The first to return, in fact." Chang didn't count Lin Anni, who'd already been escorted back to her dorm and confined there until further notice.

Chen breathed easier then, but he refused to look at Chang's face. "Yes, sir. I'll see to my work." He turned to go, but a soldier blocked the doorway.

Chang motioned to one of the terminals in Center. "We've routed the readouts here." The tech wouldn't be able to see his panels, but he could query status and receive any fault codes.

Chen glanced at the soldier in the doorway. "I am a prisoner?"

"No, no. Of course not. We've had problems with the grid. We don't know if your equipment in the Project hub is up and running." In truth, the hub was alive and active, just unmanned for the moment.

Chen looked at Chang with his eyes narrowed. He knew more about the Project's systems than he was letting on. Good. Chang had been counting on it.

"But that's not my real concern," Chang continued. "Until we clear more of your colleagues for their own duties, you won't have the support you need if an emergency arises. As you've probably guessed, we're here for the Project. It must continue despite anything else that happens. I want to make sure you have everything you need as quickly as possible."

Chen stared at Chang for a long moment, then shot a glance at the door and moved to his assigned station.

Within moments, he began keying commands and shaking his head of pewter hair.

"Something wrong, Mr. Chen?"

Chen's hands pounded his board. "Everything. We should be getting a continuous feed of data from every processor. We have dedicated comm channels and a network of satellites. It's like they're all dead."

"I'm jamming comm beyond the confines of the station."

Chen turned slowly. His gaze darted among the many illegal weapons Chang's men carried. "You said you brought me here to monitor the processors. How do you expect me to do that without a data feed?"

"Surely you have other means. Less detailed. Less complete, perhaps. This station must have instruments to monitor Venus."

"Of course, but those measure the effect the processors have on the atmosphere. They don't monitor the processors or their systems directly. If we lose one for some reason, the atmospheric spectrum may not deviate from the models for days.

"Unless. . ." Chen spun back to his board. "I could focus the sensors on the emissions of each processor as we pass over and compare the reading to baseline. It'll give me something, at least."

"Qin, take us to a lower orbit, low enough so the screen of chaff won't obscure Mr. Chen's readings." He turned back to his other duties, but Chen wasn't finished.

"You realize I can't see all the processors at once? With atmospheric distortion, I'll only get meaningful readouts from stations within a thirty-degree arc of our longitude."

Chang nodded. He considered himself to be a reasonable man . . . for an officer in the People's Army. "Let me know if you need anything."

Kelly awoke in the cramped confines of the crawlspace. The sound of heavy footsteps echoed up from the corridor beneath her with a gait she couldn't mistake. Han.

"Shit," she breathed.

Rod gasped. He slapped one hand over his mouth and pointed at her with that I-caught-you look in his eye.

Kelly ignored him. She cast a worried look at Mark as Han drew closer.

"Down the hall," he ordered. "Search the dorms."

Lighter footsteps hurried away.

Han stopped directly beneath. Kelly could hear his breathing through the floor. She held her own breath and tried to will even her heart to silence.

"Search the interstitial." Han banged the ceiling with the force of a sledge hammer.

A whimper escaped Kelly's mouth. She stifled it with her palm. Mark brought his finger to his lips. Rod's eyes grew wide as the heavens.

"That's how they got out in the first place," Han continued. "You. Find a hatch. Get up there. Now."

More footsteps.

Pipes, electrical conduit, and vent shafts crisscrossed the crawlspace. They served only habitation level six and were small in size. They hindered movement but provided little obstruction to vision. Worse, the whole space was awash in whites and grays. Kelly's bright blue shirt and pink hair would stand out like a Jovian moon in the Terran sky.

Then the banging started. Within moments, an access hatch from the floor below snapped up, the latch pounded to failure by the butt of a pistol, which came into view as a man began to climb through. The soldier need only turn to see them.

Throwing her makeshift crowbar at the man, Kelly launched herself into motion.

Han shouted from below. A burst of rifle rounds perforated the floor where Kelly had been, narrowly missing Mark.

Bullets ripped through the interstitial's ceiling, the innermost skin of the habitation cylinder, and into the vacuum of space. Air swept toward the breaches. A piercing whistle filled the crawlspace. Pressure panels snapped closed along the environmental ducts, sealing the vents. Doors slammed shut across the access hatches. The soldier pulled his legs through as a safety door sealed him into the crawlspace.

Rod slid across the smooth aluminite floor, swept by the wind, until Kelly caught his collar. She hauled him along a utility conduit toward a nearby hatch.

"Come on," she shouted over the rush of wind. Already the air was nearly too thin to breathe. Her lungs labored for oxygen.

Mark reached the hatch first. He twisted the handle and yanked it open. The pressure door beneath had a manual override, if he could cycle it in time.

Gunshots rang over the whistle of air. Han's soldier didn't rush after them or even scramble for safety. He tried to steady his aim in the crosswind and pulled the trigger again.

Kelly shoved Rod to the floor and crawled onward.

"Hold on to something," Mark shouted.

Kelly gripped a pipe with one hand and Rod's arm with the other. Mark levered the override and slid the pressure seal aside. The rush of air from the corridor below threatened to tear her away. She gulped in some of the air, but her lungs cried for more.

Doors slammed into place on the housing deck and the pressure continued to drop.

The shots of the soldier subsided. He flailed toward the holes. The pitch of the whining air shifted as his body sealed half the breaches.

Mark grabbed Rod's free arm. Together, he and Kelly heaved Rod through the hatch against the waning current.

Kelly followed. Her cells screamed for oxygen. Her mind shouted distress. All of her instincts told her to keep the treasured air she had in her lungs until her body consumed every molecule of oxygen it contained. But she couldn't. Nineteen years of safety briefings took hold. By a force of conscious will that overrode every shriek of her body, she blew out the breath that sustained her to prevent it from bursting her lungs in the plummeting pressure.

Mark crawled through the hatch and braced his feet on either side of it. The rent in his face split again and red mist streamed behind him. He muscled the pressure hatch back into place and dropped, unconscious, to the floor.

Rod crawled aimlessly near the edge of the corridor, gasping for something to feed his blood.

Kelly's own head spun. She fought to retain consciousness.

Center must have seen the pressure doors slam when Mark opened the hatch, so Han was already on his way. He might even be waiting in the hall for the air handler to restore the pressure, which it would do within minutes. Then they would be his.

Chapter 12

Air whistled past Lieutenant Han, through the interstitial, and into space. Safety doors sealed him and two of his men inside the breached corridor.

"You idiot," the sergeant beside him shouted. "You've killed us."

Han smashed the man's face with the butt of his rifle and sent him sprawling, senseless, to the floor in a spray of blood.

He spun on his other man, a mere private, to see if he had any objections to offer. The private stared as though he lacked the courage to choose his own form of death.

Already lightheaded, Han marched to the nearest safety door, his footsteps made faint by the thin air. Though the doors weren't designed as security systems, they had utility in a military context. Han had studied them.

He cycled through before the pressure dropped beyond override levels. That brought in a rush of air and slammed a second row of doors farther down the hall. Without so much as a glance at the insubordinate sergeant, he sealed the door behind him and the environmental system began to stabilize the pressure.

He cycled the next door open and found one of his men waiting for him. Han keyed the link in his ear. "Han to Center."

"Center," Chang answered personally. "What's going on out there? Maintenance reports pressure doors cycling all over the place."

"We've had a vacuum breach. I lost at least one man, but I think I've found the fugitives. Have any hatches to the interstitial cycled open since the breach?"

"Checking." Chang went silent.

When the link came alive again, Corporal Ming answered. "One cycled just after the breach."

"Where?" Han threw all his intensity into the question.

"Corridor sixty-eight. Where are you?"

"Outside dorm sixty-six, fourteen."

"Go station south and take your first left."

Han was already moving.

"Left again at sixty-eight."

He rounded the second corner and found his way sealed.

"You'll see a pressure door," Ming said. "The hallway beyond has already begun to pressurize. The door should open in a few minutes. The kids are behind it."

The air handler wasn't filling the corridor fast enough. Kelly fought down nausea and vertigo until she reached the nearest pressure door, cycled the manual override, and flooded the hallway with oxygen from the intersection on the other side.

The sudden gust knocked her from her feet and doors slammed shut down each of the adjoining halls. She turned her face to the oncoming wind, breathed deeply, and pushed herself to her feet. Already she felt better, though the pressure was still well below station normal.

By the time she got back to the others, Rod had crawled to his feet and was trying to slap Mark to consciousness.

"Too bad we don't have water," Kelly said.

"I could pee on him."

Kelly scowled. She pointed at a pressure door at the far end of the hallway she'd just opened. "You know how to open that door?"

"Duh."

"Do it."

Rod stared at Mark's face. "He's bleeding again."

"Rod."

Still no movement.

"Now, damn it!"

Rod threw his hands into the air as if to ward off her profanity. "All right already. I'm going."

Kelly felt the need to watch him, to make sure he did what he was told, but she didn't have time. Instead, she grabbed Mark by the shoulders and dragged him toward the door.

Rod forced the override lever into place and the barrier slid aside. The rush of incoming air didn't come close to what Kelly had experienced with the first door. The environmental system was catching up.

A door slammed somewhere nearby, then another. If Mark hadn't thrown the gun away, Kelly could have shot a hole through the ceiling and separated themselves from Han by a shield of vacuum. A barrier of nothing. She didn't even have the pipe she'd carried into the interstitial. The only weapon she had left was speed. She needed another. She was tired of running. It was time to fight back.

The notion seemed absurd. Fight? Ha! The only things she'd ever been good at were sex and chemistry.

What she needed was a lab. Not a university or planetary science lab, but a real lab. And she knew where to find one.

Another door slammed, this one closer.

Rod cast a worried glance in the direction of the sound.

"That one." Kelly pointed to the door she wanted.

Rod sprinted for it.

Kelly dragged Mark behind her. She left the doors they passed open so she could hear them slam shut as Han approached. Mark's head rolled to the side and a moan escaped his lips. Kelly pulled him through the door, then pointed Rod toward the next one.

Finally, Mark began to crawl to his feet.

"Come on." She put his arm over her shoulder and wrapped hers around his waist. "One more door. Then we're done." If she was right.

Another door slammed behind them. *Shit.*

The next room contained half a dozen pressure suits. Instead of an interstitial above it, a ladder led to an airlock. Beyond that, space.

"Are you serious?" Mark said.

Kelly grabbed a suit from the rack and shoved it at him. "Put this on."

"Cool." Rod pulled down the smallest suit there, though it was way too big for him.

Mark hesitated. "Have you ever done this before?"

"No. Hurry." Kelly ran up the ladder and cycled open the airlock's inner door. Like it or not, they were all going EVA.

Despite his reservations, Mark began to work his way into one of the suits.

Kelly jumped to the floor and pulled a suit from the rack. It had a hard-shelled torso with a control panel on the belly and oxygen tanks strapped to the back. An inner garment, woven with poly tubing, attached to sleeves of neoprene and flexsteel. At least the legs and boots seemed self-explanatory.

Kelly pulled them on, then helped Mark lift Rod into his pants. She lowered the torso over the boy's head and cinched a life belt around him. Mark twisted on Rod's gloves and helmet.

Another door slammed closed. Surely the air had stabilized by now. It felt normal, but even low pressure seemed more than adequate after what they'd come through.

Kelly pulled on her own torso piece, donned a belt with a pair of lifelines on retracting spools. She grabbed the gloves, rotated the wrist clamps into place, and then snapped the helmet down. A hiss of air filled the suit and the status lights flashed on. All green. "You guys green?" she asked.

No one answered.

She tapped Mark's helmet and he turned toward her.

"You green?" She asked again.

He seemed not to hear. The EVA suits must have used the station intercom, which Chang had shut down. Either that or Kelly just didn't know how to turn them on. So she settled for a show of thumbs up.

Mark returned the gesture.

Kelly queried Rod in the same manner and he indicated green as well. She prayed he was right. She hadn't come this far to lose him now.

The pressure readout on the wall said 60k. Station normal was 75, too low by Earth standards but sufficient with the oxygen-rich air mixture used on *Venus Rain*. Another ten seconds and every pressure door on the level would open, clearing the way for Han and his men.

Kelly raced up the ladder and hit MANUAL CONTROL. A warning light told her the inner door was open. No shit. She slid aside the panel labeled EMERGENCY OVERRIDE and pulled the lever. Just as the room equalized at station normal, the airlock door flew open, forced by the pressure inside the donning room.

Kelly, Mark, and Rod rocketed into space, blown like projectiles, followed by the three remaining pressure suits and all the loose gear in the room. In her haste, they'd forgotten to tether themselves to the station.

Chapter 13

Every door of the auditorium had been closed and sealed, their access codes changed from Station Center. A single guard remained to watch the thousand prisoners, who wouldn't be returned to their homes, they were told, until Mark, Kelly, her brother, and her mom were captured.

Thus the attendees of the thirtieth anniversary celebration spent the night in the auditorium. Some slept in their seats, others on the floor. Most didn't seem to sleep at all. La Roche wasn't one of them.

He could have stayed up to plan and scheme a way out during the nighttime hours, while the guard was thin. But if he escaped, he'd become a fugitive, like Kelly and Mark, running through the interstices of the station, trying on his old and battered hips to stay one step ahead of Chang's patrols.

That wouldn't serve his purpose one iota.

Instead, he worked through the problems Chang would encounter until he found one he could help with: food for the prisoners. It wasn't much, but it would allow La Roche to take another small step toward gaining freedom. The middle of the night, however, wasn't the time to bring it up.

So he slept on the corner of the stage.

The next morning, he levered himself to his feet and approached the guard. After what had happened the last time he neared the main doors, the bystanders watched him with equal measures of pity and respect. He was a slow learner, they might have thought, but he had the courage to do what they did not. In truth, he had no choice. His purpose was greater than theirs.

"We need food," he told the guard. Water was less of a problem, since the prisoners had been getting it from the sink in the lavatory.

"Impossible."

"Why?"

"We haven't the manpower to manage the people. If we bring in food and can't maintain order, someone'll get hurt."

"Let me tell you about these people." La Roche adopted the tone he used when he needed to bring his class to heel. "They're tired. They're hungry. Most of them haven't slept in over twenty-four hours."

The guard looked at him as though La Roche's litany bored him or he didn't comprehend the language.

Unperturbed, La Roche continued. "You're holding them against their will. They watched your lieutenant murder their friend and colleague. As far as they know, they're next."

Disinterest faded from the solder's eyes.

"You push these people and you'll have a riot on your hands. Then how long do you think that popgun will keep you alive?"

The guard glanced uncertainly at the rifle he was holding.

"I've heard talk among them," La Roche lied. "It's not far off. Food would go a long way toward diffusing their tempers. It would show goodwill. You can't release them to their quarters? I understand. If you can't make them comfortable, at least give them what they need to survive."

A plea entered the soldier's eyes. He wanted to help, but he couldn't. Maybe Chang or Han had ordered him not to.

"If you can have something delivered—a cartload of provisions from one of the grocery supply depots and a portable food-prep station would be plenty—I'll make sure the people don't trample one another to get it."

The prisoners nearby began to mumble amongst themselves. A few offered silent nods of support.

The soldier keyed the link in his ear and spoke a litany of Chinese words that La Roche pretended not to understand. When the guard finished, he agreed.

La Roche went into the media room, plugged the equipment back in, and turned on the microphone. Nobody watched him. Nobody cared.

Then he hobbled to the front of the auditorium and climbed the steps to the stage. The promise of food would encourage enough volunteers to distribute the provisions in an orderly manner. That would solve a problem for Chang that his solders hadn't recognized, or at least hadn't addressed, until La Roche brought it up. The action wasn't likely to escape Chang's notice.

"What is it?" Chang asked.

"Something you should see, sir."

Chang didn't want to see. Chen was going to show him data, some scan result or cryptic error message Chang wouldn't comprehend. Nevertheless, he pushed himself from his seat, bone-tired, and feigned a passing interest.

He'd been sent to commandeer the Project, to commandeer the planet without interrupting the Project, an impossible task by any estimation. *Venus Rain* housed two thousand people because that's what it took to maintain the Project—and Chang had only forty men to accomplish his mission. That's all he could cram onto the standard complement of transports, along with all the technical and military equipment and countermeasures, and a minimum of supplies. Any more ships, any more capacity for men or military gear, would have drawn notice from China's enemies. Only a single freighter had been added to the scheduled supply convoy, which President Li justified by claiming its purpose was to retrieve and dismantle Mingyun satellites in Venus orbit. Anything beyond that would have doomed Chang's mission before it left Earth, before President Li could lay the blame of failure upon the mission commander, Colonel Chang.

As it was, Chang could hope for success only if the processors ran by themselves until his men could clear a sufficient workforce to maintain them.

Now this.

Chen pointed to a false-color display of Venus, all reds and yellows and shades in between, an infrared thermal image. Each of the atmosphere processors, spaced at regular intervals on the surface, appeared as a cool blue dot.

Chen pointed to one processor that stood out, white, among the rest. "Processor thirteen is running hot."

"Why?"

"I don't know. Without a data feed from the surface, I can't check the systems. I can't determine if the pumps are running, if the thermal contactors are working, or how much coolant it has. If you reestablish comm, I'll tell you in a matter of minutes how serious it is."

"I can't do that."

Chen threw up his hands. "Then why am I here? You gave me a job. Now give me the resources to do it."

Chang almost laughed out loud. He'd made a career out of doing his job without the resources he needed. It had taught him that people rarely needed everything they thought they did. Instead, he shrugged as if he didn't care. "I'm sure you'll think of something."

Panic flooded through Kelly like a frigid wave of death as she shot past the threshold into space. She reached for the lip of the opening. Her fingers caught just enough of the edge to knock her into an endless cartwheel. Mark and Rod followed her through, both forced into space by Kelly's own recklessness. And the only one who might know they were there was Lieutenant Han, a man who wanted them dead. Kelly had just done his job for him.

Her mother's voice came unbidden to her mind. "You never think, Kelly. You know that? You run off, so desperate to destroy yourself that you never consider the consequences . . ." She'd said that just last week, after she found another tin of synth in Kelly's room, as if she had the right to care now that Kelly was of legal age. Her mother's litany went on, of course, but as always, Kelly shut it out of her mind as non-sequitur.

Her senses fought for orientation. What registered first was the lack of stars. Space, yes, all around her, but no stars. A giant pillar passed her faceplate, hundreds or thousands of meters away—she had no reference to gauge the distance. She'd launched them all into the gap between the huge habitation cylinder and the central axis about which it rotated. The immense spoke that swung past was one of many that linked the cylinder to the core.

All around Kelly spun manmade hardware, filled with life, but the light of the housing decks was shut away from her, shielded by the deck-six overhead crawlspace. The only light came from a dozen airlocks that linked the station's world of life with Kelly's universe of death.

The docking ring at the north end of the axis came into view, impossibly far away. It should have blazed with an array of flood lamps that usually lit the hatches, seals, grapples, and power feeds that serviced any ships docked there. All that remained was a single flashing beacon.

She saw the axis, the dark core of the station. Two huge, counter-rotating masses bulged from the slender shaft. The larger mass was *Venus Rain* Center. The other, toward the south end of the axis, the end that pointed toward the planet, held the station's helium fusion reactor. Between the two, stationary as the core, sat dozens of privately owned, zero-g research laboratories to which Kelly had been headed before she lost control.

Aside from the zero-g playground she'd played on as a child, the greenhouses that were required field trips in grade school, the stores and shops on the Concourse, and the teen hangouts and clubs, that was the extent of her knowledge of the station.

It was enough. Hope began to shine through her despair like the Sun through polarized durapane, a little at a time. Except for the north and south ends of the axis, *Venus Rain* surrounded her, Mark, and Rod. Unless they drifted out one end or the other, they would reach some part of the station. If they could clip their lifelines to something, they could find their way back inside.

But Kelly had a specific objective in mind. For that, she had to reach the axis.

The kilometer between it and the cylinder seemed like a light year, which she traversed by slow increments defined by her rotations. Lights inside the spokes spun past like the wheel of a giant carnival ride. But bit by bit, the axis came closer.

If she was lucky, she would get there before Chang figured out what had happened, and Han and his dogs would still be hunting for them in the cylinder.

Eventually, the central beam of the station loomed before her, close enough to make out some of the details. External ladders ran the length of it. Dark windows broke the matte surface at regular intervals. Airlocks provided maintenance access to the magnetic bushings that connected the stationary core to the rotating spokes and the counter-spinning control room and power reactor.

The closer the axis got, the more Kelly realized she was traveling way too fast. God, she couldn't even see it past her fishbowl helmet most of the time. It loomed, then was gone, replaced by the south end of the cylinder. Venus blocked out the stars. A world hotter than any other planet in the solar system. Hell incarnate. A storm of fireflies, like nothing she'd ever seen from inside the station, floated between her and the planet.

When the cylinder returned to her vision, she lost all sense of orientation. The entire ring looked the same. She grasped the clip of her lifeline and said her prayer. "We're all going to hell anyway."

Then the core spun back into view . . . too close.

She slammed against it with her shoulder and chest. The pain in her breast sent a wave of nausea through her.

Blinded by the impact, she struck out toward the ladder with the loop in her hand, hoping beyond hope that its latch would catch on something. Then she bounced away.

Seconds later the line snapped taut. Something inside her tore.

She groped for the cable as she came around, found the loop, and froze. She'd missed the ladder. The clip hadn't caught. The hoop wedged between a pole of the ladder and one of the rungs and held only until the line slackened, and then the loop drifted free. Nothing held her to the core, and she'd spent her momentum toward the cylinder. She was lost, no more than twenty meters from the axis.

That twenty meters might as well have been twenty light years.

Mark and Rod were nowhere in sight.

CHAPTER 14

The instant the airlock flew open, Mark grabbed Rod's shoulders and hugged the boy to him. Wind gathered them up and propelled them from the donning room behind Kelly. Though he'd never gone EVA, his shock resembled fear for only a moment. It felt like the thrill of his shuttle launch from Earth, sudden g followed by weightlessness and space.

He knew as they suited up, of course, that Kelly had a space walk in mind. It was the manner in which she initiated it that surprised him. She had this impulsiveness, refreshing and scary, in everything she did. That, more than anything, was why he'd fallen in love with her. And like the way she had sex, the explosive decompression of the whole donning room was intense, spontaneous, and brilliant.

Once they were outside, Rod's panicked thrashing threatened Mark's grip until he held nothing more than a fold of excess neoprene along Rod's sleeve. The boy, too small in his man-sized pressure suit, had no way to grab hold of anything when they reached the axis or the far side of the habitation cylinder.

"Rod!" Mark yelled. "Rod!" But no sound made it past his helmet. His hand began to cramp before he finally got the clip of his lifeline hooked around a loop on Rod's belt.

He shifted his grip and grabbed the boy's shoulders again. Mark hugged him until he stopped struggling. By increments, Rod seemed to realize that, for the moment at least, he was okay.

Then Mark took stock of their trajectory. Kelly tumbled away ahead of them, angled toward the south end of the axis, while Mark's path remained true. He didn't want to ponder what might account for Kelly's change of direction, but his mind gave him the possibilities anyway: she'd hit the bulkhead on the way out of the hatch, her suit or tank was venting something —oxygen or coolant—into space, or both.

Eventually, his own slow somersaults put her behind him. By then, she'd become a mere speck in the darkness.

In his mind, Mark saw her as he always had: drifting, lost and alone. Defiant and terrified. He sought some way to help her. For the moment, there was none, so he focused on Rod instead. He eased out some line between himself and the boy to increase the chance that one of them, or the line itself, would catch on something and hold them to the station.

The two had several minutes before they'd reach the station's axis. Maybe a half-hour or more—Mark couldn't tell—but the collision wasn't imminent. He had time to prepare.

He perused the control panels on the arms and chest of his suit. The buttons he could read were labeled in Chinese. Though they were back-lit, many of the markings had been worn off by years, maybe decades, of use.

Rod had drifted thirty or forty meters out by the time Mark completed his suit survey. He continued to ease out the line until it reached the end of its length. By then, the counter-rotating mass of the fusion power plant loomed close, matte black and windowless.

Mark pressed a button labeled with the symbol for shoes and a magnet icon. With effort, he forced the weight of his boots over his head and tried to come at the whirling mass feet-first. He hit it with a glancing blow and bounced away.

On the rebound, he passed near the axis and grabbed the ladder that ran the length of it. When his feet came down, electromagnets in the soles of his boots latched onto the deck.

Mark hooked an elbow around one of the rungs, clutched his forearm to his chest with his other hand, and held tight.

The lifeline snapped Rod to a stop and Mark reeled him in. On the strength of his boots' magnets, Mark climbed over the spinning bulk of the reactor toward where he'd last seen Kelly.

Kelly was six, maybe seven. She and her dad were building holograms from pre-fab subroutines with the Holomaster XL-10 at the kitchen table.

She put the head on a pink pony she'd constructed. "Run. Run, pony. Run."

The pony pranced halfway around the table, blinked out, returned as a ball of fluff more like a mutated lamb than a horse, and rolled sideways to the edge of the emitter's range before disappearing altogether.

She and her dad laughed as he reset the program. Back then, she never could get her constructs just right, which was okay. It was more fun when she didn't.

Her mom walked in and shook her head. "Are you guys at that again?" She made some tea and hot chocolate from the selection of drink packets over the stove and brought them to the table. "Let's play a game."

"This is a game," Kelly said.

"How about mahjong?" Her dad keyed the Holomaster and mahjong appeared on the table in front of them.

Kelly pouted. "I don't get mahjong."

"Chinese checkers, then." Her mom made the change.

"Cool." Kelly touched the pad, turned her pieces pink, and rubbed her hands together, smiling deviously. "I go first."

Life with her parents had been like that once, not always bitter and depressing. Kelly could admit it to herself now that it no longer mattered.

She watched the green bar on her O_2 gauge creep downward and wondered how many long-lost memories she'd have to endure before the tank finally went empty. All the while, the station's axis drifted slowly, inexorably away.

When Mark and Rod rounded the edge of the power plant's cylinder, Kelly's squeal of delight nearly pierced her eardrums in the confines of her helmet.

Mark snapped one of the lifelines on Rod's waist to a rung of the ladder and locked the reel so the boy wouldn't drift away. Just to be sure, Rod wrapped his arms around the ladder and hugged it to his chest, the way he used to hug his favorite blanket as a child.

Mark clipped his own line to a rung and pushed off toward Kelly. He came at her with his arms spread, ready to embrace her. God, he was coming fast. If he didn't get hold of her on the first try, he was going to knock her farther into space. Her heart thudded in her chest. Mark's approach was the most frightening and welcome sight she'd ever seen.

But he never got there. His lifeline snapped tight several meters short. Kelly had already drifted too far from the axis. She was already lost.

Mark hung in space for interminable seconds, impossibly far away yet close enough that she could have seen his eyes if not for the tint of his face-plate. Slowly, he turned and pulled himself back to the axis. At least Rod was safe. That was the most important thing.

If only she could talk to them.

Mark seemed to watch her for a few minutes, and then he launched himself at her again. This time he flailed his arms, as if he was trying to swim to her. Once again, his lifeline stopped him.

Kelly's heart sank as he made three more futile attempts to reach her on a tether that was just too short.

On Mark's sixth try, however, something different happened. After flailing his arms, he reached toward his belt, as if to unhook his own lifeline.

"No!" Kelly yelled. Realizing he couldn't hear, she whispered the rest to herself. "Rod needs you."

A tug at her waist yanked her from her despair. The pain that had begun to fade from her shoulder throbbed once more. She welcomed the sensation more than she would have welcomed synth. Mark hadn't unhooked his own line—he'd found hers, which she'd left dangling, lost in the darkness, behind her. He hooked it to his belt and, hand over hand, reeled her in.

Before she did anything else, Kelly looped one of her tethers all the way under the ladder from right to left and hooked it to her belt. Gritting her teeth, she trudged down the axis until she came to the first set of the ladder's anchors.

There, she wrapped her other line around the ladder on the far side of the bracket before releasing the first line. *See, Mom? I do think. I can learn from my mistakes.* She switched lines at every bracket until she came to the last airlock before the bulbous protrusions of the labs.

Mark followed with Rod in tow.

Kelly reached for the lock controls, but Mark stayed her hand with his. When she looked up, he touched his faceplate to hers and yelled, "You have any idea what you're doing?" His voice, carried from his suit to hers through the vibration of their faceplates, sounded coarse and mechanical.

"Yes!"

"As soon as you open that door," he yelled, "they'll know we're here."

"You got a better idea?"

After a moment, he pulled away and motioned to the controls.

She pressed OPEN and the chamber inside began pumping down.

She didn't have time to wait for the lock to cycle. The maintenance grid would have shown the start of the pump-down. Therefore, Chang's men were already on their way. She made sure she and Mark were still anchored to the ladder and that Rod was strapped to him—some things she'd never forget to do again. Then she pulled the override.

"Colonel, airlock ten just opened."

Chang marched over to Ming's display. A red light flashed two-thirds of the way down a diagram of *Venus Rain*'s axis. "Inside or outside?"

The light went out. "That was the outer door. The inner door is still sealed."

Chang stifled a smile that would have pained the damaged side of his face and keyed the link in his ear. "Han, where are you? We have an intruder in airlock ten, on the axis."

Han answered immediately. "All my men are in the cylinder. I didn't think the fugitives would cross the gap." He seemed reluctant to call them kids, as Chang did, which was probably wise. The fact that they were nearly children didn't change what had to be done. "Are you sure it's them?"

The signal for the airlock's inner door flashed open. "I'm sure." It was either the kids and Amanda Baker, or it was something worse, an enemy who had somehow reached the station undetected.

Han began barking orders into the pickup, directing his men to cordon off the exits from the station's core. He asked Ming to free the lifts he needed. But he was too far away. Whatever the kids were planning, they'd have it done before he got there.

Chang pointed to the guard at the door. "Get those kids. Take them to the hold, or take them to the morgue." *Bleed the innocence.* "I'm giving you a man from Center," he told Han. "He's headed to the airlock now."

The air passed Kelly in its mad rush into space. Once the airlock was empty, the three moved in and Kelly keyed the pressurization sequence. They waited interminable minutes for the chamber to come to atmosphere. *Open,* her heart said with every beat. All the while, Chang's men were coming.

Finally the door cycled and they rushed in. Kelly popped the seals on her helmet and pulled it loose, gasping for air as if her suit hadn't provided enough.

Mark pulled his own helmet free and clipped it to his belt.

"You guys all right?" Kelly shook her hair free of the collar ring and let the neon strands float in the zero-g of the station's axis. That was all the freedom she allowed herself.

Mark helped Rod out of his helmet.

"Get me out!" The boy clawed at the clasps of his suit, his voice hoarse as if his throat was raw. "Get me out! Get me out!"

"Leave it on," she told him. "We'll need them."

"No." He looked stricken. "I can't do that again."

Kelly took his face in her hands and drew his gaze to hers. "It's all right. You're all right." She hugged him until his breathing settled.

"Don't make me go out there," he said when she released him. "I can't."

She turned away, toward the corridor.

"Please," Rod said.

Kelly looked as far as she could see down the pipe in both directions. Light illuminated a section at the far end of the tunnel. One of Chang's soldiers hurried toward them. The man's clothes were dark, not white like a pressure suit. Surely by now he'd heard about the disaster Han had created on deck six. If so, he wouldn't dare pull a trigger at that distance.

She propelled herself down the main corridor by the zero-g handles. Each pull tugged at the pain in her shoulder. The only lights were those lit by motion sensors as they moved from one ten-meter section to the next.

She reached a series of side tunnels that led to half a dozen laboratories, scanned the Chinese markers at the intersection, and turned the corner.

"How do you plan to get in?" Mark struggled to keep up while towing Rod behind him on a tether.

Kelly didn't look back. "That's your job, computer guy."

"Wait."

She stopped. "What?"

"There's sensitive data in those labs. I don't have the security codes."

"Then break in."

"What are you after?"

Jesus. He sounded like her mother. But he wasn't, so she answered. "Chemicals."

"Then go to the storeroom. It'll be locked, but not as securely as the labs."

Again she'd been acting without thinking. Fortunately, Mark wasn't. She wanted to hug him but didn't have time. Instead, she squeezed past and backtracked to the main corridor.

Chang's man worked his way closer, but *Venus Rain* was huge and the tunnel was deceptively long. At least half a kilometer of corridor stretched between her and the soldier. She had a few minutes, maybe. No more. And she didn't even know specifically what she was after. She'd have to see what she could find and hope it was something she could use.

Signs led her down another tube to the storeroom door. Mark pulled his EVA suit down to his knees and dug La Roche's utility knife from his pants pocket. He cut into the panel, shorted the lock, and forced the door open.

"I'll be back in a minute." He moved toward another hatch, labeled SPARES AND CONSUMABLES.

"Stay here," Kelly told Rod in her do-what-I-say-or-I'll-kick-your-ass voice. She enunciated her words clearly. "Don't. Touch. Anything."

"Aww, man."

Then she pulled herself into the spherical storeroom. Four unlocked cabinets hugged the walls: acids, caustics, flammables, and oxidizers. She opened one of the doors. Bottles hung in rows, their caps stuffed into clips to keep them from drifting in weightlessness.

She read some of the labels and failed to recognize most of the exotic stuff, but the basics were there. Phosphoric acid. Sulfuric. She grabbed one-liter bottles of several things she thought she could use, starting with ammonia. It would explode with any number of incompatible chemicals, like the next two she grabbed: iodine and hydrofluoric acid. She stuffed the bottles into the pockets of her pressure suit without thinking past the possibility of a rupture in the vacuum of space. As bad as that would be, she ignored the consequences. In some sense, it didn't matter. She must protect herself and Rod. She had to know she could fight back if necessary.

On her way out, she grabbed a bottle of acetone from the flammables cabinet and pocketed a handful of latex gloves from a dispenser to help her handle the stuff. By the time she finished, Mark was waiting with Rod, his pockets stuffed full of hardware and tools he'd taken from the parts room.

"Ready?" Kelly pulled herself back to the main aisle without waiting for an answer.

Shit. Chang's soldier was almost on them, and he'd built up so much momentum they'd never outrun him.

Kelly launched herself across the main tube to another spur that jutted from the axis, found an unlocked door, and fled inside. As she'd hoped, the zero-g office had a window, but it faced station-south, toward Venus, the open end of the habitation cylinder. If they came loose from the station this time, nothing would stop them before they hit the planet's atmosphere.

"Lock it." She pushed herself to the desk and made sure it was bolted to the floor.

Mark swung himself in and planted his feet. Rod waddled beside him, his feet also stuck to the floor.

"How did you do that?" she asked.

Mark pointed to a control on his wrist. "Magnetic boots."

Kelly found the button on her own arm and locked herself down too. "Come here." She clipped Rod's lifeline to Mark's belt and Mark's tether to her own waist. Her line, she wrapped around the foot of the anchored desk. "Put your helmets on. And whatever you do, don't look at the window."

Mark stared at her as if she'd lost her mind, but complied.

Rod glanced past her. "No." He shook his head frantically. "Not outside."

A pounding began at the door.

"Do it," Kelly yelled.

Mark grabbed Rod's helmet, batted the boy's protesting hands aside, and snapped it into place.

Kelly put on her own helmet, then took the hydrofluoric acid from her pocket. She opened the bottle and splashed the chemical in an X pattern onto the window. Droplets splattered off and drifted in the air. She tossed the empty bottle into a corner just as two gunshots ripped through the lock on the door.

The soldier shouldered his way in, pistol ready.

Chapter 15

Words scrolled across the screen of La Roche's thinpad, "I'm giving you a man from Center. He's headed to the airlock now."

Software provided by his government intercepted and decoded Chang's transmission. La Roche could have read it in Chinese and developed a more accurate interpretation. But since he wasn't supposed to understand the language and didn't want to raise the suspicion of anyone who might catch a glimpse of his screen, La Roche accepted the imperfect translation and monitored the exchange in silence, his features schooled to neutrality.

He didn't have to bring up a schematic to locate airlock ten. He'd spent years studying this station: its layout, occupancy load, facilities, supply requirements, computing capacity, transmitting power and bandwidth . . . Some of the information he sought was company- proprietary. Some was classified and largely inaccessible unless he wanted to raise unnecessary suspicion, but over the past decade, he'd gathered what he could.

One of Chang's soldiers approached.

With a single touch, La Roche transformed his screen into a series of dynamic graphs.

"What that?" the man asked in broken English.

"Atmospheric projections." La Roche offered him the thinpad as though he thought the data might somehow interest the man. "Anybody keeping an eye on the processors?"

The soldier scowled at the screen. "Food here."

With a nod, La Roche slipped the pad into the inside pocket of his rumpled sports coat and struggled to his feet. Right now, food was the one thing he'd welcome more than data. Unfortunately, because he'd volunteered to coordinate the distribution, and because it would set a good example for the others, he'd have to wait until everyone else was served before he himself could eat.

Kelly stared down the barrel of the soldier's gun as he floated in the doorway.

Oh, God. She'd never killed anyone before. She'd wanted only to fight back, to maybe sabotage something, as Mark had done to the maintenance grid.

She fumbled with the buttons on her collar until the microphone and speaker in her helmet clicked on. "Get back," she screamed. "Get out!"

Droplets of hydrofluoric acid pelted the back of her helmet with tiny, wet slaps. They hit the back of Rod's helmet and Mark's in front of her. More floated toward the door.

The soldier shook his gun. "Take off your helmets!" His face contorted with rage. He looked like he was trying to give himself an aneurysm.

"Get out!" Hysteria filled Kelly's mind. She didn't want this man to die. She hadn't meant to kill him, but it was too late. She couldn't save him. She had to make him save himself.

The soldier didn't seem to notice the drops of acid in the air until one touched his face. Even then he wouldn't feel the symptoms right away. He wiped at the liquid with the back of his gun hand, leaving the other anchored to the door jamb.

More drops hit the back of Kelly's suit. She ignored them. Hydrofluoric acid wouldn't attack the neoprene or flexsteel. It would kill her only if it hit her faceplate. Still, she'd prefer that to getting it on her skin. On her faceplate, it would burn a hole through the durapane and the void would try to suck her through the breach, but she'd die quickly. On the man's face, it would seep through his skin until it reached bone. Then it would consume the skull's calcium, slowly, more painfully than childbirth, until there was too little bone left to contain the brain. Then the acid would attack that as well.

But this man was lucky. He would die before that happened.

The soldier thrust the gun at Kelly's head. "Take off your fucking helmet!"

A high-pitched whistle split the air, almost too high for human hearing, but amplified by Kelly's speakers until it pained her ears. Wind tugged at her slightly. Acid ate a hole through the office window large enough to trip the decompression sensors. The magnets in her boots were too weak to hold against the breach. She slammed into the window with a force that threw the breath from her lungs. Mark and Rod followed. Their bodies crushed hers until breathing became impossible. Acid splattered her faceplate in its rush to escape with the air.

Oh, God. Her faceplate!

You never think. Shit, her mom was right.

The chemical continued to weaken the glass. When the soldier hit, the force of his impact shattered the durapane and acid-soaked air swept them all into the void.

You never think. You know that? You never fucking think.

Kelly tumbled out with the force of three bodies pressing her. Venus spun into and out of view.

Always so desperate to destroy yourself . . . How many ways had her mother said those words to her? How many times had Kelly refused to listen?

Her tether snapped taut, whipped her body like a lash, and wrenched a cry from her. Mark, Rod, and the soldier swept past.

Mark's line sprang tight and yanked Kelly's other hip. Then Rod's line. At the end of the tether, her brother thrashed like a drowning man. If he was screaming, no one could hear him.

An opaque haze marked Kelly's faceplate where the acid attacked it. Space had helped. The liquid on the surface evaporated the moment the pressure vanished. But the chemical already reacting with the glass would continue to do so until one or the other was consumed.

Painfully, she groped for her retracting spool and pressed the button to draw in her lifeline. Gradually, the three returned to the office.

The air was gone, of course, as were the dangerous chemical droplets that had hung in the air. The soldier was dead, killed by Kelly's own hand. She had hoped to escape the lab before he reached the door, to trap him inside the axis. She and the guys could have gone by EVA to any part of the station they wanted. Now he was dead. Acid was attacking Kelly's own face-plate and probably those of the others.

All because she had failed to think. She'd finally done something she couldn't take back. Now she'd live or die with the consequences.

Not knowing what else to do, she levered the manual override on the pressure door. Nothing happened. For a moment, she just stared past the blemishes in her faceplate. Then she cycled the lever frantically and howled in frustration until Mark put his hand on her arm.

He motioned to a solid red light over the door. The office had lost too much pressure. Safety protocols superseded the override. They'd have to go back to the airlock.

She led them around the corner, into the same airlock they'd used earlier, and waited to see if their faceplates would fail before the environmental system could pressurize the chamber.

When the door finally opened, Kelly propelled herself through the donning room to the main axis corridor. Han and his men were nowhere in sight.

She tossed her helmet aside and reached for a fresh one.

"Wait." Mark's voice came to her through his external speaker.

"What?"

"This way." He pointed down the axis, away from station Center.

Kelly hovered for a moment. If they stayed inside, Chang could track their movements. But outside . . .

You never think.

Rod clung to a zero-g handle like he'd never let go. His helmet micro-phone was off. If he said anything, Kelly couldn't hear it.

They could replace their damaged helmets and return to the void. Then what? They'd have to come back inside sometime. Chang would still find them.

Damn it, Kelly, think. She hated when her mother was right.

Mark seemed so sure. Somehow, he knew what to do. But Kelly didn't know how to trust him.

Of all the people in the worlds she'd thought she could trust, her father had been the only one. Until one day, he simply left. Suddenly he wasn't there anymore.

After that, Kelly's mom never was either. Oh sure, her mother provided for her, gave her food and a place to live. Yet even then, Kelly understood that on a station this size, with so many of the men single or away from their families, there were other ways to get those things.

Even for an eleven-year-old girl.

Kelly never resorted to those other ways, however. She took the things her mother offered, but not because she had to—not because it was the only way to get them. She took them because it was easier than getting them the other way, at least until much later. Then she did it because she wanted to.

Since her father left, Kelly had never counted on anybody for anything . . . until now. "Go," she told Mark, then propelled herself after him.

Rod followed, bobbing and pushing himself every time he reached a wall of the tube. Every once in a while, whenever Kelly had enough leverage, she gave him a shove in the right direction. Lights winked on as they reached each new section of the tube.

Mark stopped in front of a lift and extracted the combat knife from his belt. He wedged it into the crack between the door panels and probed around for something.

Kelly looked down the tunnel in each direction. "Hurry."

When Mark finally got the doors open, he held the blade against the maintenance grid sensor.

Kelly smiled. She didn't need to make any more bad decisions, at least for now. She could let Mark think for her.

He held the door open and motioned the others through with a tilt of his head.

Kelly grabbed Rod's sleeve, propelled him into the gap beyond the doors, and then followed. Just as she passed the threshold, a light came on further down the tube, halfway to station Center.

In an instant, vertigo grabbed her. The junction collar between the rotating lift spokes and the stationary axis was a feat of engineering that had been touted as a unique feature of *Venus Rain* at the time the station was built. One wall, which contained the door that Kelly had just passed through, remained stationary. Everything else spun at the same rate as the station's cylinder. The four lift shafts that extended a kilometer to the habitation decks swept past, one every fifteen seconds. Kelly bounced off the spinning bulkhead between them. Finally, her hand found purchase on the magnetic rail mounted around the circumference of the axis.

By then she'd lost track of Rod.

Mark pulled himself through the door, found a handhold, and eased the panels closed.

Rod passed by, clinging to one of the spinning walls of the collar, followed by a shaft that contained a rapidly-climbing lift car. Within seconds, that car would crush anything caught in the collar.

"Pick a shaft," Mark yelled. He selected the one nearest Rod and launched himself into it.

The climbing lift car passed again. Kelly didn't have time to wait for Mark or Rod to come back around. She threw herself at the next shaft. The opening slammed her sore shoulder. Desperately she gripped the lip to hold herself against the spin and to prevent herself from rebounding. At last she pulled herself inside.

The car drifted into the collar and passed over Kelly's spoke with a roar and a rush of air. It slowed to a halt with the top of the car against the door to the axis, bringing the car and everyone in it to zero-g.

Kelly climbed out of her spoke and crawled to Mark, who'd pulled Rod inside his hole with him. "Down the shaft?" she asked.

Mark pulled off his helmet and nodded.

They took off their EVA gloves, hooked their helmets to their belts, and began to descend. A slight tug of gravity urged them toward the habitation cylinder. The pull would increase as they descended until it reached Earth's full gravity at the bottom. She had no idea what they were going to do when they got there.

Chapter 16

"Colonel?"

Chang raised his hand to put off Chen until Han finished his report.

"I've got four teams in the hub, bracketing the laboratory sector," Han said. "We've begun a room-by-room search."

"They're there," Chang said. Then he turned to Chen.

"I have it, sir," the Project tech began. "Or at least part of it."

Chang moved to stand behind him.

"Ever since I discovered the temperature anomaly, I've been going through the processor's maintenance records, looking for any hint of a problem, data shifts that might have gone unnoticed because they were still within tolerance—"

"Get to the point," Chang said.

"That processor was scheduled for maintenance this week. According to the logs, work began at two o'clock yesterday afternoon, but it was never closed out. Then I checked the berth assignments. One of the company shuttles is gone."

Chang scowled.

"Checked out yesterday afternoon by—"

"Amanda Baker."

Chen nodded. "Worst case, she sabotaged the processor. Best case, something else has gone wrong and she can fix it."

The good side of Chang's face twisted into a grin, but he kept the right side neutral. He marched over to Private Huang at the comm station. A cold wave overtook his heart. Amanda's presence on the surface was both an opportunity he wouldn't have hoped for and a liability he couldn't afford. "Station-wide intercom."

He waited for Huang to key the system. "Attention, *Venus Rain*. This is Colonel Chang."

"If she's still alive," Chen added.

Chang gestured for Huang to kill the link and spun on Chen. "Explain."

"Surface temperatures on Venus reach four-hundred-fifty degrees centigrade. The processors have some temperature control, but they weren't designed for more than a few hours of human occupancy, Amanda Baker's been down there since yesterday afternoon." He was careful not to accuse Chang of murder but Chang could read the insinuation in the man's demeanor.

"Sir?" Huang prompted. He'd muted the pickup, but the light on his board said the channel remained open.

"Short of hailing her," Chang asked Chen, "is there any way to find out?"

"I can continue to monitor the processor's plume. If the temperature goes down, we'll know she's responding to the alarm. If not . . ." He shrugged. "The processor will last maybe twelve hours before the tower cracks under the stress. We'll have to take it offline for a month for structural repair and panel replacement. Longer if we lack the parts."

"Surely the processor will shut itself down before that happens."

"It's supposed to, but it's already past thermal cutoff and it's still pumping gasses."

Chang didn't reply. His mind began to work through the possibilities. "How many shuttles do we have in dock that can land on the surface?"

Ming sat straight in his chair, his posture as rigid as if at attention, even when he was seated. "Two, sir."

Chang nodded, then motioned to Huang. He had nearly twelve hours to correct the problem or shut the processor down. In the meantime, he'd learned something he could use.

"This message is for Kelly and Henry Baker." His voice permeated every cubic meter of *Venus Rain*. "I know you're on this station. I also know your mother, Amanda Baker, is not. She is alive on the planet surface. But she cannot survive there much longer."

He paused to let the statement sink in. "If you and Mark Torben turn yourselves in to Lieutenant Han or any of his men, I will let your mother return to *Venus Rain*. If not, she will die on the surface. And Lieutenant Han will find and execute you. The choice is yours."

He signaled to Huang and the private killed the connection.

"Should it become necessary to talk to Amanda Baker," Chang told him, "I want to do so without compromising our jamming net."

"Yes, sir." Huang bent to his work.

To Chen, Chang said, "You have one hour to find a way to fix that processor."

Kelly and the guys had been climbing for probably thirty or forty minutes, but it seemed like forever, and they'd come only two-thirds of the way down. What had begun easily had turned more and more laborious as the artificial gravity increased.

"I can't do it," Rod said finally, clinging to the ladder with a white fist. He stared into the depths of the hole. Kelly's own arms had become too weak to hold her weight. In desperation, they each clipped a lifeline from their pressure suits to the ladder, took up the slack, and hung.

They were still there, resting, when Chang's message came over the comm.

When he finished, Rod turned a pleading look on Kelly. *Do something*, it seemed to say. But what? She looked at Mark.

"Do you want to talk to him?" he asked. "I can see if the channel is still open."

Kelly shook her head. There was too much pain between her and her mother, and too much fear in Rod's eyes for her to think straight. "I want to get out of this hole."

"Rod?" Mark asked, giving the boy a chance to decide for himself, something that would never have occurred to Kelly.

Rod's only reply was a frantic nod.

"Yes, what?" Mark pressed.

"Get out of the hole."

"Okay," Mark said. "We need to keep ourselves tied off."

They worked out a system in which Kelly and Rod clipped lifelines to the ladder for each of the three of them and then climbed down in ten-meter jaunts. Mark followed, unclipping the lines behind them.

By the time they reached the housing decks, Kelly had decided to turn herself in. Not out of any sense of responsibility to her mother, who'd never shown any toward her. "Make sure Rod gets to the dentist by four-thirty," a typical note said when Kelly got home from school. "Dinner's in the pantry." If you considered dehydrated pot roast—add water and radiate—to be dinner. Other families went out to eat at least once a week.

"I can't afford it," was her mother's stock answer to everything, whether they were asking for time or credits. Yet there was always money for school, which Mom wouldn't let Kelly drop, and Rod's doctor's appointments, which Kelly had to take him to.

Though Kelly understood the stakes of China's game—ownership of the planet Venus, Earth's sister in the solar system, the only other habitable planet—she had no means to grasp the potential political outcomes, what the countries and worlds were willing to do, or what they were capable of. One thing she did know: Venus had just passed through an orbital window for Earth. It wouldn't pass through another for a year and a half. And any travel via Mercury would take months at best. *Venus Rain* was a finite station. Kelly and the guys could hide for only so long.

Worse, Chang had probably completed the lockdown by now. If so, he and his men could focus on the hunt for her, Mark, and Rod.

Kelly had known all of this before she broke into the chemical storeroom, of course, but things had changed since then. She'd killed a man. She'd seen the cost of rebellion. This was a life-and-death game she'd gotten them all into. That didn't bother her for her own sake—she was going to burn in hell one way or another—but Rod deserved better. If they turned themselves in now, she might be able to negotiate his survival.

Mark stopped at an air vent that led to the interstitial between the third and fourth habitation decks. He anchored himself with his lifeline and unfolded a screwdriver from La Roche's utility knife.

"No," Kelly said. "Let's go down to the floor."

He gave her a long look, devoid of judgement or criticism. Maybe he'd reached the same conclusion. "You sure?"

Still, she hesitated. Chang might kill them all as soon as he had the chance. Or Han might. "Yeah."

"The voice of reason?" Mark folded the knife and dropped it into a pocket of his pressure suit. "Chang's deal is only good if we all take it."

"I don't want to." Once again, Rod's attention cycled back and forth between the older two.

"You'll do what I tell you," Kelly snapped.

"You're not Mom. I don't have to—"

"Rod!" She bit her tongue on any number of retorts, moved to the side of the ladder, and motioned Mark past her.

Mark didn't wait for the argument's outcome. He probably assumed it was already decided and that Rod would figure that out soon enough. Or maybe he thought the outcome had no bearing on his next actions. He did use the combat knife to cheat the sensor as he forced the lift door panels apart. In his own way, he was keeping their options open.

Kelly thrust a finger at Rod. "Do I need to come up there and slap you?"

Rod folded his arms over his chest as best as he could in his bulky suit and hung by his lifeline four meters above her on the ladder.

She unclipped the helmet from her belt and threw it at him. Rod had to fend it off with his hands. "Ow! Shit." He spun awkwardly away. Kelly scrambled up like a spider in a web. Rage turned the sweat in her pressure suit cold. Rod held out his hands before she could swing at his exposed face. "All right already!"

Kelly unclipped one of his lifelines. "Get your ass down there before I knock you clear to the maintenance deck."

"Geez." He watched her warily as he passed.

When Kelly climbed out of the lift behind him, she heard a soft beeping in the corridor. "What is that?" she asked Mark.

"My thinpad." The sound was barely audible through his pressure suit.

"I didn't know you had it."

Mark eased the door closed. "I don't. It's one of La Roche's."

"What do you think it means?"

He shook his head and motioned to a public lounge nearby. It would at least give them a place to shed their pressure suits and decide how best to survive their surrender.

Surrender. Even unspoken, the word nauseated Kelly. She'd never surrendered anything in her life, unless if felt good or got her something she wanted. Only Mark's tacit support gave her the courage to continue.

She unpacked and inspected the chemical bottles, which seemed to have survived their foray into space and the long climb down from the axis. Mark tossed his suit behind a cushioned chair and examined the thinpad. Kelly shed her suit as well and came along side him. One of the programs called for attention.

He keyed it.

"Kelly? Mark?" The screen displayed. "Are you there?"

The two exchanged looks. Tentatively, Mark typed a response. "We're here."

"This is La Roche . . ."

CHAPTER 17

When La Roche heard Colonel Chang address the kids over the intercom, he knew he'd gotten his break.

The food, canned goods and cereal mostly, had just about been served. Order had been maintained as well as he could have expected throughout the distribution, so La Roche left the last of the serving to his volunteers. He grabbed a can of chili, a flask of water, and a styrene spoon, and returned to the corner of the stage that he'd staked as his own personal claim.

There he popped open the can and wolfed down half its contents before slowing to pull out his thinpad. With atmospheric simulations running in the background, he keyed the comm-ware. This time, however, he wouldn't just eavesdrop. It was time to act.

La Roche selected the frequency the Chinese had been using for inter-personal communications, the only channel he knew wasn't being jammed within the confines of the station. He set the gain as low as it would go so his message would reach the local areas of the habitation decks without sending a signal strong enough for Chang to pick up and track from Center.

Even with his own encryption algorithms, which Mark could decode if he still had the thinpad he'd taken from La Roche's apartment, Chang's men would hear the transmission. But they'd probably assume it was radio-frequency noise from one of *Venus Rain*'s power systems or interference from Chang's jamming net.

Watchful for the guard, who'd remained at the entry doors since the food distribution began, La Roche typed his message and sent it continuously for twenty minutes with no response.

According to Chang's transmissions, the kids hadn't been seen since they'd killed a soldier in one of the zero-g offices. Chang presumed they were somewhere in the axis, but the layout of the core wasn't that complex. If he hadn't found the kids by now, they probably weren't there.

That would put them in one of the lift shafts or outside the station. Either way, if they were alive, they'd show up in the cylinder sooner or later. Even so, La Roche turned up the gain.

If Mark didn't have the thinpad, La Roche had already lost his means of influencing the events around him without some overt gesture, probably involving the gun from his case. And that option was too compromising to pursue until he'd ruled out everything else.

Finally he got an answer. "We're here."

Thank the heavens. La Roche resisted the urge to start keying demands. "This is La Roche," he typed. "You OK? Find your brother?"

"Yes. We're fine."

"Good." La Roche paused to make sure no one came near enough to read his screen. "Don't give location. Transmission not secure." That was a lie, but if Kelly thought he was taking a risk for her, it might help secure her cooperation.

The screen stared, dark and silent, while La Roche considered how to proceed. Kelly might not be ready to hear what he needed to say. "This Kelly?"

"Mark."

"Get me Kelly."

La Roche cursed the pause that followed. Chang couldn't decode his message. In that sense, the transmission was secure. But he might trace it to the auditorium. Or to the kids.

"This is Kelly."

"Hear Chang's ultimatum?" he asked without preamble. The soldier still hovered at the door, but the last woman in line had been served. If Han or his men wanted something in exchange for the food, they'd demand it now.

"Yes."

"Mother on surface?"

"Think so."

"How—" La Roche started typing, but before he could send the message, another line came in from Kelly.

"Rod says yes."

"Rod your brother?"

"Yes."

"How long mother on surface?"

"Since yesterday."

"What will you do?" There could be only one answer to that question. The Venusian surface wasn't considered habitable under the most generous of estimates. If Kelly's mother was still alive, she wouldn't be for long. Fortunately, in an atmosphere processor, she might extend her life expectancy any number of ways. But all of those ways were extreme. Any course Amanda chose to take would be precarious, a fact that La Roche was counting on.

"Give up." There was no pause, barely enough time for Kelly to have typed the words.

No. For the sake of the worlds, Amanda must remain on the surface. Her presence there was the lucky break La Roche had been waiting for.

If she was still alive, she was in a great deal of trouble. And the longer she stayed there, the more tenuous her situation would become. Sooner or later, she'd do something desperate, something that would cause Chang to need La Roche's help.

But only if she stayed there.

La Roche took a deep breath and forced diplomacy into his reply. "Listen, Kelly. I'm monitoring Chang's transmissions. Know you broke into office on station axis. A man is dead. You know that?"

A pause. "Yes."

Was she loathe to admit it? Did she care? The text was too impersonal. "Chang will kill you." La Roche didn't let her reply. "Mother already dead. Han to execute you on stage. Chang to broadcast as example for rest of us."

He gave her time to absorb his lies before adding what should now be obvious. "You can't give up."

There was a long pause. La Roche had just taken from them the one option that might have saved their lives and the life of Kelly's mother. He swallowed hard. His mission wasn't supposed to come to this—sacrificing innocent people. Not that he hadn't done it before when the need was great, but it was harder with people he actually knew.

"Professor, Mark again. How you know Amanda dead?"

He didn't, but the human body could regulate its temperature in air only up to fifty-four degrees centigrade, and for only a short time, before shutting down. The habitable areas of the processors ran at sixty-five degrees. "Processors rated for 4hrs occupancy. Amanda dead since before midnight."

"What if she isn't?"

"Chang try to contact her since early morning. If alive, she would've answered. It's her way home."

A soldier entered through one of the main auditorium doors and hurried toward the stage.

"Sorry." La Roche typed quickly now. "Not what you wanted to hear. Had to know truth. Only thing save your lives. Don't contact me. I'll be in touch."

Secretary Mariano's mustache stilled and his upper lip tightened, as it always did right before he delivered bad news. "Apparently they've reached an accommodation, though Zhukov didn't say what it is."

President Powers sat up in her seat and scanned the faces around her. Chief of Staff Parker shifted his bulk. Her political advisor, Anne Portman, raised an eyebrow curiously. Dan Norton's mouth twisted into a knot of satisfaction and self-restraint, as if he'd somehow been vindicated. Of the Europeans, none responded beyond the look of severe gravity they'd worn since the meeting began. Even European State Secretary Yates seemed more subdued than he had during the China Dominion Affair.

Mariano waited for the President's attention before continuing. "Zhukov has made it clear that if we launch gun ships to Mercury, Petrov will treat it as an act of war."

"He can't possibly justify such a stance." Anne Portman leaned forward, her elbows on the huge mahogany table that dominated the Situation Room. "As long as we land them at our own base without molesting any Russian convoys."

"Just launching warships constitutes a treaty violation," Mariano said.

"A treaty that China has already broken." Norton cleared his throat. "Their act of war justifies ours. If we declare China—"

"Yes, well, be that as it may . . ." Yates spoke with a British accent, which was rare in the European hierarchy. The levity in his voice belied the somber expression he wore. "Russia seems willing to overlook that particular transgression because it's to their benefit to do so. The point we need to consider is: are we willing to wait three months for another window on Mercury just because Petrov's decided to play hardball?"

"No." Four months ago, Powers had nearly plunged all the worlds into a war that would have shattered the ideals of those who'd crafted and signed the Third Outer Space Treaty—a war that would destroy any hope of a unified humanity on the surface of a new world.

When that crisis ended, she'd thought sense and civility had prevailed, but Li Muyou had backed down only to buy himself time to get his troops to Venus.

Nevertheless, American voters had approved of Powers' response to the China Dominion Affair, or they'd forgiven her for it. Either way, they left her in office for a second term. Maybe they'd known better than she that this wasn't yet over. Whatever their reasons, they'd given her a chance to play it out. She wouldn't let them down.

Powers clutched her cane and forced her next words out. "*New Hope* has enough supplies to sustain it as long as we launch a freighter through Mercury within the next seven months. We have that long to force President Li to back down. We can't waste half of it sitting on our asses, stroking the Russians."

A similar decision had escalated the conflict four months ago, but there was no doubt this time about Li's guilt or intentions. He must be stopped. It wasn't clear that war was the only way to do it, though it very well might be. Sending warships to Mercury now, before the launch window closed in two days, was the only way Powers could keep her options open.

And if Russia stood in the way . . .

"What can the European Union have ready to launch within the next twenty-four hours?" Powers asked.

Yates pushed his glasses up on his nose. "Thirty warships, including freighters and troopships; ground troops, both automated and human;

weapons, ammunition, and supplies. Whatever you need. As I said, we're prepared to offer our full support. And we're aware of the strategic timing issues. Our ships went on alert as soon as President Hunt received Li's ultimatum."

Powers turned to Norton.

The Secretary of Defense cleared his throat. "We have all four CATS, four Trainers, and a whole convoy of supply and support ships on standby. They can launch within hours of your order."

"What's the flight time to Mercury?" Powers asked Norton.

"Twenty-two days."

"Tony," Powers told Mariano, "you have that long to negotiate with Russia. Convince them we intend to use Mercury only as a stepping stone to Venus and as a means to prevent Li from using his base there as a strategic hub for China. Tell Petrov we have no plans to interrupt Russian shipping. Maybe he'll stay out of our way.

"Dan, coordinate our efforts with those of Europe. I want a simultaneous launch as soon as you can arrange it. Send everything we have. Li's had an open window on Mercury since the China Dominion Affair. He may have put troops or warships there already.

"We know he has at least three Mingyun satellites in Mercury orbit. Make those your initial targets. I want strategic and tactical plans in place to cover every foreseeable circumstance, before our ships arrive.

"Have I missed anything, gentlemen?"

Silence greeted her glare.

"Yates?" Failing to call him by his title was a breach of protocol, but Powers was too consumed by the magnitude of her decision to realize what she'd said until it was out.

Yates didn't seem to notice. He shook his head slowly and fiddled with his glasses, now folded on the table between his hands. The room was as silent as a derelict freighter. No one moved.

Powers glanced at Anne Portman. She'd left no room in her tone for her political advisor to object, but she hoped to read something in the woman's expression.

Shiny black hair hung down, occluding Portman's features.

Bereft of approval, Powers settled for support. She had no shortage of that in the room, if only because her staff's duties required it of them.

Then she lit the spark that would ignite the heavens. "Now, gentlemen."

Chapter 18

Over the years, Amanda had watched Kelly slip away without realizing it was happening. It started simply enough, a small matter of curfews, ten minutes here, an hour there. Then came the clothes, the boys, the drugs. The constant rebellion and the fights—oh, the fights.

The worst was the day Amanda had come home from work with plans to take Kelly—age seventeen—shopping to help mend some of their relationship. She rounded the corner and caught Kelly stuffing a tin into one of her overfilled drawers. "What's that?"

"What do you care?"

"Kelly."

She shrugged as though she thought it didn't matter. "Synth."

Amanda held out her hand. "Give it to me."

"No."

"Kelly."

"It's not yours."

"It is now." Amanda stepped closer. "Who gave you the money to buy that?"

"Who says I bought it?"

Amanda paused. "Oh, Kelly."

"It's not addictive."

"I don't care. I don't want you getting high. And button your shirt."

Both voices began to rise.

"No shit you don't care. You never did."

"That's not true."

Kelly wheeled on her. "Then how come you're never here?"

"Don't you dare make this about me."

Kelly headed for the door in a huff, and Amanda grabbed her arm. She snatched it away. "Don't touch me."

"You aren't walking out this time."

"Watch me."

Amanda blocked the door. "Sit."

"Fuck that."

On and on it went. The neighbors must have heard it halfway down the cylinder.

Back then, it had all been Kelly's fault. She was out of control. She couldn't be managed, tamed, or taught. Amanda could find no way to deter her from her path of eventual self-destruction. She was on a crash course with the Sun.

But now, with the clear perspective of one facing death, Amanda saw things differently. While she'd been working to keep food on the table and air in the ducts, she hadn't been home to enforce the rules. She'd been so desperate for help with Rod that she'd overlooked everything else Kelly did as long as she took care of him. Even that, Kelly had failed to do.

Amanda had sacrificed her relationship with her children because that's what it took to pay the bills. Back then, it seemed like the right priority. And she'd paid them. But, oh, the cost.

In three years, Kelly would graduate. She'd stay on station or she wouldn't. Either way, she'd be gone. And why shouldn't she be? Amanda had simply used her as a babysitter since she was ten. Sure, she'd fed and housed her, but she'd never really been there for her. Now she'd lose the opportunity to ever be there again.

If she wasn't careful, her relationship with Rod would go the same way. Then everything she'd worked for, everything she loved, would disappear.

Right there, in the noisy confines of hell, Amanda vowed to save that relationship. She would cut back her hours. That alone would cost her her position and possibly her job. If the company kept her, she'd have to give up processor maintenance and return to the machine shop for half the money.

She didn't know how to pay the bills on that kind of income, but that no longer mattered. She'd be there, physically and emotionally, for her kids. If she was lucky, she could build a conduit to span the void between herself and her errant daughter.

Somehow, she would find a way. . .

When the comm finally came through, Amanda almost missed it. The channel had been open since the previous day, hissing static. The caller's voice was nearly lost in it.

"Shshshshshsh," *crackle*, "shshshshsh, Rain, shshshshshshsh."

To silence the noise on her end, Amanda twisted closed the valve that showered her with vaporized coolant.

"Shshshshshshshsh, Baker, shshshshshsh, shshshshsh, read," *crackle*, "shshshshsh."

She ran to the comm panel, cranked up the gain, tuned the squelch.

Crackle, "Shsh, is *Venus Rain*. Shshshshsh, Baker. Come in. Over."

The voice was unfamiliar, but as sure as if it was Kelly herself, Amanda knew her kids were on the other end. This comm was the first span of the conduit.

Amanda thumbed the microphone. "This is Amanda Baker, in P-13. I'm here. Your transmission is broken. Do you read? Over."

"Shshsh, read you. Shshsh, condition. Over." *Crackle.*

"Say again, *Venus Rain*. This is Amanda Baker on Venus surface. Can you clear your transmission?"

The channel hissed nothing but static for several minutes. For a time, she thought she'd lost comm again. Her body temperature began to rise, seeding a new layer of sweat beneath those that already caked her body. Her skin felt like a carapace, chapped and brittle, as she moved.

Nevertheless, she refused to leave the comm.

When the voice returned, it was stronger. "*Venus Rain* to Amanda Baker. Do you read? Shshshshsh."

"This is Amanda Baker. Yes, I read you."

"What's your condition?"

Amanda hadn't eaten in a day. Her water had run out hours ago. Twice, she'd dipped into her shuttle's cooling system to refill her drinking flask. She'd been abandoned by those she worked for, shut out of communication, and threatened by some Chinese asshole named Chang if she should try to return to the station. She didn't know who she was talking to, but she recognized his Asian accent. "How the hell do you think I am?"

"Alive," the voice said. "Shshshsh. I'm sorry." *Crackle.* "Didn't know you were down there. Shshshsh."

She took a deep breath and tried to convince herself he was telling the truth. "When can I come home?"

"Soon."

"I'll be dead by 'soon.'"

"I'm sorry. Shshshsh."

Amanda pounded the pickup. Her ire raised her body temperature. On some level, she understood that, but that level was buried deep beneath the fear of abandonment she'd nursed for the past twenty-four hours, beneath her desperation. "Who is this?"

Crackle. "Shshshsh. Chen Tongyi."

She recognized the name. Chen worked for the Project, not for Chang.

"What's going on up there?"

"We've got a problem," Chen said. "Shshsh. Your output plume is reading hot. Chang won't shut down enough of his jamming net for me to run a diagnostic on the processor—"

Who gave a shit about the processor? Amanda had poured her life into the Project ever since she'd graduated from Planet U twenty-two years ago, but the Project no longer mattered. All she cared about were her children. She almost asked about them, but Chang, or someone working for him, was probably listening, and her tinkering had probably pissed him off. If he didn't already know she had family on station, she wasn't about to tell him.

So she tackled her second priority first. Saving herself. "No shit the plume is hot. I'm bleeding refrigerant to keep myself alive."

"Shshshshshshshshshshshshshshshshshshshshshshshshshshshsh."

The pause made her want to shout into the pickup. *And I'll keep doing it until you let me come home.* Instead, she bit her lip and waited.

"Mrs. Baker." Chen's voice was hesitant, full of sympathy. "The reactor is running past redline. You'll have to do something about it before Chang will let you leave."

To hell with that. "Let me talk to Chang."

Another pause, bloated with static.

Then a second voice came across the void, thick with a Chinese slur. "Mrs. Baker, this is Colonel Chang. I am calling shots now on *Venus Rain*." His tone was hard and uncompromising. "I am also calling shots for the Project."

"You son of a bitch." She couldn't show respect she didn't feel. He may have taken all of *Venus Rain* hostage, but Amanda had a hostage of her own. "I know why you're here." The Venus system had only one thing to offer humanity. "I can destroy this processor by the simple act of dumping the coolant. And you know I'll do it—"

"I think you already are." *Crackle.* "Shshshsh. According to Chen, the processor is already lost unless you can turn back the damage. I can't let you return until you do."

What an ass. Of course the processor was in trouble. Amanda had put it there. And she'd watched the gauges ever since. The system no longer had enough coolant to sustain it. Only one thing could save the tower now, and for that, she needed approval from one of the top three men on the Project: the executive lead, the technical lead, or the station director. "I'll shut it down until the coolant can be replenished, but I'll need the authorization code to do it."

Chang spun on Chen. "Who has those codes?"

Chen's eyes went wide. "Zhong Aoche, Shou Jijin, and Doctor Dennis La Roche."

Chang discounted Shou, who'd already refused to give Chang one set of access codes.

"Have you cleared Zhong?" he asked Lieutenant Gou.

"Yes, sir."

"Where is he?"

"In the auditorium."

Chang keyed the link in his ear. "Chang to Han. Send Zhong Aoche to Center."

He stabbed a finger at the comm panel and glared at Chen. "Tell her the codes are coming."

Thirty minutes passed before Zhong arrived. Chang spent the time organizing the reinstatement of cleared Chinese citizens to their former positions, starting with the facilities workers. It had been a full day since anyone had overseen the systems that kept *Venus Rain* alive, and Mark Torben's sabotage had demonstrated just how vulnerable those systems were.

When a pair of soldiers escorted the CEO into Center, Chang met the man squarely. "I need the authorization code to shut down processor thirteen."

The man's jaw dropped. "You have any idea what that'll cost the Project?"

Chang didn't. "Of course." He gestured for Chen to explain the problem.

According to Zhong's personnel records, which Chang had studied during his trip from Earth, Zhong had been on the Project since the processors were brought online thirty years ago. He'd hired on as an accountant, a peon among the hoards who managed the incoming money that funded the largest endeavor the worlds had ever undertaken. From there, he worked his way up to manage the financial department, then to deputy director of *Venus Rain*, and finally, four years ago, upon the retirement of his predecessor, he became the CEO on the Project.

Confident that Zhong would do nothing to damage the work he'd poured his life into, Chang let him talk to both Chen and Amanda without eavesdropping. He returned his attention to restoring the basic personnel infrastructure before some errant system, Kelly Baker, or Mark Torben could initiate a crisis he lacked the resources to manage.

But the reinstatement of each employee required both Chinese citizenship and a background check through all relevant records, which Chang had brought with him from Earth. It also included a detailed interview, conducted by Lieutenant Han's soldiers, with a prescribed set of questions and predetermined boundary conditions on the responses. Two clearance specialists in Center reviewed each interview transcript before finally clearing the employee. Colonel Chang himself dictated the priority of each citizen based upon his job function.

"Colonel?"

Chang set his thinpad aside and gave Zhong his full attention.

"I understand your situation—"

The man didn't have enough information to understand the complexity of Chang's situation. But in the context of Amanda Baker's processor, he let the remark go.

"—at least the superficial aspects of it."

Superficial?

"But that processor is a complex animal. Chen estimates that irreparable damage is *not* imminent. We can send down more coolant."

"No." Chang couldn't spare a pilot, and he sure as hell wouldn't give one of the prisoners a ship.

"Why?"

Chang shook his head. "Out of the question."

"Then I'll have to consult our technical lead before I authorize a shutdown. We may have other options."

"Dennis La Roche?"

"Yes."

"Also out of the question." La Roche was European. Chang wasn't about to let him near the Project, especially after what Chang had done to Raji Yanamandra.

Zhong hesitated. His eyes flicked to the handgun holstered on Chang's belt. He grunted. "Too bad."

Chang's hand moved to his pistol. Zhong might have had the codes, but he wasn't the only one who did. Yet there was something in the man's confidence . . .

"Look." Zhong tried to sound amiable but failed. "I didn't get where I am without knowing the value of things and learning how to bargain."

Chang matched Zhong's nonchalant manner to hide his own mounting sense of alarm. *All right. Let's bargain.* "I didn't get where I am without learning how to kill. I can get the shutdown codes from Shou."

Zhong flinched but didn't back down. "I don't care what your political agenda is. Or President Li's. I suspect they're one and the same, but it doesn't really matter. You're here for the Project. You need that processor running. The Project isn't far enough along to progress without it."

Chang gripped his gun to keep his wrist quiescent.

"Every day it's offline," Zhong continued, "we'll backslide weeks in the terraforming effort. I won't shut it down if there's another way. If there is, La Roche will find it."

Chang waved the notion aside with a gesture like the cut of an ax.

"Either that or let the gas reaction tower melt down and add years to the Project."

Chang snatched his gun from its holster, but he didn't point the weapon. He had no intention of pulling the trigger. "The alternative is to shut the processor down."

This time Zhong didn't flinch. "You can shoot me if you want to, but I don't think you will." He glanced at the soldiers who'd escorted him to Center and who now guarded the door. "This is where we come to what things are worth. Without the Project, your mission—whatever it is—is meaningless. Without that processor, you fail."

Chang's hand tightened on the grip of his gun. The bars of some unseen cage seemed to rise up around him.

"You need me to give you the codes to save the processor." He held up his hand to head off Chang's interruption. "Sure, Shou has the codes, but his responsibility is to this station, not to the Project. He holds the codes as a formality. He won't issue them without a nod from me or Doctor La Roche. Either way, you're going to have to let La Roche take a look at your problem.

"Besides—" Now Zhong's amiability sounded almost sincere— "he's been the technical lead for nearly a decade. He has almost as much invested in the Project as I have. And he's been helping your men in the auditorium. If you watch him closely, the worst he can do is destroy the tower. You've really got nothing to lose."

Chapter 19

"Got 'em. Four bogies. Three o'clock, sixty degrees down."

"I see them," Major Bill Ryan said. The ships materialized from the gray-green mass of southeast Asia and grew in his long-range display, closing fast as they left the azure ball of Earth behind. Chinese Marauders. They had to be. And they outnumbered the Americans two-to-one.

"How do you want to do this?" Eddie Metcalf asked over the secure comm channel.

Bill didn't have to think. He already knew the play. "I'll lead them on. You drop down for a jump-and-run."

"You got it." The *Cheetah* vanished from Bill's radar as Metcalf retracted his reflector plates. The stealth space fighter slipped, unseen, into the ether.

As bait, Bill left his reflector plates deployed. "Full burn, Carter. Oh-two-oh mark one-five. Let's draw them out."

Bill had met the small, two-man Marauders in simulated combat dozens of times and usually lost. The ships were fast, maneuverable, and deadly. He had identified only one weakness: their range. The more fuel he could make them burn before he engaged, the shorter this fight would be. If he was lucky, he could force the enemy pilots to limit their maneuvers to the low-energy end of their repertoire.

As the Marauders approached, the *Cheetah* stalked among them, made invisible on both radar and visual displays by its matte black, radar-absorbing cladding. Bill could only estimate when Metcalf would attack, based on the capabilities of the Covert Armed Tactical Spacecraft. Thirty seconds, give or take. "Ready, Carter?"

"Oh, yeah." Carter was not only new to Bill's crew but new to the CATS program as well, and her confidence was disconcerting. She had more of it than she deserved.

Bill watched the imager and waited. By increments, the Marauders drew nearer. "Fifteen."

Carter shifted in her seat. Her ebony hands tensed over her controls. "Wait for it."

Behind them, gunner Duane Townsend scanned space for additional targets.

Eight seconds later, a blip appeared on the radar, a streak in the sky, as missiles from the *Cheetah* raced toward the enemy, guided by infrared lasers.

Damn. Seven seconds early. Metcalf's burn must have been brutal for him to have reached his targets so quickly. But what bothered Bill wasn't the timing, it was the missiles themselves. Metcalf should have known better. The Marauders scattered from them like streamers from a Fourth-of-July rocket.

Bill gripped the arms of his g-seat. "Now."

Carter yanked her joystick to the right and Bill retracted the reflector plates. While the Marauder crews were distracted by their own evasive maneuvers, the *Black Panther* changed course and vanished from the sky.

"Ready missiles." Eddie Metcalf forced the words past the pull of hard g as the flat disks of the Marauders grew larger in his display. The *Cheetah* wasn't close enough for guns.

"Ten seconds," he said as the counter ticked down.

Lieutenant Branson readied the missiles, all conventional bees with high-explosive stingers and a variety of fusing options. Unfortunately, the enemy would see them coming.

Metcalf fed the countdown to Branson's display.

His gunner locked a targeting laser onto each Marauder, one by one, and programmed the missiles to seek those spots.

At mark minus one second, the doors under each wing slid open, and missiles catapulted from the launcher. As soon as they cleared the bay, their rockets propelled them toward the enemy.

The Marauders broke formation and spun away at nearly right angles to their former heading.

Metcalf's muscles tensed. "Hold them."

"I got it. I got it." Ire crept into Branson's voice in response to the unnecessary order.

But Metcalf wasn't questioning Branson's ability, and the targeting system wouldn't lose a Marauder once it locked. He feared the limitations of the missiles themselves.

One of the Marauders sped toward them.

"Ready guns," Metcalf said.

"I got it."

The enemy ship pulled up as it reached the missiles.

"Damn," Dubrock, Metcalf's pilot, said.

The missiles fanned out in an attempt to follow the Marauders, but they were hampered by their own design. "Remote," Metcalf ordered.

Branson punched the red button in the corner of his console before all the Marauders could escape. At once, the missiles exploded.

One Marauder spun away. Metcalf zeroed it in his long-range imager. A stream of debris and venting gas trailed behind it. Well, that was something, at least.

A sharp silver streak cut across the display.

The rattle of cannon fire shook the *Cheetah* as her guns roared to life. Tracer rounds left streamers in the void, but the Marauder crossed their firing arc undamaged. "Damn," Metcalf said. They'd never catch that one. "The choice is yours, Dubrock."

The pilot picked another target and brought the ship around to a new heading. "Hold on to something."

A low roar filled the crew cabin and thrust buried Metcalf in his seat.

Two hours passed before they came for La Roche. When they did, Lieutenant Han approached him personally. One of the two men with him spoke fluent English. "Colonel Chang has requested your presence in Center."

La Roche sat on his corner of the stage. He looked up from the atmospheric simulation scrolling across his thinpad, which predicted the rate of CO_2 growth in the atmosphere in the event that one of the processors went down. He didn't have to feign suspicion. "Why?"

"He needs your expertise."

"In Center?"

"He's running the Project from there."

La Roche frowned. "Again, why?"

Han shoved his soldier aside. "Come. Now."

La Roche glanced at the gun hanging from Han's belt and shrugged. He put on the sports coat in which he'd hidden the items from the case and climbed painfully to his feet. "The lifts get cold for my old bones."

He clicked off the simulation and slipped the thinpad, as casually as he could manage, into his pocket, and then gestured toward the door.

When Han led him out of the auditorium, his pair of pups followed behind as if they thought an arthritic old man could somehow threaten their lieutenant.

The halls of the station were deserted. Every door was closed and, according to their status displays, locked.

It was just after 5:00 P.M. Stores and businesses should be closing, employees and patrons alike should be heading home to their families. It was shift change for both the Project and Station Operations. Kids would be out of class. Restaurants and clubs on the Concourse should be starting to fill. This was the busiest time of day anywhere on *Venus Rain*. The halls should be teeming.

Instead, they were empty. Not even a patrol of Chinese soldiers passed them on their way to the lift. The pastel walls, each painted in a soothing shade of mauve, chartreuse, canary, or lavender, seemed to glare in the harsh illumination of the solid-state lighting panels that shone down from the ceiling.

Escape options ran through La Roche's mind as he passed the benches, planters, and food-vends that appeared at intervals along the corridors, but he discarded them all.

When he got to Center, one man other than Zhong lacked the uniform of the Chinese Army. He wore the orange-circle emblem of the company. Apparently he worked for the Project.

Ten soldiers surrounded Chang. Far too many for La Roche to oppose, even if he could count on help from the civilians in the room. Two men guarded the door, obviously more concerned about what the Project men might do than about an attack from outside Center. Chang himself sat at the command console, fully occupied by his link and the list of names that scrolled on the terminal in front of him. If he noticed La Roche's arrival, he didn't react to it.

"Doctor La Roche." Zhong motioned him to the terminal manned by the Project worker. He spoke in English, which elicited a frown from Han.

La Roche enjoyed Han's discomfort without reaction. "What's going on?"

"We've got an employee in trouble," Zhong said. "Not to mention a processor."

"An employee?"

"Amanda Baker. She's one of our—"

"I know the name."

"She's on the surface. She was doing the monthly maintenance on processor thirteen when this whole thing started."

"She's still there? Alive?"

Zhong nodded.

In that case, La Roche's mission depended as much on what he could talk Amanda into doing as it did on whether he could save the processor, which he had no intention of doing. If he could bring down the value of Venus, China might be willing to negotiate with his government.

Chen summarized the condition of the processor, then motioned to Chang. "He won't let us access the data stream from the processor."

"Why not?" La Roche asked the colonel.

"Because I would have to shut down my jamming net to do it. But you can talk to Mrs. Baker. Ask her for information you need."

The duty officer at the comm panel opened a channel, and a speaker near La Roche squealed with noise.

Chang glanced at a private named Huang, two terminals down.

"Sorry, sir," the soldier said in Chinese. He slid his chair along the track to the next terminal and began typing codes.

La Roche removed his glasses to promote the illusion of blindness and began to wipe them absently in a fold of his rumpled shirt. The truth was, even though he was seventy-four, his eyesight surpassed that of most young and healthy men. Unlike the bad hips that nearly crippled him, his formerly poor vision had been thought to be a mission liability. European Intelligence had corrected it to 20/10 with corneal implants before La Roche left Earth. From three terminals down, he watched Private Huang key his passcode.

When the channel cleared, La Roche replaced his glasses and stepped up to Chen's terminal. The temperature of the output plume flashed at the top of the screen. He keyed the comm. "Mrs. Baker, this is Doctor Dennis La Roche. Can you hear me?"

The whine of the jamming signal floated in the background of Amanda's voice, but filters suppressed the noise enough for La Roche to make out her words. "I can hear you, Doctor. Welcome to my tragedy."

"How are you? How's your body temp?"

"I'm okay."

"Then I'd say your story's not a tragedy yet."

"I've been bleeding coolant to counteract the heat. There's not enough left, I'm afraid. I need to shut the processor down so I can come home." The strain in her voice suggested fatigue. Or desperation.

For a moment, La Roche forgot about escape and focused his attention on Amanda and the processor. "Maybe not. We might have some time."

"I'm still bleeding coolant. I intend to do so until Chang gives me permission to go home. If that kills the processor, that's his problem."

La Roche looked at Chang's hard, bloody features. "I think he understands that, but you have a lot more to lose than he does. Don't do anything rash."

"I can't do anything at all without the shutdown codes."

"Read me the gauges. Start with the first stage of the tower."

"Three, eighty-seven. Three, seventy-seven. Three, twenty-four . . ." She read off all sixteen numbers, which La Roche typed into the console.

"And the liquid helium?"

"Twenty-six bar."

La Roche let out a low whistle. The problem wasn't as bad as he'd hoped, but the worse he made it sound, the more leeway he'd have in his choice of solutions. And the more credible it would be when the whole thing exploded.

"Any spare tanks?"

Amanda grunted. "There were yesterday."

"Maybe Chang will let me send down another bottle." For the sake of credibility, he had to ask.

Chang shook his head. *Thank God.*

"Then again, maybe not. But we still have options. Stand by." La Roche sat down in the seat next to Chen's and brought up the technical specs for the entire processor, including the power plant beneath it.

He inspected the plumbing diagrams for both cooling systems for several minutes, then perused an inventory of spare parts and consumables listed as being on site at the processor.

"I need access to the Project computing hub," he told Chang.

"Access your systems from here."

"I can do that, but they'll run faster from the hub."

Chang's right hand oscillated like a gyro on his wrist.

La Roche waved at his terminal. "It took me several seconds just to pull up a schematic, for Pete's sake. She's running that processor in a parameter space it's not designed to run in. I need to do some characterization. That means simulation, teraflops of simulation."

He took a breath to let Chang's mind catch up, and then he continued. "Your men have the systems bogged down here. It'll take hours to do what I can do in minutes from the hub."

Chang stared at La Roche. His raw visage revealed neither incomprehension nor deliberation. Yet he said nothing.

"Besides," La Roche continued, forcing strain into his tone. "I need to modify some of the routines. All of the source code resides in the Project database. I can upload the programs, but that'll take more time.

"Send the guards with me if you like." He stabbed a finger at the men who'd walked him to Center. "But if you want me to save the processor, I'll have to do it from the hub."

Chapter 20

Three of the Marauders regrouped. The fourth, at the edge of the radar display, followed the erratic vector of a ship beyond control.

"Radar pings," Duane Townsend reported from the weapons console.

The stealth cladding of the CATS was good, but not perfect. Sacrifices had been made to shield the CATS from the heat of atmospheric reentry. "How often?" Bill asked.

"Every three seconds." Too fast for the kind of resolution the Marauders needed to pick them up.

Bill keyed the comm and made sure the encryption light was on. "*Black Panther* to *Cheetah*. What's your vector?"

"Transmitting coordinates and bearing. Enemy engagement in two minutes, twelve seconds."

"Take us in, Carter." He deliberately left the timing out of the order and failed to specify where he expected Carter to take them. "Let's see what we can do." *Let's see what* you *can do.*

She programmed an approach vector that would get them to the Marauders seconds before the *Cheetah*. She had indeed come a long way. Just weeks before, she'd have asked for specifics. It would've cost them time, even if only a few seconds. But in combat, they might not have those seconds.

The *Black Panther* spun on its vertical axis. Main thrusters kicked in and pushed the crew into their seats. From there, Carter began a gradual arc to intercept the Marauders, who had begun a search pattern, seeking ships they knew were out there somewhere.

"This is the fun part." Bill's fierce grin made his jaw ache. The CATS could have gone anywhere, behind a space station or beyond Earth's horizon. The enemy would have to check every satellite in orbit just to make sure the CATS hadn't taken refuge in the radar blip of one of them. "Ping rate?"

"Holding at three," Townsend said.

As long as the Marauder crews didn't catch sight of them through a window, the enemy would never see them coming.

"Time to target?"

"Forty-eight seconds." Carter's focus on her board was absolute. Her shoulders were more tense than Cory Abrams' would have been during such a routine maneuver. But he had been the best pilot the CATS program ever had, until the day he gave his life for his duty.

Right now, though, Bill just hoped Carter was up to the combat before them. In a dogfight, the whole crew absolutely counted on the pilot. No one could do her job for her. Maybe he should have taken a pilot from one of the other crews, one who had years more experience than Carter and whose ship wasn't as likely to be deployed into combat as the CATS flagship was.

"Ten seconds," Carter said.

"Ready guns." Bill keyed the radar. The Marauders would be scanning for that very signal, but by the time they triangulated its source, it would be too late. Townsend needed real-time information for this strike.

"Ready," Townsend said.

Three Marauder blips loomed in Bill's display. "Fire."

The percussive roar of the *Black Panther*'s cannon, firing twenty rounds a second, filled the ship. One of the Marauders exploded. A chunk of the enemy's port thruster struck the *Black Panther*'s belly with a jolt.

"Careful," Bill yelled. "Damn it, Carter." She should have pulled up sooner. Townsend could align his weapons to the target. Carter didn't need to align the ship's course to it.

"Sorry, sir."

Another Marauder exploded as the *Cheetah* made a pass behind the *Black Panther*. The third pulled up and away at the top of its thrust.

That's it. Burn your fuel, you bastard. "Go after her, Lieutenant."

Carter dropped into her most formal tone. "Yes, sir." She sounded like a beaten puppy. Bill could have softened his tongue, but he didn't have time to train her gently.

The *Black Panther* turned to pursue and the Marauder pulled hard to the side. Stealth cladding could no longer help them. The enemy had them on visual.

"Stay on her."

Carter made no reply.

"I got your wing," Metcalf called through the comm.

Good. Bill noted Carter's response to the Marauder's movements, evaluating her. Grading her. "Ready guns."

"Ready."

The Marauder wavered across Bill's field of view and Carter struggled to keep it within Townsend's firing arc.

"Evasive!" Metcalf yelled. An explosion rocked the ship and a hailstorm of debris peppered the back of the *Black Panther*.

Bill wrenched his attention back to the radar screen. The fourth Marauder had returned. Pieces of the *Cheetah* formed a widening starburst in his display.

The lead Marauder performed a flat spin before them, sacrificing evasive maneuvers to train her guns on the *Black Panther*.

"Pull up," Bill ordered.

"We've got him," Carter said. The Marauder was a sitting duck—all Townsend needed was a second to lock targ. But the *Black Panther* didn't have a second. Without evasive maneuvers, she'd die like the *Cheetah*.

Bill had no time to argue. He thumbed the command override, grabbed the auxiliary stick—an act he should never have to do unless he lost his pilot in combat—and pulled the ship up. With luck, they could lose themselves in the black and swing around for another stealth pass.

As they flew over the Marauder, its front turned up like a flipped coin. High-energy lasers tore into the *Black Panther*'s exposed belly and traced a line of ruin straight to the auxiliary fuel cell. Bill hauled the controls to the side, but too late. The tank exploded.

The whole cockpit flashed an angry crimson and the windshield went blank. The controls on every console went dark. A faint buzzing from the back of the cabin announced mission failure.

Lieutenant Carter turned to him with fire in her eyes. "With all due respect, sir, what the hell was that?"

The CATS simulator settled into its cradle. When the motion stopped, Bill punched the door release. He spun on Carter, his temper piqued as much by the knowledge of his own mistake as by her insubordination. "Later, Lieutenant."

"After you've had time to cool your thrusters—?"

"That's enough—"

"—and realize that you were wrong?"

Bill locked eyes with her, his fists shaking at his sides, until she looked away. Her buccaneer attitude matched his own more than he cared to admit. But she was only twenty-two and had trained for only three months. She just wasn't up to combat.

"I said." He enunciated his words carefully to keep from yelling. "That's Enough."

Carter stared at her feet. "Yes, sir."

Townsend busied himself with nonexistent duties at his dead weapons console until Carter walked slowly from the cabin to join Metcalf and his crew, who stood on the far side of the sim room, waiting for Bill to debrief them from the exercise.

When Bill reached the bottom of the simulator steps, Major Dana McCaughey was waiting for him. Straight blonde hair framed her smooth face to shoulders that proudly displayed the gold oak leaf of her new rank, which she'd earned for her heroic performance during the China Dominion Affair.

He glanced at the screen above the controller's console, which showed an image of the interior of the *Black Panther* simulator. "How long have you been here?"

"Long enough." Disappointment showed in her clear blue eyes.

"She disobeyed a direct order."

Dana held out her palms defensively. "I didn't say anything."

"You were going to."

Her eyes held his for a moment. "All right. Yeah. You screwed up."

Unlike Lieutenant Carter, Dana was no longer Bill's subordinate. She could say things like that without fear of reprisal. The fact that she was his girlfriend made her criticism hurt that much more.

"She disobeyed a direct order."

"I'm not defending her."

"Suppose we held together long enough for Townsend to take out the Marauder. Do you think we'd have survived flying through its wreckage?"

Dana shook her head.

"We were dead. If I'd have let her go, we'd have failed the mission anyway."

"That's your point, and it's valid. But—"

"Besides, what the hell was that at the end anyway? Every time they ratchet up the difficulty on these exercises, the Marauders pull some new trick out of their ass. Sometimes I think the programmers just make this stuff up."

Dana folded her arms across her chest and waited.

"What do we know about the Marauders anyway?" Bill continued.

"That's not the point."

"Her disobedience would have killed us all in real combat."

"*My* point is," Dana said, "how will she ever learn that if you don't let her make the mistake?"

Bill ran his fingers through his thick brown hair. Dana was right, of course. Maybe he should have taken Miller for a pilot and let Dana train Carter. She was better at this sort of thing, but then he'd have to trust Dana's life to a rookie if this thing at Venus broke out into open warfare. He'd worry about her. It'd distract him from his own job.

"I'll rerun the simulation on hologram. Show her what she did wrong. Then I'll bust her ass for insubordination." He shook his head. "She's a good pilot, but damn."

"The lesson will stick longer if you run the scenario again. You can start it just before the *Cheetah* came apart."

Bill checked his watch. "We'll miss our reservations."

"I think they'll find us a table."

Bill sighed. They'd planned to celebrate her promotion now that the paperwork had finally gone through. Nobody deserved the rank more than she did. Not even himself, and he'd held it for years.

The truth was, his performance had declined since his accident. It had taken two months just to get Medical to clear him for flight status, and since then he'd done nothing but train Carter. He'd forgotten how far Abrams had come, and how much training it took—even for a pilot with the innate skill of Lindsey Carter—to achieve some level of proficiency in a system as complex as the CATS.

"Thanks," he told her, not just for her advice, but for waiting until his crew was out of earshot before offering it.

She smiled.

Bill put his fingers in his mouth and whistled. The sharp sound echoed across the sim room. He waved at both crews to join him. "We're going back in," he hollered. "We need to run it again."

But before they got halfway back, the comm link in his ear chimed. All of the CATS personnel, including Dana, stopped to listen to the massage.

"Attention all crews. Report for duty. This is not a drill. Repeat. This is no drill . . ."

Chapter 21

When Kelly was fifteen, her mother walked in on her and some boy whose name Kelly could no longer remember. He launched himself from the bed, taking the covers with him, scooped up his pants, and bolted from the room.

"What do you think you're doing?" her mother shouted.

Kelly was supposed to be watching Rod, but she'd downloaded enough *Rocket Bob and the Sputniks* to keep him entertained in his own room for hours.

"What did you expect?" Kelly sat up and swung her legs off the side of the bed. She made no move toward her clothes because she knew her nudity would upset her mother. "You started me on contraceptive injections when I got my first period."

"I didn't give them to you as permission. I did it in case you disappointed me." Her mom picked up Kelly's jeans and threw them at her. "Obviously you have. We'll talk when you're dressed." She stormed from the room and chased the boy out the front door.

Kelly pulled on her clothes and marched through the living room.

"Where do you think you're going? We're not through."

Rod stood, eyes wide, in his bedroom doorway.

Kelly ignored him. Her mother was home, for the moment. She could watch him. If she had somewhere else she needed to be, that was her problem. Kelly turned to her mother with more calm than she ought to have felt. "Yeah, Mom. We're through."

And they were.

The truth was, Kelly could barely remember a day when she wasn't trying to get back at her mother for something. She didn't know how to stop being angry. Now that her mom was gone, Kelly fumed at her for finally leaving the family for good. An unfamiliar ache in Kelly's heart deepened her rage, yet it crippled her ability to respond to it. So she just sat, cold and quiet, in the women's lavatory on the third level of the cylinder, where she and the boys had taken refuge from Chang's search parties.

Mark lay beside her, his relaxed features battered and bruised because he'd had the courage to help. His soft, regular breathing suggested an inner peace, as though he was at ease with himself and his reasons for getting involved with Kelly and her brother.

And for the first time since she hit puberty, Kelly began to feel an inner peace as well. She felt connected to Mark like she'd never been to anyone before. She began to belong, if not *to* him, then *with* him. Maybe he could provide some sense of order in her chaotic, impulsive universe, a gravity well about which she might find a stable orbit. In time, maybe she could even love him.

Rod sat nearby, hugging his knees, rocking back and forth, uncharacteristically silent ever since he'd heard about their mother.

"Rod," Kelly said.

He just sat there, rocking.

"I'm sorry. I know you were closer to her than I was."

"Not really," he muttered without looking up. "You're the only one who was ever home."

"I'll take care of you," she said. "You know that."

He looked away. "Nobody's ever taken care of me."

"That's not true."

"Whatever."

No. Not whatever. She wanted to take him by the shoulders and shout, *You look at me when I'm talking to you.*

Instead, she put her arm around his shoulders and hugged him to her side. He was probably right. But it would be different now, for all of them.

Mark couldn't sleep on the hard, cold floor of the lavatory. He dozed a couple of times, but never long enough to get the rest he needed.

When the thinpad beeped, he rolled over and keyed the program. "What?"

"This is La Roche, out of auditorium. Amanda sabotaged processor. I'm to save it, but don't think I can. Instead, working to save you guys. You must leave station."

"Who is it?" Kelly asked.

"Who do you think?" Mark showed her the text, then replied to La Roche. "How?"

Rod lifted his head off his knees. His eyes were red, like he'd been crying, though Mark never heard him do so.

Kelly knelt behind Mark and watched the screen over his shoulder.

"Shuttle," La Roche wrote.

"Won't last long on surface."

"Not going to surface. Mercury."

"Launch window?"

"No standard window for 10 days. Low-energy flight longer. 36 days. Mercury catch up."

"36 days? Shuttle designed for short flights. To surface and back. <12 hours."

"Not using company shuttle. Commercial ship *Eclipse*. Arrived with convoy day before yesterday."

Kelly clenched Mark's shoulders until her nails dug into him.

Then the rest of the message came through. "You'll be safe. But I need help."

"Name it," Mark sent.

"Need into Chang's systems."

Mark's brow furrowed. "Tall order. Why?"

"Reprogram *Eclipse*."

"Send parameters. I'll do it on board."

"Chang'll track you. Shoot you down. Need to disrupt operations. Send system codes and architecture. I'll run smoke screen."

Mark typed quickly. "Don't have access. Can reset codes on some systems. Not operations or security. Can lock accounts, then nobody gets in. Including you."

"Good enough. Contact when ready."

Mark started shaking his head.

Kelly turned him to face her. "What is it?"

"He's not making sense."

"Lock out the accounts. What do we care?"

"As soon as I log on," he said, "Chang will know where we are."

"Just for a minute, right? Get on and get off before Chang, Han, or anybody else can get to us."

"I don't like it," Mark said after a pause.

"Why not?"

"How will disabling the accounts help him? Or us?"

"If it gets us out of here . . ."

Mark took a deep breath and released it slowly. "What if he's setting us up?"

"Why would he?"

"I don't know. Maybe he made a deal to get out of the auditorium."

Kelly's look was incredulous. "You think he'd do that? Sell us out to Chang for his freedom?"

"Why would he help us? Chang will probably kill him for it."

"Why would you help me and Rod? If we stay on-station, Chang will kill you for that."

Mark went silent. That was a question he couldn't answer. His compulsion to help people had never gotten him into this kind of trouble before.

"Our mother's gone." Kelly glanced at Rod. "I'm all he has. I have to keep him safe and I don't know any other way to do it. Is La Roche asking too much for his help?"

After another long pause, Mark levered himself up and pulled Kelly to her feet. "No. He's not."

La Roche had schematics for the atmosphere processor and its buried fusion power plant showing on several screens. On another, he ran temperature projections for the reactor, the processor, and Amanda Baker's body. He rolled his chair from screen to screen, as comfortable in the Project hub as he was in his own living room. Though the guards monitored him from the doorway, they let him use his equipment and whatever programs his Project codes would allow him to access.

In truth, though, La Roche didn't need the computing power he claimed. He'd run every conceivable self-destruct scenario in the past. Now he just confirmed the result for the one he intended to use. Because the soldiers could see his screens, he did so with tabulated readouts only, sans graphs. He pretended to run secondary calculations on his thinpad as a way to talk to Mark.

The conversation had gone well enough, until Mark asked why. That had forced him to improvise. He didn't know, or really care, what kind of access Mark had, or what he was willing to do. La Roche was familiar with the system architecture, and the codes were irrelevant. Chang would have changed the important ones as soon as he came on board, regardless. What La Roche needed was a smoke screen of his own. He needed Mark to create a diversion long enough for La Roche to get into Chang's military database.

In the meantime, Chang's men patched a comm channel from the Project hub, through Center, to Amanda.

"All right," La Roche told her. "I've got a procedure for you. You need to check your stores. Look for cryogenic piping, fifteen-millimeter diameter. You'll need about a hundred meters of it." Then he described what he wanted her to do.

"You want me to pull coolant from the power plant?" Amanda replied. "Say again. That didn't come through clearly."

"Yes, Amanda. We're going to pull coolant from the fusion reactor. Just enough to replenish the processing tower to minimum levels."

"Is that safe?"

He certainly hoped not. "The reactor specs include a tremendous amount of margin."

"That's not what I asked."

"I wouldn't tell you to do this if it wasn't safe. But you have to start now and shut down your own bleed in the meantime."

Ill-filtered static from Chang's jamming satellites filled the pause that followed. La Roche wondered briefly if he could squeeze out a coded transmission to Earth on Amanda's frequency, but decided he couldn't. His thinpad's transmitter was much weaker than those of *Venus Rain* and processor thirteen. He'd have to get control of one of *Venus Rain*'s comm antennas, surely among the most secure systems on the station.

As for the processor, it was true the power plant had far more coolant than it really needed and that Amanda could bleed off it for hours before the system would even notice, but all of the coolant, at some point or another, passed through the chiller. And if the chiller overheated . . .

"Okay." Amanda's voice shook. "Tell me what I need to do."

Chapter 22

Major Bill Ryan climbed into the cockpit of the real *Black Panther*, one of America's four Covert Armed Tactical Spacecraft. Originally, he'd flown the *Puma*, one of *Black Panther*'s predecessors. Flown it, and crashed it. This time, he vowed, it would be different.

He settled the bulk of his full pressure suit into the command seat next to Lindsey Carter. Duane Townsend climbed in behind them.

The ship's systems—boosters, thrusters, navigation, control, communications, vacuum integrity, temperature, atmosphere, radar and tracking, sensors, power, backup battery, targeting, and weapons—all read green.

"Missiles?"

"Twenty-four," Townsend said. Six times the quantity they'd been permitted to carry on their last mission.

Bill grunted. "I guess we're expecting trouble."

He donned his secure headphones and signaled his men to do the same. Together, they listened to their final orders before launch. Until that moment, they knew only that they were to launch for Mercury and that the mission was genuine. Now they heard the rest.

"You will proceed to Mercury in advance of US/EU convoy. Hostile enemy contact is expected in Earth orbit. Do not engage. Repeat. Do not engage enemy in Earth orbit."

Bill glanced at his crew. Townsend raised an eyebrow, but nobody said a word.

"You must escape from Earth and enter Mercury space undetected. When you arrive, assess the threat and prepare a path for the safe arrival of the convoy. Details follow."

Bill listened to a litany of mission specifics, including Mercury's orbit parameters, transfer orbit from Earth to Mercury, ship names, specs, and manifests for the entire convoy. The briefing also listed known Chinese and Russian assets in the Mercury system, with the caveat that the Chinese threat might be grossly underestimated. "China had a window from Earth three months ago, during which they might have transferred troops and weapons to Mercury. Intelligence reports at least three Mingyun satellites in Mercury orbit. Russia is not, at this time, considered to be an enemy of the United Sates. If engaged by Russian forces, however, return fire with all force necessary to defend yourselves and the convoy."

Individual targets were not assigned by ship, as they had been four months before, which meant Command didn't really know what they'd find when they got there.

"Ten days after you arrive, you'll be joined by an additional supply caravan." According to the briefing, that caravan launched a few hours before on a lunar trajectory with no military escort. It would land at Lunar Alpha under the guise of a regularly scheduled shipment, refuel, and then burn for Mercury.

By then they'd be three full days behind. They'd miss the standard launch window, which contributed much to the ruse, and would need every bit of fuel on their own tanker just to catch Mercury.

But if the battle lasted that long, they would need the supplies. And China had let the convoy go—their first mistake. Bill prayed they'd make many, many more.

"Two minutes, guys," Carter said from the pilot's console.

The huge doors that hid the underground launch platform separated with a loud pop and squealed open.

Bill initiated the final countdown. As commander of his ship, he was the only one authorized to do so. Even the pilot, responsible for both flight and navigation once the ship entered space, couldn't activate the sequence that would launch it from Earth—a launch that, upon the direct orders of the President of the United States, would violate international law.

The *Snow Leopard* sat beside Bill's ship. Its matte black exterior was broken only by the ship's name stenciled in white beneath the cockpit, along with the silhouette of a sprinting jungle cat and the fifty-four star American flag. The huge wings, which could support the ship in the sparse atmosphere of worlds like Mars, stretched twenty-five meters from the awkward, radar-absorbing angles of the ship's body.

Bill braced himself for takeoff as the system counted down the last ten seconds in audible beeps.

The solid rocket booster strapped to the belly of the *Black Panther* roared, pressing Bill into the back of his g-seat with a force three times that of Earth's gravity. The ship cleared the lip of the launch bay and sunlight streamed through the windshield, muted by the polarized durapane.

Three minutes later, thrust waned. With a thump, the booster rocket detached and fell away. Any tracking radar could see it fall, but without it, the *Black Panther* became invisible. Carter, her hand on the joystick, rolled the craft over and the giant beach ball of Earth came into view, growing ever smaller. Dana's ship, the *Snow Leopard*, burned toward space behind them, along with the other two CATS and three cargo ships from Cape Canaveral, a hundred kilometers west of MacDill. Burn trails rose from launch sites all across the country as additional ships joined the convoy.

Thrust kicked in again, lifting the *Black Panther* into a stable orbit until she came around to her window for Mercury. With luck, their launch had been lost in the wave of sudden activity that ignited the skies over both the United States and Europe.

Blips filled the display, not from his own instruments—his radar would have given his position away—but from America's orbital tracking net. All the usual markers were there, the closest being *Freedom Station*, *Cosmique*, and the *Protocorp Medlab*.

European blips showed as well, at least a dozen of them, any of which could represent two or more ships in close formation. China could not mistake the intent of the Western powers. The worlds were going to war.

"Major," Townsend said. "Command was right. We've got company."

⊰⟪○⟫⊱

La Roche talked Amanda through the procedure. When it came to which line to draw coolant from, he sent her to the chiller rather than to the reactor. Once she drew from that, the reactor's own helium would boil. The pipes in the hottest part of the line, the reactor's fusion core, would rupture. And Chang's precious processor would go up in a flash of incandescent brilliance.

"Ready."

La Roche stared at Mark's message for a second before he typed his reply. "Good. Log in. Don't disable accounts 'til I say go. When done, take circuitous route to docking hub."

"Got it."

"Start the bleed," La Roche told Amanda when she finished plumbing the connection. "Slowly." He wanted to give her as much time as he could. "Just half a liter per second. You should see the tower's temperature begin to drop within the next four and a half minutes."

He told the same thing to the soldiers. "Contact Chang and let him know. But this is a delicate process. I'll need to monitor it from here until the system stabilizes and we can shut off the bleed."

One of the soldiers nodded and keyed the comm.

La Roche turned back to his work. "I'm in," said a message from Mark on his thinpad. La Roche listened to everything the soldier told Chang. When he was sure the link was closed, he pulled the 9-mm handgun from his pocket. Using his body to block his actions, he fitted his silencer to the barrel and rounded on the guards.

La Roche pulled the trigger and the first soldier fell with two quick rounds in his chest. The other's gun cleared its holster, but that was as far as it got. La Roche pumped three slugs into his torso, and with a spasm of the soldier's hand, his weapon clattered to the floor.

La Roche checked the bodies to make sure they were dead.

When he came back to the terminal, he slid a data card into the console and programmed a trajectory from *Venus Rain* to Mercury.

Then, with the code he'd stolen from Private Huang, he logged into the control computer. He stabbed his thinpad into the terminal's I/O port and uploaded his own program. As soon as it was in, he sent a one-word message to Mark. "Go."

≈⟨ O ⟩≈

A swarm of Marauders rushed to engage the American and European convoys. Bill tapped the radar screen with his finger. "Not our problem."

"Major—" Townsend began.

Bill craned his neck against the ship's acceleration to see around the edge of his seat. "You heard our orders. Those ships are not our problem."

Townsend met his gaze for several heartbeats before breathing a rough sigh into his microphone. "Yes, sir."

"Nevertheless . . ." Bill turned back to his board and increased the resolution of the scan. "Ready the missiles." The Marauders were closing fast on a vector that would intercept the European convoy. Several banked toward the American support ships as well. None, however, came for the CATS.

The American Trainers, the only fighting ships the United States owned besides the CATS, raced to intervene between the enemy and the unarmed convoy.

As the data net refined the images, individual Marauders came into view. "Christ." A dozen closed on the Americans.

Dana's voice came over the encrypted, short-range channel. "Bill, you watching this?"

He opened his mouth to censure her for breaking radio silence, but the ships below were yammering all across the military channels and only the CATS comm-ware could decode Dana's message. Space stations called out, some in a near panic, for information or protection. They could see what was happening on their screens as easily as Bill could read it from the tracking net, but they didn't know what it meant.

If they did, their calls would be much more frantic.

"Yes." He couldn't say more. His voice caught in his throat. The longer he watched the display, the more he saw his friends about to die.

"We have to do something," Dana said. Though her rank matched his, he was the wing leader. Only he could give such an command. And he alone would face the consequences of defying a direct order.

"I know."

"Majors." It was Captain Etre, on the *Jaguar*, another veteran of the China Dominion Affair. "We can't engage. We have our orders."

174

"Oh, I'm not going to engage," Bill said with levity into the comm. "Are you going to engage, Major McCaughey?"

Carter glanced over, her mischievous smile white against her black skin, her eyes sparkling with anticipation.

"No, sir," Dana said. "I'm not."

"Well, then, it's settled. We'll have to let our missiles do it for us. Townsend . . ." He gave the order to his gunner but left the comm open for the other ships to hear. "Target the Marauders. Point of interception fifty thousand kilometers ahead of our convoy. Proximity fusing."

The orders he'd received had contained the words, "Do not engage," but those did not define his mission. His mission was to "escape from Earth and enter Mercury space undetected," with the authority to "assess the threat and prepare a path for the safe arrival of the convoy." The convoy couldn't arrive safely if it never made it out of Earth's orbit. And Bill could help them as long as his means didn't betray the CATS.

Before he closed the channel he added, "Stealth munitions only."

Townsend didn't even bring the targeting computer online. Instead, he tapped the navigation system and programmed the missiles' course based on their thrust-to-mass ratio. That made the targets much more difficult to hit, but to do more might have alerted the enemy. When he was ready, he launched six and wasted no time in closing the missile-bay doors.

The need to incorporate long-range tactics had become apparent to someone in Washington during the China Dominion Affair, and since then, designers had kludged together a stealth variety of missile. They took standard missiles and clad them in the same radar-absorbing material used for the CATS.

They'd failed to redesign the body style, however. From behind, their heat trail lit up an infrared scan like a solar flare. From the side, they stood out like a comet in the night sky. But from the front . . . that was a much nicer story. One Bill was counting on now.

The CATS crews had taken to calling them "no-see-ums." He hoped the name was apt.

Chapter 23

"Colonel Chang," Ming said. "Mark Torben just logged onto the telnet."

Chang sat up in his seat. There'd been no sign of the kids since they'd killed his man in the axis and he'd begun to think they might have died there as well, killed by their own actions or by his soldier. But his gut told him it wasn't so. It was too easy. And in war, nothing was easy. "Where?"

"The Concourse."

Chang keyed his link. "Han, get to the Concourse. Mark Torben is there."

"We just lost security," Lieutenant Gou said.

Chang wheeled his chair to face the man. "Explain."

"Scanners, checkpoints, alarms, everything. The operations firewall just crumbled."

"The grid's out too," Ming added. A sheen of sweat shone on his neck, beneath his military cut.

Chang's hand shot to his link. "Han! Talk to me."

"Entering the Concourse now."

"Shit." Gou's nudged up the bridge of his glasses and returned his hand to his board. "Someone's mining the control database."

Good. Torben had to stay put until he found what he was looking for. "Direct Han to that terminal."

"I don't think it's Torben. It's a ferret, and it didn't come from the Concourse."

"What?" Someone else, then. But who? Every dorm on the station had a telnet terminal. And with the firewall down . . . "Kill it."

"I tried. It's passcode protected."

"Then keep an eye on it. Find out what it's after." Chang turned to Private Qin, sitting idle at the helm. "Trace it back. Find out where it came from."

The man tapped his board. His face screwed into perplexity and he tried again. "I can't get in. The system won't take my codes."

Chang flew from his seat. He marched to an empty terminal and typed his own code. INVALID ACCOUNT. "Who's still logged in?"

Two hands went up: Ming and Gou.

Gou played his board like a blind pianist, his head up, watching the screen while the sightless proficiency of his hands worked the panel. "Damn, this thing's good. I'm trying to block it in, corner it in a database we don't need and shut it down."

Chang ignored him. "Ming, Han's on his own. Give Qin your terminal. Trace that thing to its origin."

"It's into our data."

Chang wheeled on Gou. "*Our* data?"

"Yes, damn it. *Our* data. Troop counts, supply and ammunition manifests, satellite orbits, countermeasure deployments, comm frequencies, encryption codes—"

Chang pounded the board in front of him. "Are you *sure* it's not Torben?"

Without slowing his hands, Gou said, "No, sir. I'm not. This thing could route our data to any unsecured memory location for him to retrieve later."

Or Torben could have programmed it to infiltrate from another hub. "Qin?" Chang's tone turned ominous, promising demotion or worse to anyone who failed him.

"No good. The ferret's covering its trail, storing the data in a temporary file, then putting it back into its original registers once it leaves. I can't tell where it's been."

Chang gripped the back of his chair to quell the spasmodic cycles of his wrist as his control of *Venus Rain* eroded around him. Then, as quickly as it started, it was over.

"It's out," Gou said. "The ferret's gone."

"Tell me you didn't lose it."

"No, sir. I didn't. But it got out with the data."

"Where?" Chang asked through clenched teeth. Sweat began to sting the burnt half of his face.

"The Project hub."

Doctor La Roche. He should have known.

"Burn!" Captain Eddie Metcalf yelled through the comm to the other three Trainers. Because the Trainers had taken off from a runway instead of a launch tower, their trajectory hadn't nearly matched those of the supply and troop ships they'd been assigned to protect. Furthermore, the launch had cost them much of their maneuvering fuel. And they had to burn most of the rest to get to the Marauders before they reached the convoy.

The trip would take at least twenty minutes, so Metcalf split his attention between the radar display and his data terminal. Specifications, more likely speculations, of the Chinese ships scrolled past. The designers had sacrificed the Logan ion drive, storage space for interplanetary provisions, and one crew member—relative to the CATS complement of three—to make the Marauders fast and maneuverable. They boasted two 33-mm machine guns and a forty-megawatt laser with a sophisticated tracking system to hold the beam stationary on its target for the fraction of a second that it took to burn a hole through the skin of a ship or breach a fuel tank.

And, as Metcalf had learned in the simulators, Marauders were nearly impossible to hit with conventional missiles.

But if they could keep the convoy alive for the first few minutes of combat, the Marauders would have to turn back or resign themselves to drift in space for want of fuel. To do that, the Trainers had to get close enough to use their guns.

"Major Ryan to Trainers, stay on an intercept course with the Marauders, but do not engage before I give the order. Repeat. Do not draw the Marauders off their current targets. Over."

Metcalf keyed the comm from the Trainer *Calico*. "Copy that." He tried to keep the bitterness from his voice. Command had assigned him to a mere Trainer, when he'd worked for years to fly a CATS—that alone was a kick in the pants he and his crew hadn't expected. Then Command ordered the Trainers into combat and told the elite fighters to flee without engaging. "If you want us to fight," he'd told Colonel Davis, "at least give us the fighting ships."

Now, even if Metcalf reached the convoy ships in time, Ryan had ordered him not to save them.

It was a ludicrous order.

Yet Metcalf would follow it. Not because Ryan was better at what he did than anybody else, though he was. Not because Metcalf had faith in Ryan's expertise and judgement, which he did. And not even because the order had been issued by his friend, Bill Ryan. None of that would get him to follow such an order.

He'd follow it because he, Captain Eddie Metcalf, was an officer in the United States Air Force. He'd follow it because that's what he was trained to do.

He put the Marauders on the long-range imager and watched the gap close, their radar traces nearly hidden behind the lumbering freighters and a single troop transport that carried over a hundred and fifty men.

Then something else appeared on the radar screen. Not blips really, just a haze that covered a full quadrant of the display. But it remained for only an instant. When the sweep passed the quadrant again, it was gone.

The Marauders scattered. Three—no, four—exploded on the spot. Another spun in a wide arc, tumbling out of control. In a flash, a dozen enemies became seven, and those thrown off course by evasive maneuvers.

"Trainers, engage," Major Ryan ordered over the secure link.

The enemy still outnumbered them nearly two to one, but Metcalf welcomed the odds.

The *Calico* gave chase to the nearest enemy ship. G yanked at the corners of Metcalf's vision. The whine of the targeting laser sounded in his ear. And frantic chatter screamed over the link.

"You've got him, Harry."

"He's on me, he's on me!"

Metcalf could make out a few of the words, but the overlapping voices became indistinguishable.

"Yes! Take that, you crazy fucker."

One down.

The fleeing Marauder passed the *Calico's* windshield in sporadic intervals.

"He's pulling away," Dubrock said.

Branson's fingers hovered over the initiator. "Stay on him."

The pitch of the targeting system changed to a steady wail and, because they weren't close enough for machine guns, Branson launched a pair of missiles.

The Marauder spun away and the missiles flew wide.

"Mayday. Mayday." The voice of Colonel Davis overrode the mayhem. "We're under fire."

Shit. The Marauder had pulled them too far astray. Metcalf scanned the data from the tracking net. "Charmichael, get over there." Another Marauder sped at the *Calico*.

The decompression klaxon went off as a searing green beam of coherent light shot through the cabin. Dubrock rolled the ship to protect the fuel cells, but the Marauder's beam destroyed everything it hit.

Air streamed through the breech and escaped into space. One of Metcalf's scanner displays went dark and several sensors blinked errors on his board. "Brake!" Metcalf yelled over the screech of a dozen alarms.

Dubrock rotated the thrusters and hit full braking throttle. A roar vibrated through the weakened hull and shook his board, overlaid by the pulse of machine-gun fire.

It didn't matter if the *Calico* held together. The Marauder that had ripped a hole in their side was on a collision course at speed.

CHAPTER 24

Heavy-booted steps echoed down the corridor, accompanied by barked Chinese commands as Han cast his net around the whole section of the Concourse, the large shopping and entertainment sector that formed a wide belt around the waist of the habitation cylinder. Kilometers of public walkways and service corridors threaded their way through a maze of shops, arcades, restaurants, theaters, gambling clubs, and other businesses.

"Hsst," Kelly hissed over her shoulder. "He's here."

Mark tapped a few keys and shut down the public terminal, which was nestled between a clothing store and an ice cone stand, just off one of the Concourse's six main plazas.

Kelly ducked back as Han strode into view.

Mark hadn't picked this terminal at random. The row of store fronts had a service corridor that ran the length of the block behind them.

Kelly, Mark, and Rod slipped into the alley, which looked nothing like a space station should. It reminded Kelly of the grotesque slums in Earth's largest cities, whose inhabitants turned up dead, night after night, on the newsblips.

The smell of cooking grease and rotten meat was especially bad behind a fry-bowl stand. "Gross." Rod turned up his nose, then clamped it between his thumb and forefinger. Only the creative design and delicate balance of the environmental system, which swept air out of the public areas and into the service ways, kept the smell from permeating the whole deck.

The three moved quietly. Even Rod kept his mouth shut, probably so he wouldn't inhale some rank disease.

Mark stopped them at a junction and peered around the corner. Without a word, he shook his head and pointed back the other way, but Han's footsteps clomped behind them.

With the laser in La Roche's knife, Mark cut the padlock from the back door of a haircut place midway down the block and the three slipped inside. Kelly locked the door behind them.

A moment later, they heard voices. "Expand your search," Han said. "Check the shops."

Kelly's heart jumped as somebody tried the door. It didn't settle down until the voices faded away.

When they emerged ten minutes later, Han was standing in the alley, waiting for them.

The Marauder slipped past the front window and the *Calico*'s machine guns ripped it apart, scattering it to the eight planets like so much stardust. Shrapnel pelted the *Calico* like hail as the Trainer passed through the debris.

Another Marauder stalked them from behind, approaching fast. Silent muzzle flashes highlighted its guns.

"Come about one-eighty. Forty degrees down. Full burn."

The Marauder zipped by to join the one that the *Calico* had been chasing. While Dubrock stabilized the ship, both Marauders started a broad loop toward the American troop ship, which had pulled away from the freighters. All remaining Trainers were converging on these last two Marauders, but only the *Calico* was close enough to intervene.

One, the *Angora*, appeared nowhere on the tracking net display, which could mean only one thing. Metcalf tapped his clenched fist on the edge of his console, but he kept the news to himself. Death was a reality in combat. But the crew of the *Angora* had been friends to all of them. He didn't want it to distract his men.

The *Calico* was punctured and blind on one side, save for the satellite feed from the tracking net. Her front had been peppered with debris, whose damage Metcalf could see in the marred windshield. And an unnatural shudder vibrated ever more strongly throughout the ship. Still, she raced alone against two Marauders to save a hundred and fifty men.

"Targeting is down," Branson spat through the speaker.

Wonderful. Just wonderful. "Keep at them, Dubrock."

"Doesn't matter," the pilot said. "We won't catch them anyway."

Metcalf watched the tactical display for a moment. "Yes, we will." Even with the runway launch, the Trainers had more fuel reserves than the enemy, and the Marauders had burned hard from takeoff to intercept the Americans. To compensate now, they'd chosen a low-energy vector toward their target. "But it's going to be close.

"Ready guns."

Branson keyed his console to comply. "We took quite a beating on our front end."

"Acknowledged. Stand by."

A minute later, the trailing Marauder cut across the *Calico*'s path.

"Fire."

Branson keyed his board and the barrel of one of *Calico*'s guns exploded. A shudder rocked the cockpit, but a sensor stopped the feed of ammunition to save the Trainer from destruction.

The other gun fired a few rounds before it jammed. One hit the Marauder and it spun away, out of control.

They had nothing left for the second Marauder as it closed on the transport.

"I could fire a blind missile volley," Branson said. "We might get lucky."

"Or we might hit the transport."

Dubrock held an intercept course. A collision course.

"It's up to you now, Dubrock," Metcalf said, somber but not disappointed.

The pilot nodded once, firm with resolve.

"Branson?" Metcalf wouldn't do this without the full consent of his crew.

Branson hesitated only for a moment. "Shit."

Seconds later, the Marauder filled the windshield and Metcalf's world vanished in a painless flash of valor.

≈《○》≋

As soon as his ferret returned, La Roche unplugged his thinpad from the terminal. He knew better than to think it hadn't been detected or followed. He grabbed a second thinpad from the desk and shuffled from the room as fast as his aged gait could take him.

He didn't go far. The corridors weren't safe for a hobbled old man and he wasn't sure how quickly Chang's men would respond. So he rounded the first corner, descended a staircase to the facilities deck, and tucked himself away among the machinery.

The gravity was only slightly greater here than on the university deck, but La Roche's old bones could feel the difference. Or maybe he'd aged since he killed his guards. Either way, it didn't matter. He'd reached the point of no return. La Roche would be a fugitive until he escaped the station or died on it.

He unfolded the Gauss driver from his utility knife, detached the back panel from both thinpads, and swapped the memory chips. Using the spare thinpad, he copied Chang's data, ferret and all, to a data card, then restored the original chips.

Now he had to find the kids without using the thinpad's transmitter.

Fortunately, Mark's login had provided La Roche with more than one kind of help. First it aided the ferret. Now it aided La Roche. He needed only to monitor Han's communications to locate the kids.

"La Roche is gone," someone reported. "His guards are dead."

"Find him," Chang, or maybe Han, replied. If La Roche turned on the audio, he could have recognized the voice, but he didn't take the risk.

"Recover my data." That must have been Chang. La Roche had definitely gotten his attention. Maybe that would give the kids a chance.

He tossed the spare thinpad into the first waste incinerator he passed and tucked the data card into his pocket for safekeeping.

As Chang's men coordinated the search over their comm links, La Roche used the transmissions to thread his way through the gaps of the tightening net.

Adrenaline drove him on.

"Tell President Petrov our ships will secure Mercury only against *Chinese* military occupation and *Chinese* shipments to Venus," President Powers told Secretary of State Mariano. "Assure him we've made no decision to stop Russian helium."

"We haven't made a decision? That's supposed to reassure him?" Mariano's look was almost pleading.

"Tell him we have no plans to blockade Russian shipments of any kind, to Venus or anywhere else."

"Do we?"

"Tony." Powers met his gaze with as much sincerity as her old, sleep-deprived body could muster. "We have no plans. *I* have no plans. What we do with Russian shipments depends on Petrov."

"Madam President?" Her aide stood in the doorway. "Secretary Norton—"

"Send him in."

Mariano turned to leave, but Powers stretched her cane across his path. "You'll want to hear this."

Norton strode into the Oval Office as if he hadn't needed permission to enter.

Powers sat down behind the desk without offering him a seat, but not just to remind him he was addressing a superior office—she wanted to take this news sitting down. Once she was settled, with her cane lying flat across her lap, she wrapped her hands around it to keep them from shaking. "Report."

Norton grinned with fierce satisfaction. "The ships have burned for Mercury. As expected, Chinese Marauders intercepted the convoy. We suffered losses, but not enough to jeopardize the mission. Our troop ship survived, as did the European transport; our refueling tanker; eight US and European supply ships; half of the robotic troops, including the airborne surveillance and strike drones, robotic infantry, and several remote defense stations; and the bulk of the ammunition and supplies. We lost two Trainers. A third was diverted to *Freedom Station*, too damaged to survive atmospheric reentry. Six out of twelve European fighters and our remaining Trainer, the *Siamese*, now provide escort for the convoy. The surviving Marauders have returned to Earth or to Chinese orbital stations.

"As far as we can determine, the CATS themselves remain undetected."

Powers couldn't suppress a heavy sigh. "Any satellite activity?"

"No, ma'am."

Mariano's face had gone ashen between his dark mustache and brows. He appeared sickened by Norton's passionless enumeration of death. "That means we were right about China not having Mingyun satellites in Earth orbit."

Norton seemed to enjoy Mariano's discomfort. His grimace turned into a sneer. "Oh, it means a lot more than that."

"Indeed it does." With hardened resolve, Powers took up her cane and pushed herself to her feet. If the European Centurion satellites hadn't engaged, it could only mean Hunt was trying to conceal them. President Powers' job had just grown infinitely more complicated. "Indeed it does."

Chapter 25

Before long, Amanda began to see a change. As she sat back in the sweltering heat, the tower's temperature begin to decline.

Her own body temperature rose. It had been a half-degree below normal. Now it was four degrees high and climbing. But she didn't turn her jury-rigged mist generator back on. At this point, her survival depended more on the processor's temperature than it did on the temperature of her own body.

What she didn't know was how far the temperature of the plume had to drop to convince Chang his precious processor was safe. Or how long it would take.

Suddenly, klaxons blared around her. The lights dimmed and red strobes flashed from the walls.

Amanda raced to the status panel. She'd seen a processor redline before, heard every kind of alarm and buzzer it was designed to produce. But she'd never heard a klaxon like this before.

Her eyes raced across the board. All the sensors and lights showed green or yellow, except for the tower temperature, and that was still dropping. The processor was fine.

Blood drained from her face, maybe even from her heart. Despite the heat, her hands and feet turned cold. Her breath caught in her chest. She got that awful, sinking feeling she'd felt only once before—when her son's hand had been mauled in a sonic blender at the age of three.

Instantly, instinctively, she knew what had happened. She didn't have to run downstairs to check the power plant. She didn't have to see any of its gauges or sensors. As sure as if she'd been set adrift, naked, in the void, she knew she wouldn't survive this day.

Yet she had to try.

She flew down the steep, grid-metal staircase, flight after flight, barely touching the steel handrail anchored into the bare Venus bedrock, until she reached the reactor deck fifty meters underground. The temperature gauge flashed High Limit and a shrill whine sounded from the depths of the machinery.

Somewhere inside, an overheated coolant line had ruptured.

She didn't try to fix it. She didn't know how. Her expertise included the atmosphere processor, not the power plant. But she understood the inevitable outcome. Fusion cores didn't melt down like fission piles. They exploded. And when they did, they blew with a force that rivaled the thermonuclear weapons of the previous century.

Exertion and panic drove her body temperature past tolerance. Her head pounded, the staircase listed to one side, and she fell against the railing. She pulled herself upright and barreled on. Amanda had taken the required course on heat stroke. She recognized the signs. The muscles in her legs cramped from need and dehydration, but she drove them on.

She raced up the stairs, out to the shuttle bay, and punched the evac button on the wall. A pressure door slammed down between the maintenance chamber and the bay. The pressure began to increase toward that of the Venus atmosphere. Amanda climbed aboard *VR-2* and slammed the door behind her.

The startup sequence would take a half an hour if she followed the checklist, but she didn't have that long.

She powered the drives first. Whatever else happened, they needed time to stabilize, for the fuel injection orifices to expand to their steady-state size. If she fired them too early, they could crack under the pressure.

She powered the comm. "Mayday. Mayday. Amanda Baker to Center. La Roche was wrong. The reactor's gone critical. Request emergency permission to launch."

The only reply was the squeal of jamming noise.

Shit.

She went down the board, toggling every system at once—power, environmental control, life support, navigation, helm, and a dozen others. She checked none of them. If they'd gone bad in the day and a half of withering Venus heat, she didn't have time to fix them.

She didn't have time for anything.

The klaxons continued, loud enough to filter through the pressure door, the hangar, and the walls of her shuttle. The sound became deafening as the pressure in the hangar rose.

Amanda tried the comm again, shouting over the noise.

No reply.

Chang had made it clear he would shoot down any ship in the Venus system. So her choices were simple. Stay and die, or launch and die.

The hangar door swung open.

Amanda ignored her preflight checklist and launched *VR-2*, trusting her fate to the mercy of a ruthless tyrant rather than to the fallibility of the laws of nuclear physics.

Kelly swung the cushion case full of hazardous chemicals at Han's head. The bottles inside were plastic, but they carried weight.

He blocked the blow, grabbed the neck of the sack, and yanked Kelly into the wall behind him. His other hand reached for his gun.

Kelly took the blow on her sore shoulder and twisted away.

Mark dove at Han, using his full body weight to plow the Chinese killer into the wall. Han kneed his gut and shoved him aside.

Rod followed with some kind of fancy, flying kick. He caught Han in the jaw and slammed the man's head into the wall with enough force to dent the aluminite. The smack of the impact echoed down the service aisle.

"This way," a soldier yelled from somewhere nearby.

Han's eyes blinked twice, tried to focus, and then he staggered to one knee.

Mark collected Han's gun from the floor and fired several shots in the direction of the approaching soldiers.

Kelly retrieved the cushion case and took off down the alley. When she looked back, Mark and Rod were right behind her.

They raced through the alleys of the Concourse at least one turn ahead of the soldiers. As they ran, the pull of air increased. The hum of the air handlers grew louder until they reached the garbage collection point. Decades of grime coated the floor. The corroded walls hadn't been painted in years.

Kelly rounded the next corner into a dead end. The far wall contained a bank of three-meter-high filters, through which the air from this whole sector of the Concourse was drawn.

Mark stuffed the gun into his belt, ran to the last filter in the row, and wedged his fingers beneath its edge. "Help me with this."

Kelly and Rod joined him.

"On three," Mark said. "One. Two . . ."

Together they tore the panel loose from its moorings. Behind it—too close behind to allow room for a person to hide—stood a floor-to-ceiling fan, its metal blades humming. Its draw was so great that Kelly nearly stumbled into the fan. "Now what?"

Mark pulled from his pants pocket a grounding strap he'd salvaged from the lab's spare parts room. It looked like a steel-weave belt, just long enough to fit Kelly's waist. He thrust one end into the fan to stop it. The blades bit into the strap and ripped it from his hand, leaving two bloody grooves across his palm. "Crap." Blood dripped onto the floor.

Kelly snatched the gun from his belt. "Find a way through that thing."

Rod rolled up his left sleeve as she walked by.

The immediate corridor was clear, but she could hear Han shouting orders to his men. "Cover the alleys. You, over there. The rest of you, that way." His voice took on a tone of confidence. "We got them. There's no way out of there."

Shit. How did he know that? She focused her attention on the alley, ready to shoot anything that moved, until she heard Mark's frantic shout behind her.

"Rod!"

She turned just as her little brother reached into the fan, as if he thought he could stop it with his bare hand.

Kelly's heart stopped. She forgot the corridor, Han, and his men.

The blade bit into Rod's wrist and yanked off his forearm just below the elbow. The fan screamed with the acid shriek of a metal grinder. Chips and chunks of prosthesis flew back into the room like shrapnel. With a loud clang, the aluminum rod that gave strength to her brother's false arm caught on the fan's frame and brought the blades to a halt. Its fingers twitched in a parody of lost life.

Mark stared, pale and breathless, at the stump of Rod's arm.

Soldiers peeked around the corner, cautious. Kelly tried to shoot, but the trigger stuck. The safety was on.

She shoved the gun sideways into Mark's chest, hitting him hard enough to knock him out of his shock, scooped up her bag with one hand, and shoved Rod into motion with the other. By the time Han's men ventured into the garbage collection site, she and her brother had squeezed between the blades.

Mark clicked off the safety and fired down the corridor while he climbed through the stalled fan. With the butt of the gun, he knocked the rod loose and set the blades free.

"You all right?" Kelly asked Rod as soon as they were through.

He rubbed his truncated stump. "It hurts, but the arm let loose when it was supposed to."

Kelly searched his eyes for a long moment.

Finally, she fished the iodine bottle from her cushion case and loosened the cap. Running, she dribbled iodine like blood down the corridor. When they reached a side passage, she rolled the bottle down the adjoining hall, leaving a trail of drops behind it. The chemical was a little too dark and purple to look authentic, but if Han was in a hurry, it might buy them a few seconds.

With her teeth, she ripped a strip off the hem of her open shirt and shoved it into Mark's injured hand. "Bind that." The ruse wouldn't work if they left two trails of blood.

From there, the three raced down the broad, featureless shaft of the return air duct without a clue in the worlds where they were going.

A bright flash filled the sky as Amanda burned for space. The shock wave from the nuclear blast reached her high in the Venusian stratosphere, where the low atmospheric pressure sapped much of its strength. Still, it rattled the ship with a bout of turbulence such as she'd never felt before. Her head and arms were battered against her seat. Instruments shook so badly she couldn't hope to read them. Her status board flashed warnings all across the panel. She could only ride the crest of the wave and pray that *VR-2* would hold together.

Somewhere along the way, she lost thrust.

When the shock wave passed and the tumult subsided, most of her instruments returned to green, but the ship drifted in a dead, off-axis tumble.

Tentatively at first, then more firmly as she regained her own personal bearing within time and space, she ran a series of computer diagnostics. She needed data. She didn't know how to make a decision without it. Maybe that's why she'd been such a bad parent.

Hull integrity read good. Several of the ship's sensors had been shaken loose or damaged. Comm was down, either due to a hardware malfunction—probably the dish—or because of the jamming signal. She wasn't sure the computer could tell the difference. The navigation panel survived, though the few sensors left working picked up ghost images that clouded most of the screen. Main thrusters were dead.

No, not dead, just offline. The automatic launch sequence had shut them down when the ship reached orbit. Maneuvering thrusters read normal.

Her ship remained intact, at least enough of it to limp back to *Venus Rain,* within range of Chang's missile satellites. For the moment, though, she was okay.

With the sky full of false readings, the computer couldn't fix her position. She had to navigate manually. Circumstance provided two distinct points for her to work with, Venus—particularly the mushroom cloud hovering over the known longitude and latitude of processor thirteen—and the Sun. The computer supplied the location of *Venus Rain* based on the station's standard orbit. With that, she programmed an intercept vector and engaged thrust.

On the way, Amanda tried the comm again. Perhaps the destruction of the processor would get Chang to talk. Again, all she got back was static.

The thrusters pushed her higher until she reached the station's altitude. Her sensors hadn't reported false readings after all. They'd reported truth. Where the station should have been coasted an unimaginably vast cloud of foil ribbons that confused her radar. The sparkling display gave her the sensation of flying into the dust of a fairy's wand.

Once inside, she couldn't see beyond the sunlight reflecting from the chaff, so she relied on her computer to provide her coordinates based on time, velocity, and Venus's gravitational pull. Her only comfort was that, inside the cloud, Chang might not see her coming. Maybe he didn't know he'd lost his processor, or that *VR-2* was in flight. By the time he discovered her presence, she might be too close to the station for Chang to target her with his missiles. Maybe, just maybe, he would let her dock.

Unfortunately, it didn't work out that way. When she arrived, the station was gone.

Amanda checked her coordinates and those of the station again. Yes. She was sure of it. This was the right spot. Chang had moved *Venus Rain*.

And Amanda had no way to find it.

CHAPTER 26

Mark, Kelly, and Rod found their way from the return air chase to the nearest lift, where Mark defeated the sensor, pried open the door, and stepped in. As luck would have it, the lift car was on the Concourse deck.

Unfortunately, it was locked into place. Even if it wasn't, they couldn't have used it without it showing up on the grid.

As soon as the panels closed behind them, Mark boosted Kelly onto his shoulders so she could reach the doors in the car's ceiling, which normally opened only when the car rose all the way to the station's core.

They were in for another long climb to the axis, and then to the docking hub at its north end. If La Roche was right, they could all escape the station from there. This time, though, they'd climb uphill, against the pull of the station's artificial gravity, without safety lines, and Rod had only one hand.

"Can you climb?" Kelly asked him.

He nodded but looked up the shaft with trepidation.

"You guys get started," she said. "I'll catch up."

Mark motioned for Rod to go. "What are you going to do?"

She fished the bottle of ammonia from her sack. "Keep Lieutenant Triggerfinger from following us up." She uncapped the bottle and dropped it to the lift floor. The pungent, suffocating fumes began to fill the car.

She let the vacuum-tight door slide shut and snapped the pressure door into place over the car's vent shaft. "Let's go."

With his eyes already red and watery from the escaped fumes, Mark grabbed hold of the ladder and started up.

By then, Rod was several decks ahead. He climbed slowly, hooking the short nub of his missing forearm around the back of one rung while he pulled himself up to the next.

With some confidence that they'd given Han the slip, Kelly tried to be patient with her brother's disability. Their only saving grace was that the pull of gravity became weaker as they climbed higher. It diminished as they grew tired.

La Roche monitored Han's communications. He shook his head and chuckled out loud when the kids somehow got hold of Han's gun and escaped. With luck, they'd make it all the way to the axis.

But once they got there, Han's gun wouldn't be enough to keep them alive. There simply weren't enough hiding places in that long, wide shaft. Even if La Roche kept all of Han's men occupied in the cylinder, Chang had enough in Center to hunt down the kids himself.

La Roche had to get there first.

He picked his way by slow, painful steps to a vacant stairwell and made the harrowing climb to level six. With the lifts locked and his own body too feeble to climb a kilometer-long ladder, La Roche needed another way to reach the axis.

That was why he'd shut down the maintenance grid and security scanners, so Chang wouldn't see him cycle out the airlock.

Han kicked the iodine bottle farther down the passage and cursed his gullibility. He led his men out of the airshaft, back into the pedestrian walkways. The fugitives could be anywhere by now, and with the grid down, Chang could provide little help from Station Center. But the point was, the fugitives weren't "anywhere." They were somewhere: in the interstitial, in one of the quarters, back on the Concourse—they could have taken a stairway to another level. He just had to find out where.

He checked the nearest lift. According to the panel, the car was right where he'd left it, locked into place.

"Start checking quarters," he ordered his men. Two he sent into the interstitial. He contacted the rest on the comm and organized patrols on each level. Every soldier who wasn't in Center, except a single guard in the auditorium, was engaged in either the search for the Bakers and Mark Torben or the search for La Roche. Han waited by the lift in case the fugitives showed up there.

For twenty minutes, he paced the corridor and listened to the futile progress of his teams. Finally, he pounded his fist against the wall with an oath and punched the lift controls to make sure the car was, in fact, there. With the grid down, the panel might not report a change in status.

The screen displayed: SECURITY LOCKOUT. USE ALTERNATE LIFT.

Two of his men came into sight down the hall, so Han hailed them. Then he contacted Ming. "I need lift four." It was time to check the axis.

The reply came after a longer pause than usual. "Lift four released."

Han punched the panel again. The door yawned wide and belched acrid fumes into the hall.

His lungs filled with gas. His chest and eyes burned, and his head felt as though it had been split by an ax. For the second time in an hour, he staggered to his knees. Violent convulsions twisted his stomach and everything inside it came up onto the floor. Once it was empty, he crawled away. Dry heaves continued until he was sure his stomach ought to be dangling, inside-out, where his tongue used to be.

Somewhere along the way, the lift door closed and the environmental system cleared the air.

Both of his men were down, but they'd been farther from the door when it opened. They recovered quickly.

When he could, Han gasped into his link. "Axis." His voice was a hoarse, painful rasp. He coughed up a chunk of rations from his windpipe and spat blood onto the deck. "Go."

After several minutes of despair, Amanda forced herself to think things through. She cast aside thoughts of drifting, lost in a cloud of fairy dust, until her air, power, or sanity ran out. She forgot she could neither navigate nor use her sensors to locate *Venus Rain*. And she ignored the fact that even if she did find it, Chang would destroy her for doing so. She set herself to the task of survival.

Where would the station be? Would Chang have hidden it in the chaff cloud? If he had, Amanda was already lost. Therefore, she had to start with the assumption that *Venus Rain* was not in the cloud.

Outside it then, but where? If Chang rose above the cloud, his radar could scan outward and see anything coming in from Earth, Mercury, or anywhere else, while *Venus Rain* would remain invisible against a backdrop of glitter.

Yes, that made sense. The argument was sound enough to buoy her spirit. And the one object she could actually see through the cloud, the planet itself, would guide her. She put that reference point directly astern and engaged thrust.

It took forty minutes to clear the cloud with maneuvering thrusters alone. Once she was out, she turned on her radar, found it working, and pinged every sector of the empty sky.

Venus Rain was gone.

Amanda clenched her fists and growled through her teeth. Her voice rose by decades into a scream of primal rage as she bloodied her fists on her instrument panel. "You son of a bitch!" she screamed over and over into the black. "Where are you?"

No one answered. Her raw throat and pulverized hands began to wear their way into her consciousness. Her rage dissipated, replaced by an intense sorrow that stabbed her heart like ritual suicide.

Suddenly she couldn't remember how old her kids were. She had to count forward from the year of Kelly's birth. Nineteen. That's right, nineteen. She didn't know when she'd last celebrated her daughter's birthday, but it was sometime before their father had left. She just couldn't be there on this or that particular day. It seemed like she'd always have time later. The bills had to come first.

When Kelly turned eighteen, Amanda squeezed out a day off, but by then Kelly was already gone. "I don't want your cheap gifts and phony affection," Kelly had said. Amanda remembered, exactly, the words that had cut her where she'd never heal.

Somehow Amanda blamed their father for that. He was the one who'd left them. After he did, Amanda had done everything she could to keep the rest of the family together. But it was never enough. Never nearly enough.

CHAPTER 27

To La Roche, weightlessness felt like a dream, a chance to rest his weary bones as he drifted from the cylinder to the axis. The view of Venus from his pressure suit somehow had a more awesome quality than it did when he saw it from one of the lounges at the southern end of the cylinder.

It was especially different today. The burn trail of Amanda's shuttle streamed from a cloud of destruction that marred the planet's surface. She'd escaped. That was something, at least.

And the processor was gone. As far as the European Union was concerned, the Project was nothing more than a cover for La Roche's real job, which he was doing today. But he'd poured too many years of his life, too much of himself, into the Project to take any satisfaction from the damage he'd done.

Oh, the Project would recover. It would rebuild the processor and make up for the backslide its destruction would cause in the schedule. But now, every day the conflict wore on, the remaining processors would fall a little further behind. And every day would cost the Project just a little more time than the day before, in an exponential progression of delay.

Time was no longer on China's side. If the Western powers decided to blockade Venus—and they almost certainly would—China would be forced to deal.

As important as that small victory was, however, it wasn't the one La Roche had been sent to achieve. He had much more to do and he was running out of time.

When he reached the axis, he clipped a lifeline to the ladder and dug the thinpad from his pocket.

He couldn't punch the keys with his fat gloves, but he'd already set it to display the text of Chang's communications. It failed to reveal the kids' location but told him Han's men were on their way to the axis and that Han himself was going to the infirmary.

La Roche scanned the windows of the nearby spokes until he found the rising light of a lift car. In another, closer spoke, he saw the kids. Han's men were going to reach the axis first. When they did, they'd have the corridor covered. The kids would be trapped.

La Roche shoved the thinpad into his pocket and scrambled to the nearest airlock. When the door opened, he pulled himself in, slammed it shut, and initiated the vent cycle. As soon as the pressure reached a safe level, though not yet full atmosphere, he began shedding his pressure suit.

The inner door cycled open. La Roche kicked the suit into a corner of the donning room, took up his gun, and scanned the axis.

The soldiers' lift had just arrived. One of them floated into the corridor and La Roche put a bullet through the man's chest. The man drifted, pumping droplets of blood that hung in the filtered air. Cautious, the rest of the soldiers remained in their lift car.

Minutes later, Mark pried open a closer door.

La Roche beckoned him with a frantic gesture. "Quickly."

Mark pushed himself across the corridor to the zero-g handles. Then La Roche fired his last four rounds down the hall to keep Chang's men at bay while Mark scrambled into La Roche's donning room.

Rod crossed next.

La Roche jettisoned the spent magazine and slapped in his spare clip. Once Kelly crossed, he opened fire again until the four of them, and his discarded pressure suit, were crammed into a room designed for three.

"Is that thing loaded?" La Roche gestured to the gun in Mark's hand.

"Yes."

"Give it to Kelly and listen to me."

Mark clicked off the safety and handed it to her.

"Cover us," La Roche said. "Shoot at anything that moves." It didn't matter if she hit. Even wild gunfire in a corridor that size would keep Han's men from approaching. The walls, constructed from an alloy of carbon steel and titanium, provided the structural backbone for the entire station. Nothing she hit here would cause a vacuum breech.

To Mark, La Roche said, "The *Eclipse* is moored in dock seven. The manifest says she's carrying the standard allotment of emergency rations. With only three of you, the supplies should last long enough for you to reach Mercury."

"You're not coming?" Kelly asked over her shoulder.

La Roche ignored her. "According to Chang's communications, two of his men from Center are guarding the security checkpoint."

That checkpoint was the only way to get to the docking ring.

La Roche handed Mark a data card. "This contains all of Chang's military intelligence. Get it to the European Defense Agency. Deliver it yourself, don't give it to a middle man." Gunshots blasted in La Roche's ear. He focused all his attention on Mark. "Do you understand?"

Mark nodded.

La Roche handed him a second card. "Download this program into the shuttle. It'll take you to Mercury. I'll cover you as long as I can."

"Come with us," Kelly said.

"You're just kids. Chang might let you go, but not if I'm with you."

Kelly bit her lip for a moment until La Roche motioned for her to watch the corridor.

"Shit," she said when she looked back. She fired a few startled rounds. "I think I hit somebody."

"Good. It'll make them more cautious. Ready?"

"Almost." Kelly pulled a white plastic bottle from a cushion case and handed it to La Roche. "It'll flash if you can find an ignition source."

He read the bottle. ACETONE. Excellent. "There's a pressure door a few meters down the pipe. Close it behind you. It'll give you some time." He took Kelly's place near the opening, braced himself on a zero-g handle, and heaved the bottle down the corridor. When it had almost reached the soldiers, he shot it, spraying acetone in a cone down the axis. Droplets and vapor hung in the zero-g air like stars in a nebula

"Good shot," Mark said. "Now what?"

"Get ready." La Roche watched the corridor.

Slowly, carefully, the soldiers came into view.

As soon as the first one emerged completely, La Roche pushed off from his handle, out into sight. The solider fired and a bullet ripped into La Roche's shoulder. The muzzle flash ignited a conflagration that filled ten meters of the axis. The flames looked like some writhing, agonized beast trapped in its own death throes, consuming acetone droplets as they evaporated in the heat.

"Now!" La Roche shouted over the roar of the flames.

Kelly, Mark, and Rod raced down the tunnel toward the docking ring, stopping only to close the pressure door behind them. By the time the acetone was consumed and the flames gone, La Roche had returned to the relative safety of the donning room.

Bleeding from his wound, he held the surviving soldiers off until he'd spent half the rounds in his gun. Then he let them come into the corridor again.

When they were too far from the lift to take cover, he rounded the corner in a banzai charge down the axis. He hit three men before their bullets tore into his own body. His last thought was that every man hoped to die in his dreams, but he was content to die in weightlessness.

⤙《○》⤚

Kelly and Mark flew past the open pressure door. Mark waited for Rod to pass before he keyed the manual sequence and the iris twisted closed.

He took the gun from Kelly and checked the magazine. "Two guards, two shots. I'm not that good."

Rod clung to the wall near a fire extinguisher box. "What are we gonna do?"

"I have an idea." Kelly yanked the extinguisher from its clasp and read the label. CARBON DIOXIDE.

If memory served, the security checkpoint, just around the corner in a short tunnel that connected the docking ring to the axis, was always closed off by security doors at both ends, unless a shuttle was actually boarding.

"Hold this." She thrust the extinguisher at Mark and crossed to the environmental vent. It was too small for even Rod to fit through, but that didn't matter. She pressed her body against the vent and stuffed the untucked hem of her shirt between the slats of the grate. Inside the duct, the fabric flapped toward the security room. "We don't have to shoot anybody. Here."

Muffled gunshots erupted beyond the pressure door behind them.

Kelly took the extinguisher, pressed the nozzle against the grate, snapped the seal, and squeezed the handle. A cold spray of the non-toxic gas flooded the duct. "If it displaces enough oxygen at the checkpoint, it'll asphyxiate the guards."

"How will we know if it works?" Rod asked.

"That's the problem. We won't. Not until we open the door." It took about thirty seconds to empty the bottle into the vent.

As soon as she finished, Mark turned toward the checkpoint.

"Wait," she said. "It'll take a minute."

In maybe half that time, the gunshots behind them subsided.

Mark shook his head. "We haven't got a minute." He fired his last two rounds into the pressure door's control panel to keep the soldiers at bay a little longer, then discarded the gun and pressed his ear to the door.

"He didn't have to do that," Kelly said.

Mark pushed himself away from the iris. "Yes, I did. They're coming."

"Not you. La Roche. We could have found another way." A way that didn't stain Kelly's hands with more blood.

"It's done," Mark said. "We have to go."

He was right. "We're all going to hell anyway." She rounded the corner and cycled open the checkpoint door.

Both guards floated, unconscious, in the middle of the room, but the air handler was already feeding them fresh oxygen. The men would recover, albeit with splitting headaches, in just a few minutes.

Mark and Rod confiscated the men's guns.

"Give me that," Kelly told her brother.

"But . . ." He looked toward Mark for support, found none, and handed the gun to Kelly.

She stuffed it into her belt and pushed herself through the security-scanning pipe. Sirens blared in response to metals and explosives. Kelly ignored the alarms and continued toward dock seven.

When they got there, Mark keyed open the *Eclipse*'s door and headed for the navigation panel.

"Do you know how to fly one of these things?" Kelly asked.

"They're pretty simple—" Mark tapped a few keys and eased himself into the command chair— "if you program them right." He slid La Roche's card into the slot and downloaded the program.

"Rod, go check the stores. Make sure there's food and water."

"Looks like it's ready to go," Mark said a moment later.

Rod returned from the hold. "There's food."

"Water too?" Kelly asked.

He nodded.

"Okay." Mark snapped his safety harness. "Strap in. We're leaving."

"La Roche is dead," one of Han's soldiers announced through the link in Chang's ear. "We've got the data."

"Bring it to me." Chang was still operating off two terminals. "And get those kids."

His wrist swiveled at the end of his arm. He no longer tried to control his nervous habit and the constant pain in his face had diminished to background noise. Events had gone too far beyond his control. Until he knew his data was secure and the kids were either dead or captured, he had too much else to think about.

He waited several interminable minutes for the next update. It came from young Private Qin. "Sir, I'm showing a departure. The *Eclipse*, from dock seven."

It could only be the kids. Where the hell did they think they could go? "Increase altitude. Take us out of the chaff and put them on radar. And clear the comm channels. I want to talk to my satellites."

"Yes, sir." Qin turned to his board.

One of Han's men came in with La Roche's thinpad and handed it to Chang, who passed it off to Huang. He didn't have enough terminals to do everything he needed to do. "Find out where my data's been."

Huang took a seat and began keying commands into the thinpad.

Gravity shifted to an awkward, undulating vector as the steady thrust of orbit transfer joined the spin of Station Center. The sensation turned Chang's stomach. He closed his eyes and gripped his seat to keep from becoming ill. After a moment, however, he banished the nausea to the back of his mind with his burning face and nervous wrist.

"We're clear," Private Qin announced. "I have the *Eclipse* on radar."

Chapter 28

Amanda took her shuttle to a higher orbit, putting the chaff cloud as low on her horizon as she dared, and parked there. The station lay below her, submerged in a sea of chaff at least as expansive as the Indian Ocean. And probably as deep.

Searching a cloud that size would be worse than fruitless. It would be impossible.

So Amanda drifted, all alone, in the cold vastness of nothing, wondering where her life and relationships had gone, and what would become of her family.

When Kelly was nine, her father had taken her to Amanda's last promotion ceremony. Kelly ran around the room, telling everybody who would listen, "That's my mom, *my* mom." Back then they'd been so proud of one another. Yet somehow it had all come down to this.

A solid blip appeared on Amanda's radar screen. Her head snapped up. Out the window, she saw nothing against the backdrop of glitter, but to her radar, it was there. And it must have come from *Venus Rain*.

She tried hailing. All she got back was jamming noise. Nevertheless, the ship was a data point. She fed its coordinates into her nav panel and engaged thrust. The point at which it rose from the cloud gave her a place to start. She could trace back its trajectory.

Then *Venus Rain* emerged, dawning like the Sun to burn off a cloud of despair. She didn't wonder why Chang had come out of hiding, or care that he might destroy her just for being there. It only mattered that the station loomed, real as life, before her.

The crackle of static on her open channel went silent. Before she could respond to the sound's sudden disappearance, she received a comm.

"*Venus Rain* to *Eclipse*. This is Colonel Chang." *Eclipse*, not *VR-2*. "Return to dock or you will be fired upon. Acknowledge."

Amanda descended toward the station. Chang must know she was there, but for the moment, his attention was on the other ship. She meant to take advantage of the opportunity. Once she got close enough to the docking ring, Chang wouldn't dare target her with missiles. The problem was, she'd never docked with a station under thrust before.

"*Venus Rain* to *Eclipse*. This is Colonel Chang. Acknowledge."

He hailed on all comm frequencies. Unless the *Eclipse*'s receiver was damaged, the occupants could hear his warning.

"Mark Torben. Kelly Baker. Henry Baker. You have sixty seconds to cut thrust, or I will open fire."

"We can't." Amanda didn't recognize the voice. It must have been Mark Torben's. "Our trajectory is pre-programmed. We don't know how to shut it down. Please don't shoot." There wasn't quite enough pleading in his tone to sound sincere.

"*VR-2*, keep distance. You are not authorized for approach. Acknowledge."

Amanda had almost reached the station. Five kilometers to go. With *Venus Rain* still rising, the gap closed rapidly. Some part of her mind told her she should cut thrust, but that part was buried in panic. Her children were on that shuttle. She didn't know how or why. But they were there.

And they were in trouble.

Amanda scrubbed her face with her palms to make herself think. She had to protect them. But the voice she'd heard from the shuttle belonged to neither of her kids. Her mind screamed for confirmation.

"Thirty seconds, *Eclipse*." The cold voice of Colonel Chang froze Amanda's blood as if she'd been infused with liquid helium.

"Chang, you son of a bitch," she screamed into the comm. "Don't you dare. They're just children."

Kelly replied. "Some of us aren't children anymore, Mom. It's about time you realized that."

Shit. That wasn't helpful.

But Kelly wasn't done. "As for you, you Chinese piece of shit. Take your best shot. We're all going to hell anyway."

A dozen ports were mounted around the stationary docking ring. From a hub in the middle hung four booms, each laden with antennae for radar, sensors, and transmitters, one of which swiveled into motion, seeking a receiver somewhere in space, one undoubtedly connected to a missile satellite.

Amanda aimed her ship at the transmitter. "I got it all wrong, Kelly. Everything." She fired full thrusters—not the maneuvering jets, but the launch boosters—the ones used to propel the ship from the surface of Venus. "Forgive me." Sudden g threw her back into her seat. Her vision darkened around the edges. It was all she could do to keep her bloody hand on the joystick.

The comm dish was still turning when she hit.

Venus Rain rocked with the force of the impact. Everyone who wasn't strapped in tumbled to the floor of Station Center.

Chang climbed to his feet, using the back of the command chair for support. The spin of Center felt off-kilter, even more than it had under the thrust of orbit transfer, but it might have been his imagination. He could no longer distinguish the station's movement from his own vertigo.

"Damage report." He twisted into his seat and secured the g-harness.

"Working on it, sir."

"Damage report!" Nothing would cause his mission's failure faster than the loss of *Venus Rain*. Around him, all the sensor readouts were dark.

"Communication down. Radar down." Ming paused. "Hell, every sensor on the hub is down."

"Structural integrity?"

"The docking ring has been breached. Everything else is holding."

"Orbit?"

"Don't know, sir. We lost navigation with the sensors."

"Sir," Qin said. "The comm hub at the south end is still functioning. If we turn the station around, we can get a nav reading."

"Do it."

Within seconds, rotational thrust joined the spin of Center and the station's lateral acceleration to form a cocktail of g that overwhelmed Chang's senses. For the duration of the maneuver, all he could do was sit with his head down and his eyes closed until the sensation passed.

When it did, the station felt as though it bobbed like a cork on the open ocean. But it was just in his mind.

"All thrusters off," Qin said. "Orbit is stable. If you want, sir, I can still contact the satellites. If the *Eclipse* really is following a pre-programmed course, we should be able to hit it."

"Have they got my data?" Chang asked Huang.

"No, sir."

"You're sure?"

"Yes. The transmitter and data port haven't been used since the ferret escaped. It's all right here."

Chang went silent for a time. He could have fallen asleep with his eyes open, he was so tired. He'd been at his station for thirty-six hours, and with the crisis behind him, his adrenal glands shut down like a failed thruster.

"Colonel?" Qin asked. "What shall I do about the *Eclipse*, sir?"

Chang dismissed the question with a flap of his hand. "Let them go. They're just kids. They'll die out there anyway."

When it happened, when her mother flew into the station, Kelly felt nothing. Maybe a little shocked or a little empty. Mere shadows of emotion compared to what she should have felt. All she'd ever known were strife and rebellion. But how do you rebel against someone who's gone? Worse, how do you tell them you finally understand? In the lonely confines of the cockpit, she whispered, "I forgive you."

She searched her pocket for synth, but her mind barely registered its absence. It was gone from her system now and didn't leave addiction in its wake like a real drug would. Only the motion of her hands was habitual, not the stuff itself.

Now it was gone, and that was for the best. She would have to take care of Rod. Start over. Find a place to live. Maybe the European government would pay them for La Roche's data card. Maybe not.

Either way, she was finished with synth. Mark didn't approve of it, and Kelly was far from through with him.

She monitored the sensors long after the explosion and tried to convince herself that she'd be able to see her death coming. It wasn't until two hours later, after the *Eclipse* had make its long burn for Mercury, that she finally considered the three of them safe.

By then, Mark had moved to the passenger compartment with Rod to keep Rod's mind off missiles and Mingyun satellites. Rod couldn't have been able to hear the comm from back there. He didn't have to face their mother's death all over again.

Finally, Kelly joined them.

"That's why they call you 'Rod'?" Mark was saying. "Because of the rod in your arm?"

"Yeah." He chuckled. "Go figure."

"It looked real. I would never have guessed."

"It was top of the line." He showed Mark the stump of his forearm, which had a series of metal contacts grafted to the tissues. "Some are nerve contacts, but these two are just steel pads. They mated to a pair of battery-powered electromagnets in the arm. And like the micro-manipulators in the hand, I could control them through nerve impulses—"

"Just like the real thing." Mark held Rod's truncated arm and admired the technology. He had Rod talking, really talking, for the first time since La Roche had told them their mother was dead.

"I get a new one every year as I grow," Rod continued. "Or I did, anyway. It's part of the reason Mom never had much money."

Kelly smiled in spite of herself. Mark was a good man, not at all the type her mother would disapprove of. She actually looked forward to being stuck in a shuttle with him for the next thirty-six days.

Rod, on the other hand, would be bored beyond help within a day or two. But he was Kelly's responsibility now. With their father gone and their mother dead, he had nobody else.

She collected the cushion case she'd taken from the station, sat down, and upended it onto the seat. Only the latex gloves remained. She'd spent everything else to purchase their survival.

Even so, the gloves weren't a complete waste. She could always blow them up into balloons or puppets to entertain her brother.

Epilogue

The CATS wing of the US Air Force decelerated into orbit around Mercury. With an average surface temperature of 350 degrees centigrade, most of its surface couldn't support life. As such, the only three inhabited bases on the entire sweltering planet—Shengming, the Chinese base; Gagarin, the Russian base; and Deep West, the joint US and EU base—sat less than a hundred kilometers apart near the north pole.

On the surface, each consisted of a series of landing pads and a handful of small, concrete bunkers. Deep West included a solar array and research tower centered at the pole itself. Everything else was buried deep within the planet's silicate bedrock.

As the *Black Panther* approached, Bill studied Shengming through his long-range imager to make sure its hangars didn't suddenly yawn wide and spit a swarm of Marauders to intercept the convoys, mere hours behind the CATS.

The Russians, for their part, might disapprove of what the Western powers were doing, but unless they had foreseen, or been forewarned of, China's attack on *Venus Rain*, they'd have had no time to deploy warships here. Still, that didn't rule out some form of Russian response.

Both bases, however, remained quiet. Deep West, on the other hand, had a mining robot the size of a small shuttle sitting on one of its landing platforms. That perhaps wasn't so strange, except that the markings on the robot were Russian, and it seemed to be mining the platform. Crablike claws, designed for gripping rock, struggled for purchase on the tungsten-steel surface that capped the elevator shaft beneath it. Cutting lasers slagged the metal and a giant coring drill attacked the mountings.

"Pass over Deep West," he told Carter. As they got closer, he could just make out an object strapped to the back of the miner, an oblong device the size of a one-man hover car. But before he could determine what it was, the platform gave way and the robot, load and all, tumbled into the kilometer-deep shaft.

The flash that followed, brighter than the Mercury sun, nearly blinded him. A mushroom-shaped column of smoke emerged where Deep West used to be.

The story continues in:

MERCURY SUN

WORLDS ASUNDER: BOOK III

About the Author

Kirt Hickman was born in 1966 in Albuquerque, New Mexico. He earned a Bachelor's degree in electrical engineering in 1989 and a Master's degree in opto-electronics in 1991, both from the University of New Mexico. Since then, he has worked in research and manufacturing fields related to high-energy lasers, microelectronics, and micro-machines, fields that he leverages to enrich his science fiction. Kirt has also published the science fiction thriller *Worlds Asunder*, the writers' how-to *Revising Fiction: Making Sense of the Madness*, and the children's book *I Will Eat Anything*.